Steel Waters

Volume 1 of the continuing adventures of
Glen Wilson…

Other books by Ken Coffman

Fiction

Alligator Alley, by Ken Coffman and Mark Bothum
Twisted Shadow, by Ken Coffman with Mark Bothum
Glen Wilson's Bad Medicine
Toxic Shock Syndrome
Hartz String Theory
Endangered Species
Fairhaven

Nonfiction

Real World FPGA Design with Verilog

The Armchair Adventurer
www.ArmchairAdventurer.net

Books can be ordered from:

www.bytechservices.com
1500A East College Way #554
Mount Vernon, WA 98273

About the author:

Ken Coffman is a Field Applications Engineer and Member of the
Technical Staff at Fairchild Semiconductor.

He is the coauthor of six patents, a member of the standards association of
the Institute of Electrical and Electronics Engineers, and a guitar player. He
plays golf exactly the way his boss wants him to: very poorly.

For the latest news, see www.kencoffman.com

This book is a work of fiction. Names, characters, places and incidents are
the products of the author's fevered imagination or are used fictitiously.
Any resemblance to actual events, locales or persons (living or dead) is
entirely coincidental.

ISBN 0-975-43141-2

Published by:
The Armchair Adventurer
1500A East College Way #554
Mount Vernon, WA 98273

Dedication

For my mother, Carolyn Edwards, from whom I inherited my love for reading everything and anything. Cereal boxes, romance novels, everything.

For literary inspiration, I thank Charles Willeford, an interesting man who led an amazing life. His humorous dissections of the quirky depths of human behavior are greatly missed. RIP.

I want to thank my "editorial board" for encouragement, guidance, proofreading and commentary.

Judy Coffman	Barry Otterholt
Stacey Benson	Maureen Blando
Ken Lomax	Mark Collins
Dock Brown	Tommy Lee Bolser
Gary Croft	Mike Irvine
Mark Bothum	Craig Ranta
Dale Edwards	Karen Wespi
Mick Wilson	

Notes on the Revised (2009) Edition

First of all, I would like to thank the growing legions of Glen Wilson fans. His audience grows year-by-year and I love the arguments and questions his tales generate. There is no greater joy than interacting with readers who take seriously his adventures and foibles; those who comment, commend or argue when he thrills or upsets them. This is awesome, it thrills me and buoys my spirits when I'm toiling in the basement dreaming up the convoluted twists and turns.

Many consider Glen to be my alter ego; the literary expression of some secret, inner me. I don't see it that way. Sure, Glen and I have a special telepathic connection, but he does what he wants while I follow him around and document what I observe. I'm aware of how mad that sounds.

But often, Glen's antics are just as much a surprise to me as to you. I swear on my honor that this is true.

I hope you noticed the jazzy new cover. My old pal Franz Hajnal is an accomplished photographer and he took the photograph. The "hand model" is another friend, Bill Lepoidevin. He has deformity that was reminiscent of Glen's wounds. I asked him if he was up for it. He said yes. So, we gathered in a conference room, spread out a map of Bolivia, turned on hot flood lights, and tossed in my old pearl-handled .38 and some cartridges. The striking image is the result. Well done, Franz and Bill. Thank you. Guy Corp assembled the final cover design. Talented artist Pav Kovacic created Glen's image. I'm lucky to have talented friends always willing to answer my call and help with my mad schemes.

I'm slowly and painfully improving my writing craft. A big part of my evolution is due to encouragement and feedback from my online writing group, the Writin' Wombats, hosted at gather.com. I assure you, they have done their best to cure me of many evils; molested adverbs, soul-stealing passive voice and insidious comma splices. For the incompetence I stubbornly cling to, please don't blame them. They've done their patient best with my hopelessness.

In particular, I tip my hat to Pat Shaw, Lisa Fredsti, John Philipp, Pat Bertram, James Rafferty, Judi Fennell, Jill Lynn Anderson, Rand Phares, Jamie Chapman, Sia McKye, JK Sather, Vivian Archer, Ann Barks, Sherrie Super, Beth Hill, JC Alexander, Steve Prosapio, Dale Cozort, Gina Robinson, Dave Saari, Wendy Christy, Sy Garte, Dana Fredsti, Brenda Vander Linden, Adina Pelle and Mike Stromer. These folks are great fun to hang with. They flogged me when I wrote wrong (heh) and encouraged me when I drifted low.

To my friends gathered at The Hicken and Spleen… The next round? It's on me.

- Ken Coffman January, 2009

Note on the First Edition

When Mark and I wrote Alligator Alley (Volume 2 of the continuing adventures of Glen Wilson), there was never any thought about doing this prequel and the sequels. However, the characters simply demanded more life. If things go as planned, there will be eight books in the series when the story is finally told.

You can email me if you have questions, complaints or comments:
kcoffman@sos.net

Let me ride on the Wall Of Death one more time
Let me ride on the Wall Of Death one more time
You can waste your time on the other rides
This is the nearest to being alive
Oh let me take my chances on the Wall Of Death

Richard Thompson, *Wall of Death*

From Shoot Out the Lights

INTRODUCTION

Tuesday, May 11, 1982

I could hear meadowlarks singing in the pasture. They make beautiful music; music to enrich the soul and fill a man's heart with love. However, at this hour of the morning, I'd like to smash their noisy heads with a hoe.

Linda was turned away from me holding the comforter tightly clamped between her legs. She'd get up and make breakfast later... Around lunchtime unless I figured a way to wake her up. An airplane crash in the front yard might do the trick.

Outside, my neighbor Modine hollered—that didn't improve my mood. I knew what Modine was mad about... Roscoe had been at his chickens again. I loved that brain-damaged old black Lab, but this is farm country and you can cuss about Democrats or slip your hand down the front of little Suzie's flannel shirt, but your fookin' dog better stay away from the fookin' hen house. That's the way I heard it in my head with Modine's clipped, hard-scrapple, Lutefisk-on-special-occasions Minnesota accent.

"Corn's comin' in good fer this time a'year," Modine had said.

"Yes," I replied, "the corn is looking good."

The carrots are looking good. The apples and pears and rhubarb and alfalfa are all looking good too. There, I fast-forwarded the next half-hour of conversation for you.

Modine leaned on our shared split-rail fence, looked over the field, and picked his teeth with a kitchen match.

"I'm a'scared we're gonna have to put down that damned black dog a-urine."

"Roscoe? Roscoe's all right. Not too smart and he don't see too good anymore, but he's a good old dog."

"That may be. But he's been at my chickens and it ain't the first time neither."

"Well, fine. I'll get Lin to write you a check with a little extra thrown in for your inconvenience."

Modine discarded the match and switched to cleaning his fingernails with his Buck knife. Half a lifetime of Minnesota winters leached from him any sense that time had value. Trying to prod him would backfire and we'd end up spending an hour talking about the best hardwood for smoking venison or some old boy out by Table Rock who raised a two-headed goat back in ought-six. He trimmed his nails with the old knife. The blade was so sharp that horny little crescents effortlessly fell free. When his manicure was done to his satisfaction, he turned, hopped up on the fence, and looked me directly in the eye.

"I thank you muchly for the offer. I know Roscoe's mostly been a good old pooch. The thing is, once they get a taste for fresh fowl, you can't keep them away. They gotta be put down. There's no other way."

This whole conversation and the way these ranchers could never come to the point without taking a turn or two around the horn pissed me off. The fact that he was right made it worse.

1

"You touch a single hair on Roscoe's head and I'll..."
I looked around for something suitable. I'd been mixing
mortar for a barbecue pit. "Ram that wheelbarrow straight up
your ass."

Modine scratched his neck and chuckled.

"Wheelbarrow? That's fine, Wilson. You're gonna
poke a wheelbarrow up my keister. Anyhoo, it ain't my
place to shoot your mutt."

He leaned back and lifted his legs over the fence. After
hopping from the fence like a teenager, he walked a few
paces, then stopped and spoke over his shoulder.

"If that dog is at my hens again, and he will be, you'll
put him down yourself."

With that, he spit and walked back to his tractor.

Since then, I tried to keep Roscoe at home. He chewed
through rope, pulled up the stake I chained him to, dug a
hole under the run fence and rubbed raw bloody patches into
his neck with the collar when I finally attached the chain to
something that wouldn't give.

Now, morning sunbeams stream through the windows,
meadowlarks sing, and Modine's by the fence hollering
about his goddam chickens. I pulled on my boots and jeans.
From the wall of death I took down a .222 squirrel gun and
poured a handful of cartridges into my jacket pocket. The
wall of death, that's what I called the section of wall where
we hang the guns; a name I stole from a lovely Richard
Thompson song.

I had plenty of time to prepare for this morning, but
that didn't make it easier. The biggest problem wasn't
Roscoe. It was me. Me and Roscoe were in the same fucking
boat. As I stood in the doorway working the Remington's

bolt, I watched Modine raise a fuss and thought about my life.

On my own since I was sixteen, I'd spent a couple of years working for a rattletrap carnival traveling up and down the left coast. San Diego, California to Portland, Oregon. The carnies were an interesting bunch: manic madness fueled by cheap beer, speed, and greasy corndogs. Entertainment included a betting pool to guess when the roller coaster would fly apart and trading sex with teenage girls for free cotton candy and rides on the Twister.

It was a life that ended when the Hammer disintegrated and killed three civilians. Ten minutes later the owner drove off in a Ford Fairlane with a steamer trunk full of cash and we carnies hit the road with pockets filled with change and carpetbags packed with as many candy bars as we could carry.

As far as I know, the equipment still rusts in Chico and the locals still look for someone to sue. I hitched a ride on I-5 and ended up in Medford. With nothing better to do, I signed up with an Army recruiter and found myself at the University of Saigon for two years. I majored in black marketing, dirty deals, and military bullshit.

Over the two years of my Saigon tour working for Master Sergeant Steve Stephens, I built my stash of Baby Ruths into a leather suitcase full of twenty-dollar bills. In addition, I came home with three notches on my Colt .45, straight razor scars across my chest, and serious case of been-to-hell-and-held-the-beating-heart-of-a-meaner-motherfucker-than-you-in-the-palm-of-my-hand-no-mood-to-kiss-your-ass bad attitude.

Because I signed on in Medford, that's where I mustered out.

I met Linda at an Eagles dance. She'd recently inherited 25 acres off Dead Indian Road and I thought her spaced-out summer-of-love-is-a-drug attitude was cute. She liked my carnie stories, my salad bowl haircut (go figure) and my eight hundred and seventy thousand in cash. So, we were married in Ashland by a grumpy Justice of the Peace. Linda spent a lot of the money on chinchillas and a dozen llamas, smelly South American camels. The market for chinchilla fur never panned out but I liked the gentle-spirited llamas and couldn't bring myself to sell them or worse, eat them. So, we had 25 acres of rock garden and pet llamas. The only cash came from a section leased to Bobby, an entrepreneur growing southern Oregon's number two cash crop: hemp, marijuana, Cannabis Sativa, whatever you care to call it. The only reason corn is number one is because it provides good cover for the dope.

Linda and I were comfortable with each other and didn't have much to worry over, but that is not enough. I came across an old list of tasks scribbled on the back of a receipt. The chores were complete except for replacing cedar shakes on the barn, which I'd been meaning to get to real soon.

The problem? I could tell by the date on the receipt that I'd been meaning to get to that roof real-soon-now for over six years. This scared me. I couldn't get a grip on what happened to the years. What achievement could I point to beside cheating on my income tax and collecting a USDA subsidy for not growing barley, which didn't grow worth a shit around here anyway? Not enough. After 'Nam, I thought I wanted a quiet life. But I was wrong. It ain't enough.

Outside, Modine got madder and threw rocks at the tin roof of my pump house. Roscoe lay in the shade looking innocent. His act would be more convincing if he didn't have bloody pinfeathers painted on his jowls. *Shit.*

"Come on, Roscoe, old boy," I said gently to the dog. "Fuck off, Modine," I shouted across the field waving the rifle. Modine, apparently satisfied, strode away.

I grabbed a spade and led Roscoe through a stand of Lodgepole pines. From the top of a bump on our property we had a peek-a-boo view of Mount Ashland. We buried the chinchillas up there and figured we'd be buried there ourselves some day. Roscoe knew something was up. Nervous, he lapped at my hand and looked around for an excuse to run off.

The sky was a milky blue and though the morning air was very cool, I could tell it would be one of our first really hot days. I could see the snowy flanks of Mount Ashland and the brown stain from smudge pots drifting above the tree line. This was the one place on the farm I would miss most. How many times had I shared a bottle of wine and a joint here with Linda, worked her overalls off, and found myself a home between her thick, white thighs? I almost changed my mind.

"Come here, buddy," I said when I found a good-enough spot.

Roscoe got up from his place in the shade and padded over. I chambered a cartridge and without further agonizing, shot him directly in the forehead. He dropped with his legs splayed and did not move.

Two minutes later, the first bottle fly found him. I clawed and scraped a hole big enough, dragged him in and covered him up. I piled lava rocks over the grave to make a burial mound like the Indians left here and there.

Sweating profusely by this time, the salt made my eyes burn. I was not crying. I shouldered the Remington and climbed an oak tree. From twenty feet up through the 10X scope I could see Modine turning up rocks with his tractor.

I scanned his chicken coop. Modine had a prized wild turkey the chickens raised as one of their own until it got too ugly even for them. The range was 200 yards and the air was still. I squeezed off a round and the turkey exploded into a snowfall of brown feathers. Modine's fat wife came out of her kitchen drying a cast iron skillet. I didn't shoot her. I didn't even consider it. She ran into the field still carrying the skillet until she realized how stupid that looked and set it down. It would take her a while to get Modine's attention. I walked back to the house in no particular hurry.

I was already packed. After tossing my suitcase in the back of the old Dodge pickup, I woke Linda to say goodbye.

"I heard shots?"

"I put Roscoe down."

"It had to be done. Once they get at the chickens—"

"I know," I interrupted.

"We'll get another dog."

She sat up and grabbed her pipe without looking. She lit up and took a drag of what was left of last night's bud.

"I'm leaving, baby."

Her cotton nightgown was bunched around her waist. I soothed my blistered hand on her silky panties. Her full breasts strained for freedom through thin cotton that had been washed and hung outside to dry 100 times too often.

"Going to town? Can you get chocolate chips? I'll make cookies."

"No, Lin. Listen. I'm not coming back. The papers for the USDA are in the desk. Fill those out every year. I talked to Bobby and he'll look in on you. I think that's it."

"Glen?"

"I'm sorry. I took half of the money."

She drew deep on the pipe and coughed. Her eyes flooded with tears.

"What's wrong? We're doing fine. I love you."

"And I love you too, baby. But the years melt away and I have things to do. Besides, I shot Modine's turkey."

"Shit. He'll be pissed."

I stood and kissed the top of her head.

"Is it me?" she said, "Did I do something?"

"No, it's not you. It's me. I just have—have to go. You be well."

She put the pipe aside and worked her panties off.

"Well, one last time before?" she asked, looking up at me.

Animal magnetism pulled me. Hard. But, if we made love, I'd never leave. Afterward, I'd drift into sleep, she'd make homemade bread and a huge batch of greasy bacon, smooth things over with Modine, and that would be it. The barn roof would get fixed, the years would pass, and eventually, Farmer Glen would be buried with Roscoe on the bump. I didn't trust myself to speak, so I turned and walked out. I heard her jump out of bed.

"You fucking prick!"

I walked onto the porch. Modine rolled toward me at full speed with black diesel smoke pouring from the exhaust pipe of his tractor. Fortunately, full speed on the old Massey-Ferguson was 10 miles-per-hour. I was halfway across the yard when Linda pegged me with a waffle-soled boot.

"Get out of here, bastard."

I could tell from her anger that she'd be fine. There is no better therapy than having someone else to blame for your problems. As I started the engine a flat iron shattered the windshield and bounced onto the hood. My last view of

Linda was her red and contorted face as she concentrated on nailing the truck with a concrete paver.

As I fishtailed over our bridge, Modine roared through the fence. Split rails smashed into splinters. With this scene in my rearview, I slid onto Dead Indian Road at about thirty and ground through the gears until the Dodge topped out at 60 MPH. I had 40 miles to travel before getting to I-5. That gave me plenty of time to decide if I would head north or south.

CHAPTER 1

Wednesday, May 12, 1982

The Dodge gave up at the top of Tejon Pass. I stopped to piss at the rest stop and climbed the trail to the top of the hill to look out over the LA valley smog. The Dodge was a trooper. I'd been nursing it with a cheap, two-gallon can of paraffin-based oil for the last five hundred miles of flat hundred-degree wasteland while ignoring a jackhammer racket from under the hood. But, when I got in, it wouldn't start. It coughed and belched clouds of black smoke, but that was it. I got out and said a few comforting words to help guide its soul to the next world, and then kicked a big dent in the door.

Couldn't make it another 50 miles, pig?

I hauled my dusty suitcase out of the back and caught a ride with a Mexican driving a stake bed truck full of strawberry flats. It was a good time for me to practice my Spanish (*Es muy calor por este parte de ano,* yes it's damn hot for this time of year. Variations on this theme can sustain a conversation all day). I helped César unload at the Farmer's Market in Santa Monica. I gave him the last of my pack of Camels and he gave me a sweating bottle of Carta Blanca and *chorizo* wrapped in a tortilla. The sausage was laced with red peppers, which I picked out and discarded as soon as I was out of sight. I hiked to Sunset Boulevard and spent the afternoon lugging my suitcase around and looking in the windows of the souvenir shops and second hand stores. As the sun sank into its bloody pillow I sat on a bus stop bench and ate a Pink's chili dog washed down with a quart of Miller's High Life bought from a 7-Eleven with the last of my pocket cash. I chatted with the whores about how hot it was and whether I wanted a three-some for a hundred bucks (not right now, thank you for asking).

I waited. For what? I don't know. How did I know something would happen? In the same way Tom Selleck knows he won't sleep alone unless he wants to. Some things are inevitable.

I was ready to take Ariel (she said her name was Ariel, but looked more like a Susie or Cathie) up on her offer of a quick one for twenty dollars if she'd extend me credit. She was still pretty, not long off the bus from Cedar Rapids, and in a good mood because she'd had a recent fix. She had a pretty smile and an attractive little roll of baby fat between her cut-off jeans and sleeveless blouse.

Like everyone in LA, she was almost famous. She'd had a try-out for a walk-on part on the TV show Family Ties and had partied with David Lee Roth. She was sure that many more great things waited around the future's corner. I liked her and was about to ask her to marry me when a big, white stretch limo pulled to the curb. We watched it idle in the bus zone for a minute or two, admiring ourselves in the reflection of the opaque windows. A door opened and a nervous Jewish kid came out. He wore black zip-up disco boots and a Nehru jacket.

"Hey guys, what's happening?" he said while looking up and down Melrose Avenue.

"You want me or him? Or both?" Ariel asked brightly.

"Just the guy. You can take off."

He tried to act tough. Ariel winked at me and gathered her bag. She blew me a kiss as she strolled off.

"You look like a guy who knows his way around," he said hesitantly. "What's your name?"

"Glen Wilson." He offered an effeminate, half-hearted handshake. "And you?"

"Bryan. That's with a 'Y'. But who cares, right? It's not like you're going to write me a letter, right? Hee-hee."

He had an annoying half-laugh used to punctuate his sentences. He would get to his point or I would kick the shit out of him. Hee-hee. Perhaps he sensed my impatience.

"Things have been weird around here since Belushi died. Hee-hee. There hasn't been much dope around, and what we can find has been shit. My boss wants twenty grams of China White, good stuff, no crap. He'll pay five thousand in straight-up cash. Can you do it?"

China White? What the hell was that? I didn't have a clue.

"He'll pay my special introductory price of six thousand. I can get it in a couple of hours. Stuff so good his brain will melt. After that he pays a five hundred a gram like everyone else."

"Five hundred? We're talking volume, not tenths. We're not paying retail."

He was trying to Jew me. If people don't want to be stereotyped, they should stop acting stereotypical.

"If you want Drano and baby powder, say so and take your business up the street. I've got the best, hardly stepped on at all. Just off the boat."

The kid glanced back at the limo and up and down the street.

11

"My boss, my client, he's A-list famous if you want an autograph or something."

"Then he can afford the best stuff. And he can afford a thousand down payment," I said with my hand out. The limo horn blatted. An MTA bus crept up in traffic.

"Damn it," the kid said. "We have a bungalow at the Beverly Hills Hotel, you know, Hotel California, hee-hee. Can you be there in an hour? Gotta run, hee-hee."

He put tightly rolled bills into my hand and darted back into the limo. The limo merged into traffic. The bus pulled to a stop and the pneumatic doors opened. I waved the driver on.

"City property, asshole. If you ain't riding the MTA, then park your ass some where else."

I didn't blame the driver, I too would have a bad attitude if I had to wear one of those ugly brown uniforms.

"Fuck you," I called out in my friendliest voice.

"Fuck you, too," she replied as she closed the doors and left me gasping in a cloud of greasy diesel fumes.

I stood and stretched my back which was stiff from the uncomfortable bench. I rotated my torso and warmed up a little. I had an hour to figure out what China White was, where to get some, find my way to the Beverly Hills Hotel, and make the delivery. I checked my watch. Perfect. There was time enough to grab a beer at Rudy's before I went to work.

My friends at Rudy's (I bought a round of Coors for the diehards slumped at the bar) weren't much help. However, a couple schooners of working-man's medicine took the edge off the day. I felt just right when I left. I walked up to the Georgia Hotel and peeked in the windows of the cabs hovering outside. I looked for a hungry cabbie. I found an

Armenian driving a beat-up United Independent (you'll just go nuts if you think about it) Taxi. The name on his license was unpronounceable. One of the Indian drivers up the line pounded on the window and screeched something about taking the cab at the front of the line.

"Eat me," I said helpfully. The driver acted like he would throw me out until he saw the c-note I offered. In one smooth motion he hit the meter and drove out of the line at lightspeed. He grazed the cab in front only a little.

Nice driving.

"What's your American name?" I asked.

"John," he replied as we rolled up Melrose. "Where to?"

"Listen John, do you know what China White is?"

His eyes flicked between the road and me in the rearview mirror.

"Heroin."

One mystery solved. I should have known, but the Jewish kid seemed more like the cocaine type. I was more familiar with the brown product from Cambodia.

"Well, John, I have about twenty minutes to buy twenty grams and make a delivery to the Beverly Hills Hotel. What do you think?"

He was about to tell me get out of the cab but changed his mind when I tossed two more c-notes onto the seat beside him.

"I think I know a place," he said.

We rolled through West Hollywood's scattered, boarded-up storefronts mixed with gay bookshops and used clothing stores. John turned off the main drag and pulled to a stop in front of a rundown two-story house. This neighborhood had seen better days. The palm trees used to be alive, for example. Across the street, a pair of brown-skinned young men drank beer and argued in Spanish about something under the hood of the '63 Chevy Impala they worked on. My Spanish wasn't great, but like a dog, I could understand even if I couldn't speak. Something about the whore-pig carburetor or the rat-bastard fuel filter. My guess was the stinky-ass choke was stuck.

John nodded when I asked him to wait. I walked up the stairs and knocked at the door. From inside, Yes's Tales of Topo Oceans screamed at jet-engine decibel level, but someone had the job of watching the door, so it opened. A huge biker-cliché filled the doorway. He was six-feet tall and had to weigh over 350 pounds; all rolling belly and multiple chins behind a long wispy beard. Arms the size of baby Sequoias.

"Excuse me. I'd like to buy twenty grams of China White and I heard your establishment might have some in stock."

"You look like a fuckin' cop."

I had an automatic habit of trying to place accents. *Sure, this guy was from Texas, that was easy, but what part?* Up in the pan handle. Perhaps one of the little towns around Amarillo. Regarding the cop comment, I couldn't argue. Because Linda thought it was sexy, I kept the Army hairstyle with a mustache trimmed to the corners of my mouth.

I looked like a cop, so what?

"So what?" I said, "I look like a cop, but I'm not."

"Maybe I rip your head off and see if you bleed cop blood?"

This inspired an interesting image, but I didn't have time to play.

"Check me for a wire and gun and let's get on with our business, okay?"

14

He reached for my head when someone behind him started chuckling.

"Down, Bear. Do as he says. Check for a wire and let the man in."

This voice was a mix of Long Island and Beantown. *Perhaps a Melville native with a couple years at Boston College?* I peeked around the Bear and caught a glimpse of a much thinner man in his mid-thirties with long, feathered hair and a deep tan, dressed in a red satin dressing gown and a turban. Bear mauled me and pronounced me clean.

I *was* clean before he placed his sweaty hands on me.

"Come in, Mister...?"

"Wilson," I replied.

Bear turned sideways, but that didn't leave enough hallway for me to squeeze through. So, he retreated. I followed him into a big room, foggy with incense. The thin guy turned down the stereo and shook my hand. I had to look twice before I believed he really wore Arabian shoes with curly toes, like Aladdin's genie. He was day-time-drama handsome and looked lean and wiry beneath the robe. I was surprised that he looked healthy, not strung out.

"I'm Doctor Zalooq, which rhymes with toke, but you can call me Walter if that is more comfortable," he said.

I offered my hand to shake but the Doctor shook his head no and waved my hand away.

"Perhaps we can touch later. After I get to know you better."

The Doctor waved me to a beanbag chair and sat in a polished high-backed oak chair, almost a throne. The beanbags were arrayed into an audience around his chair.

"You appear to be on a quest. Perhaps I can help with your journey."

"Maybe I'm in the wrong place, but I understand you can supply twenty grams of H."

"I have a theory. Wherever you are, you're never in the wrong place. But nevermind that now, I sense urgency. H, heroin, horse, the soul of the poppy. I will help you, but I want to ask questions first and I request that you indulge me. How much time do you have?"

I checked my watch.

"Ten minutes."

"I don't believe the stuff is for you…"

"No, I'm going to resell it."

"And the end customer? An addict or recreational user? Snorter or shooter?"

"I can't say for sure, but I'm sure the client is not an addict. I think this will be nose candy. Party favors."

"A sophisticated consumer?"

"No, a spoiled actor looking for a thrill."

"Okay, very well." Zalooq addressed Bear. "Please bring the yellow box." He turned back to me. "I'll give you synth that friends brewed up in a chem lab at Berkeley. This is a special deal, once only. Okay?"

I nodded. The Doctor began speaking quickly in a machine-gun staccato.

"Very well. This is a phenol and serotonin acetylcholine mix with trace elements I can't mention. We call it PSK. It's only slightly radioactive and I advise you keep it away from ultraviolet light. It costs about two-hundred-thousand a gram to synthesize and there is no possibility of getting more. Period. As you can imagine, human subject testing is problematical. We can't exactly go to the FDA for approval for this type of stuff. All I ask in return is a full report, in writing, as much as you can tell me about the effects. The drug is not physically addictive and will not satisfy a heroin addict. That said, it is liable to be very popular, if you get my drift. A one-hour orgasm in powder form. What were you going to pay for twenty grams of heroin?"

I mentally calculated how much was left in my pocket, leaving a hundred or so for pocket change.

"Five hundred bucks."

The Doctor laughed. "Five hundred dollars? You amuse me, Wilson. You know I'm not stupid, so I assume you're optimizing your profit margin. I appreciate that. I'll take the five hundred and offer free advice in addition. Don't let your client inject this stuff, that would be spectacularly fatal. And don't try this stuff yourself. It will result in the best hour of your life with no hangover. Sounds good, right? However, I think its better not to know where the pinnacle of your life is. Follow me? That way you can always hope for something better."

I don't know if it was the incense or the beer, but the Doctor made sense. Bear appeared with a gleaming yellow box. It looked golden. Bear's fat arms strained with the weight. The Doctor slid a small table from beside his chair and Bear set the box down. The Doctor pulled a ring of keys from his dressing gown and located a yellow key. He opened the box and removed a beaker of white powder with a yellow stopper.

"I suppose this sterile laboratory beaker will not do?"

I nodded in agreement.

"Bear, bring polyethylene bags, what are they called?"

"Baggies," I said helpfully.

"Baggies," the Doctor sighed. "That's right, Baggies," he said with distaste.

The Doctor passed out surgical masks and filled a Baggie. He tapped the beaker and residue drifted out cleanly.

The stuff was ultra-white, as if containing UV reactant like laundry detergent. He carefully sealed the zip-lock, double sealed the Baggie inside another, and looked at me expectantly.

"I believe you said something about five hundred dollars?"

I dug out the money and handed it over. The Doctor would not touch it; he motioned for me to hand it to Bear who licked his fingers and counted the bills carefully. It took him two tries to get to five.

The Doctor handed me a business card. Doctor Zalooq, Better Living Through Chemistry, Inc. An address with a POB was the only other information. I put the card in my pocket.

"Can't I just deliver my report back here?" I asked.

The Doctor laughed.

"You'll be the most popular man in town. If you knew where to find me, then it would be me attaining that level of popularity. That's not a role I relish right now. I suggest you take your profits on a trip, perhaps South America would be far enough. Perhaps. You'd better scurry, you have four minutes."

"Whatever, Doc," I said. I slipped the dope in my pocket and rose. I didn't digest what the Doc said until later. It was Vonnegut that said you should be careful what you ask for.

I emerged, blinking in the sunlight and skipped down the stairway. The Mexicans still argued about the car. I ran over, slammed the automatic choke with the handle of one of their greasy screwdrivers, and shouted *"Arranca!"* to the pretty girl behind the wheel. She was startled but turned the key. The engine started with a roar and a vast cloud of blue-black smoke. It needed valve work real bad but they'd get another thirty thousand miles out of it.

One of the mechanics shouted "Gracias" as the other looked for something expendable to throw. I slammed the taxi door as a spark plug ricocheted off the windshield. John and the mad mechanic exchanged curses in Armenian and Spanish, respectively, in an interesting acapella song familiar to me. I've been cussed in many languages. I checked the time.

"Can you get to the Beverly Hills Hotel in three minutes?"

It took twelve minutes, but I can't blame John for the Rolls Royce and '66 Ford Comet collision that bogged things down at the corner of Wilshire and Beverly Glen. I enjoyed my view of the chauffeur and the sixteen-year-old waitress screaming at each other while cops held them apart. You could buy thirty of those old Comets for what it would cost to repair the Rolls.

I tossed bills at John after we rolled up the hotel driveway. He seemed altogether too glad to get rid of me considering he pocketed several hundred more than the meter. The baggage clerk tried to take my suitcase and we struggled over it for a few seconds before he gave up. I gave him twenty bucks and he pointed out the route to the bungalows. I was only fifteen minutes late, so I stopped for a quick cup of coffee and a scone in The Tea Lounge. The waitress, Yolanda, almost believed I was a somebody, or a soon-to-be somebody. We chatted about famous guests. John and Yoko, the Duke, and others. She was cute and I wanted to marry her, but I had a schedule to pretend to keep. I should wait for Linda to divorce me before I married again, though bigamy might be alright in California, I'd have to check that out with a lawyer. I hugged Yolanda and left an obscene tip which ate most of the rest of my pocket money.

I walked to the bungalow and knocked at the door. It was opened quickly by the Jewish kid. He looked both ways down the walkway before grabbing my sleeve and pulling me in the room. The room was neat and nice, decorated with orchids and finger food. An ice sculpture Yoda, nestled in flowers sculpted from watermelons, sweated in the corner. A carved yellow sunflower caught my eye, it appeared to be made of butter. I snagged a shrimp from a crystal bowl and dipped it in cocktail sauce.

"Dammit, that's for the guests. The party starts in half an hour! Where have you been?"

"Well, Byron..."

"It's Bryan." He held up a hand to stop me from speaking. "Did you get the stuff?"

"Yes, I did. Unfortunately, the town is very dry and I spent extra money to get good stuff."

Bryan looked tense. There was no time to make another connection and we both knew it. "How much?"

"Ten K, but it's the best in the country. Real clean, worth twice what you're paying. I had to pull strings for you guys. It wasn't easy. If you want me to take it down the road and make a lot more money, then just say the word, my friend."

Bryan rolled his eyes and waved at me to stop.

"Ten thousand?"

"Ten thousand," I replied, "and one condition."

"All right, but sign a receipt for catering so I can put it on my expense report."

I nodded. That was reasonable.

Bryan found a book of receipts and scribbled unintelligible stuff on it. After I scribbled a name (I think I signed Karl Marx, but I don't remember, it could have been Fidel Castro. I was in a worker's paradise sort of mood), Bryan counted out hundred-dollar bills from a bank bag. I handed over the baggie and slipped the bills into my suitcase. Not bad, I'd added fifty percent to my net worth in a couple of hours. Easy money.

"Wait a minute," Bryan said looking at the Baggie, "you said something about a condition? What kind of bullshit is that?"

"No big deal. I want an invitation to your little party."

Bryan still sputtered when the Star walked from one of the bedrooms. He was perfectly dapper in a double-breasted suit; all gleaming teeth and manicure. I recognized him from several movies. He was in one of Kubrick's films and, according to the Variety rolled up in my jacket pocket, got three-million and gross points for his next film. He was a hot property though shorter than he looked on the big screen.

I stood and extended my hand for a shake. He took it in both of his hands and gave a few hearty pumps.

"A pleasure to meet you, Mister...?"

"Wilson, Glen Wilson."

I admit I was star struck. I know these guys poop and puke like other human beings but still—Bunny Wilkins, his most famous role in Mobster's Honor, was a Golden Globe winner and a shoo-in for an Academy Award, if not this year then the next. Live and in person.

"A genuine pleasure to meet you, Glen. Are you in the business?"

"No, I just rolled into town on a Mexican's strawberry truck."

Bunny laughed heartily. "Very good, Glen. A strawberry truck. I assume you are a friend of Ridley's or Steven?"

21

"Not exactly, but I would like to stay for your party, Bunny."

Bryan whispered into Bunny's ear. A dark, unattractive, petulant cloud swept over Bunny's face. It took him a second to regain his good humor. He shook his head.

"A fucking dealer. Very funny. I'm meeting an actress being considered for my next film. She's not well known and won't be if I don't like her. This party is my way of getting to know her. Do you think you can be amusing and stay out of trouble for a few hours, Glen?"

A few hours? I'd never stayed out of trouble for that long, but I was willing to try. I shrugged and nodded.

"Fine. You can be an extra in our little production. You can even call me Bunny if you like. I'm flattered you know my work, but please keep in mind that was a fucking character I played in a fucking movie ten years ago. Got me? It was an acting job. I'm not really Bunny Wilkins."

Bryan flushed and hissed at Bunny. Bunny waved him off and poured whiskey from an expensive-looking bottle. "He can stay," he said tonelessly.

I slipped my suitcase behind the couch and grabbed more shrimp. The doorbell chimed. Bryan shot me a warning glance over his shoulder as he walked across the room. Having me around was not good for his blood pressure. I waggled a shrimp at him and popped it into my mouth before he answered the door and the party officially got started.

CHAPTER 2

Later on Wednesday May 12, 1982

The Party

Only 48 hours earlier, my idea of a party was a slab of beef ribs on the grill, a couple cases of Budweiser, and several hours of talking about the weather with the neighbors. I wasn't prepared for Hollywood glamour. It took several minutes to get used to talking about the weather with a famous face from TV. I met Ginger from Gilligan's Island and the second Darren from Bewitched. I met one of Hemingway's grand-kids, a stunning young woman who drank too much too fast and passed out in one of the bathrooms. I met Popeye from The French Connection and the guy who mixed up the fake blood poured on Carrie. I watched Superman smoke a joint.

Bryan spent the first part of the evening watching me to make sure I didn't stick a hand up Ripley's dress, but I was good, regaling all who would listen about Vietnam (I could see the draft dodgers sucking up my stories for use in stupid movies that would get almost everything wrong). Bunny's future possible costar, Alexis, was a former porn and soap opera actress; basically a nice girl from Scranton,

Pennsylvania underneath all the makeup. I instantly liked her and tried to warn her off the PSK but she'd try anything to get the part in Bunny's movie. Some stars drifted in and out. Steven and his people popped in for about ten minutes and Michael filled a jacket pocket with Bunny's Cuban cigars and left with a different woman than the one he arrived with. As the party wound down, there were six men and only two women. One of the guys was uninterested in the ladies and left a few minutes later.

Now the score was five to two. Bryan noticed this, and, as gracious host, made some calls. Twenty minutes later, all the guys had girls and all the girls had guys. Even me. I was introduced to a young lady named Korry with a K and two R's. Korry wasn't beautiful; she looked as if she had trouble sleeping. Dark circles under her eyes were partially disguised by hastily-applied makeup. She had a nervous twitch. Still, I liked her natural Wisconsin accent, which emerged after a couple of glasses of Scotch. She was good with voices and, while sober, claimed she could imitate any accent in the United States within a hundred miles. I couldn't get enough of her rude limericks as sung by the black maid from Gone With the Wind. I laughed so hard I almost choked on the lobster claw I chewed on.

It was nearly midnight when Bunny dimmed the lights and turned down the music. He changed into a plush Beverly Hills Hotel robe and pointed out that room service had brought robes for everyone. I helped Korry change. I undressed her and neatly folded her clothes and hung up her dress in a guest room. Before I could get the robe on her she raised her arms and did slow naked circles, moving her hips in time with the faint music. I liked her tan lines and didn't mind the faint stretch marks and liposuction scars on her belly. They only made her more real to me. She slipped into the robe and I tied the sash.

In the main room, Bryan nuzzled a blonde and Bunny paced. I guided Korry to a corner and slipped my clothes into my suitcase. The guests reclined around the room in their robes, watching expectantly. Bunny performed a speech from one of his movies, a preacher busy with falling from grace. I thought the role was an overplayed cliché, but, under the circumstances, I wasn't going to mention it. At the climax of his speech, he brought out the baggie of PSK and waved it under the noses of his guests.

"I have something very special for my friends. On good authority, this is the best stuff in the United States."

He glanced at me with a look I couldn't read. *A warning perhaps? Like this stuff better be damn good, or else?* I wondered myself. Doctor Zalooq had an interesting game going. For all I knew, I bought twenty dollars worth of animal tranquilizer and corn starch. My instinct, which was right often enough to keep me alive so far, told me otherwise. Bunny passed out makeup mirrors and straws cut into three inch lengths around. When he got to me he whispered in my ear.

"This stuff is expensive, might I convince you to refrain? You probably have plenty back in your apartment, or your pickup, or wherever it is you live."

I was happy to oblige. Bunny glanced at Korry sleeping in the corner with her head cocked at an unnatural angle, before continuing around the room. Bryan grinned at me and reflected lamplight into my eyes with his mirror. I flipped him the bird and leaned Korry on my shoulder to make her more comfortable. After the mirrors and straws were distributed, Bunny poured powder on each. The radio played *Life in the Fast Lane*. Bunny motioned for everyone to wait until Joe Walsh's guitar break, and then everyone snorted powder.

They sat around waiting for the kick. After thirty seconds or so, they wondered if they were missing something. They reminded me of fundamentalists on a mountain top a few minutes after the world was supposed to end. It was funny the way they wondered how long to wait before giving up and going back to pot or something they knew would work. The Eagles stopped singing and The Doobie Brothers started on *Black Water*. Bunny glared at Bryan, and Bryan shot me murderous looks, but the other guests looked amused. Five minutes after snorting the stuff, it hit. It started with itching, they must have felt like they were wearing heavy clothes in the Mojave because they couldn't shrug off the robes fast enough. Their bodies writhed like dolphins; wriggling and undulating. Their eyes rolled back in their heads and their mouths stretched wide. It started getting messy, so I carefully led Korry though the bodies and into the guest bedroom. I shut the door on them. I put Korry under the covers, smoked a cigarette and read a month-old Time magazine until I joined her in sleep.

The clock said seven when Alexis walked through to use the bathroom. When she came out I motioned for her to sit on the bed. Alexis glanced at Korry, and then averted her eyes. The satin sheet had bunched up. I covered Korry's nakedness and Alexis felt more comfortable.

"What was it like?" I asked.

"It was great. Like an endless rippling orgasm from head to toe. And I feel good now, my skin is tingly and I feel rested. That's great stuff. I'd ask for more, but I've got to get to work."

"Good luck with the part," I said softly.

She gave me a kiss.

"I'm sure I got it," she said while bearing a wry smile.

After she left I gently woke Korry and did what I could to give what I got. After, when she went to the bathroom, I relaxed and idly wondered why Alexis used the guest bathroom instead of the master. It hit me. I got up quickly and slipped on the robe. Outside, Bryan knocked on the master bath door.

"Come on, I gotta pee, damn it," he said.

I kicked the door open and we looked at Bunny slumped on the toilet with his works still hanging out of his arm. His face was constricted and he was very dead. Bryan turned to me.

"You bastard, this is your fault."

I wasn't going to argue with him. I pushed him into the shower and punched him in the belly as hard as I could. I ran to the bedroom, pulled Korry's clothes out of the closet, and pushed them into her arms. We rushed through the main room, stepping between the sleeping bodies. I grabbed my suitcase from behind the sofa and we ran out with robes streaming and bare legs pumping. We dived into the nearest taxi.

"Where to?" the driver asked.

"Just go," I said, "her husband came home early. Give him an address near your house," I whispered.

She called out an address in Santa Monica as I dragged my clothing out of my suitcase. As we struggled to dress, the cabbie got an eyeful, but Korry laughed. I helped her fasten her bra and button her blouse.

When the cab stopped at the corner she selected, she got out and kissed me through the window.

"Will you call me?" she asked.

"Probably not," I replied. She was hurt, I could see it in her eyes. "I'm sorry," I said.

Ken Coffman

"No problem, thanks for a fun evening," she said mistily. She waved once and headed south.

She was a beautiful sight, walking down Pico Boulevard with rumpled clothes, her bathrobe clutched tight to her breast and her hair a matted mess.

I gave the driver the address of Doctor Zalooq's place. I checked. Thankfully, the Mexicans were still asleep. I knocked at Zalooq's door. The place was dead silent. I tried the door and it was open. The place was completely empty, with just a faint smell of incense to remind me what it was like the day before. I walked through the place without finding anything interesting. In the kitchen, a dozen eggs and a quart of Hamm's beer waited in the refrigerator. I rinsed out a Mason jar and made a cocktail from eggs and the beer. I looked for Tabasco in the cupboards but found only mice turds and chewed-up boxes of macaroni and cheese. I carried my breakfast back to the taxi.

I got in, leaned back, and took a drink.

"Where to next?" the driver asked brightly. I think this was an interesting fare for him so far.

"The airport," I said.

"Which one?"

"LAX," I replied, while draining my beer. I looked over the city as the cab rolled. Bums and skateboarders, old folks wearing Reeboks and white slacks walking their dogs, whites and blacks and browns and yellows all going about their business in imperfect harmony. I didn't know what I would do next, but the drug business seemed like a good way to make a lot of money fast. It treated me well for most of the prior 12 hours. Zalooq said something about South America. That seemed like a good destination.

Somewhere in South America, perhaps Bolivia?

I was ready except for one small detail.

28

"Stop somewhere on the way so I can buy shoes," I told the driver.

"Whatever you say, boss," he said, grinning at me in the rearview mirror.

"Shoes," I heard him mutter. At stoplights, he scribbled in a notebook. I had the feeling that my life was being recorded for his screenplay. It didn't bother me.

"That's right, my man. I gotta get shoes before I go to Bolivia."

He thought about it, but didn't write that part down.

CHAPTER 3

Thursday, May 13, 1982

Los Angeles

Leaving On a Jet Plane

I found a postcard in a gift shop at LAX. Two pigs humping, Makin' Bacon. It was stupid, so I couldn't resist.

> Doctor Zalooq
> POB 1107
> West Hollywood, CA.

> Here's your scientific report, Doc. The subjects snorted about a tenth-gram. They got off good. There wasn't any hangover. Bunny Wilkins shot up, you can read about it in the paper. If I see you again, it will be hard to resist the impulse to kick your ass.

> Many Regards;
> Glen Wilson

I paid cash for an American Airlines ticket to La Paz and had a couple of hours to kill. Except for a nagging ache in my brain stem, I felt fine. For lunch, I bought a couple of hot dogs and a beer at a stand-up bar and leafed through the LA Times. From habit, I watched the crowd and picked out the undercover cops (the same faces a few too many times, clean jeans, and roaming eyes). Then I saw Bryan-with-a-'Y' appear by the Pan Am concourse. He was with a couple members of the Hollywood Mafia wearing slick haircuts, expensive suits, and Middle Eastern noses. So much for my plan for slipping out of town quietly. I wasn't sure if they wanted more dope, to beat me up, or both.

I found an old black guy cleaning the urinals who had an intelligent look on his face. His nametag said Chester.

"Hey, Chester, they told me I would find you down here." He took in my rumpled clothes, the dirty suitcase, and my lack of socks. "I'm the new guy and they told me you'd help me find a uniform and show me around."

"That ain't the way it works," he said.

I tossed a hundred into his garbage bag. Then I tossed in another. I had to toss in one more before I saw what I was looking for in his eyes.

"I guess I'm not going to argue with the genius's upstairs. But if you're gonna cause trouble...?"

I gave him my most innocent look. *No trouble here, boss.*

He didn't look convinced but three hundred bucks was probably a month's take-home pay. He led me to an "Employees Only" door and unlocked it with one of the 900 keys on his belt. We wandered through a couple of hallways and entered a locker room. He handed me a soiled set of overalls, a baseball cap decorated with the company logo, and a broom. He found a TEMP nametag and I hung it on my pocket. I stuffed my suitcase in the trash can on my cart and we went back to the public area. I spent a couple of hours pretending to sweep and picking up the shit people leave in the chairs. Magazines, soggy Kleenex, cigarette butts. People are such pigs. Chester wouldn't let me out of his sight, so when he went on break he took me with him. He shared hot coffee from a battered Thermos and I shared my Camels. The walls were stained yellow from the hazy smoke. He gestured with his cigarette.

"The do-gooders are going to make us smoke these things outside," he said thoughtfully.

"Bullshit," I replied. "They can't do that, this is a free country."

"You watch," Chester snorted. "Are you going to tell me what's up?" he said, changing the subject.

"Just trying to keep a low profile for a couple of hours."

"The dudes in the suits?"

I nodded.

"Hey, Marty," Chester called out to a security guard trying to shake a free Snickers bar from a vending machine. He'd had practice because he got one in about two seconds. They exchanged a complicated handshake. Marty looked at me suspiciously. I hadn't noticed before, but I was the only white guy in the room.

"He's alright," Chester said. "Did you notice the suits running around in circles today?"

Marty sat down. He broke off half his candy bar and gave it to Chester.

"Shit, Chester, you know the man don't tell us nothin'." Marty grinned and chewed his candy. "But I hear they's looking for a dealer."

"What do they want him for?" I asked. They looked at me sternly.

I'm just a temp, I guess I'm not supposed to talk.

"What do they want him for?" Chester asked redundantly.

"Killed a movie star," Marty replied.

"Who?"

"The guy that played Bunny Wilkins. You know... 'Don't make me cut off your little dickie'".

"You'd like that, wouldn't you."

"Yeah, punk. I'll mount the little fella on the wall."

They laughed at each other. The dialog was from one of Bunny's famous scenes.

"Bunny kicked off. I can't believe it. What did his last picture do? A hundred and twenty million?"

"Domestic. Another thirty million international."

This was LA. Even the airport cleaning staff knew the film grosses. This was as bad as listening to the Oregon farmers lie about the size of their damned watermelons.

"The radio said he died of natural causes, but the suits are looking for—a person of interest."

"Well shit, we better get some work done," Chester said, standing and putting the top back on his Thermos. "And if I see you around here again..."

"I'll cut off your stupid Mama's face."

Marty finished the quote and they laughed.

It was funny in a stupid sort of way.

I walked over to the candy machine and hit it just like Marty did but nothing happened. They thought that was funny too.

"White guys gotta pay," Marty called after me.

I pushed my cart around and even passed Bryan a couple of times. I'm always surprised at how invisible a guy wearing janitor's overalls can be. I dumped an ashtray at the departure gate as they started closing the door.

"Hold on," I said. The attendant looked up, startled. None of the suits were around when I produced my ticket and worked my suitcase out of the garbage. The attendant looked at me curiously as I wriggled out of the overalls and stuffed them in the can, but she took the ticket. Apparently, even in LA they haven't quite seen everything.

"Have a nice flight, sir," she said politely as she tore off my boarding pass and shut the gateway door behind me.

I handed out blankets and pillows to make room for my suitcase in the overhead bin. The plane was moving before I was in my seat, but I finally settled in. I ordered two doubles of Gin and Tonic and tipped the little bottles of Beefeaters into my cup. Did I mention that I don't fly well? The drinking takes the edge off the anxiety, or makes it worse. I've never flown sober, so I'm not sure.

Mr. Headache became bored while bouncing around in my skull like a firefly in a jar, so he amused himself by driving spikes into my temples, then shifted to jack-hammering my frontal lobes before settling down to repetitively stabbing an ice pick into the back of my eyes, all perfectly synched with the metronomic beat of my pulse. He liked a heavy backbeat, go figure. When that grew tiring, ol' Mr. Headache rang up a couple of pals, and by the time the plane reached cruising altitude I had a better than nodding acquaintance with Mr. Mouthwatering Nausea and his bratty brother, Gut-Wrenching Stomach Cramps. I hosted a power trio of pain, stomach cramps and misery and I hadn't even tasted South American tap water yet.

A rivulet of sweat worked its way into my left eye and I blinked it away, then wiped a hand across my forehead. The airsick bag lay within easy reach, teasing me while tucked into a pouch on the back of the seat. I eyed it warily, grateful for its presence but dreading the possibility of actually using the damn thing.

I studied the horizon through the tiny window. When that didn't distract me enough, I shifted my attention to the flight attendant's ankles. She wore a thin gold chain under her nylons and there was a crude tattoo above her ankle. Black pumps squeezed her toes into an odd sort of cleavage. I let my eyes rove slowly over interesting curves until our eyes met. Her figure was a bit overfull, but nice enough. Everything seemed to be in place. I wasn't completely snared until I noticed a scar starting at her left eye and curving up her head until disappearing into her black hair.

We shared a raised eyebrow and it felt like the leading edge of one of those magical moments that happen to people in romance novels and Hollywood screenplays. Maybe I'd soon be enmeshed in a crackling firestorm of adventure with this sultry Latin bombshell named, according to her nametag, Concépcion. Connie. I liked the sound of it.

I felt nearly alive when the plane dropped three feet while my stomach dropped only two, leaving my gut a foot higher in my chest than I generally keep it. I instinctively deployed the airsick bag and deposited drool before my ass fully settled back in the seat.

Mortified, I stared into the cheery yellow barf bag and contemplated the chances of latching my seat belt without spewing gin and peanuts onto fellow travelers. It seemed like a worthy endeavor, since another air pocket like the last could easily toss me out of my seat and into the lap of a startled neighbor, and I happened to be wedged between stoic Latinos who looked as if they could use a good strip search. They might be clergymen of course, bade by a greater power to go forth disguised as bitter and angry men with eyes empty of all but the glittery promise of a vicious response to the slightest slur, but I preferred to play the odds and assume they were cold-blooded killers returning from a blood-splattered convent assault.

I managed a hard swallow and a deep breath and fumbled for the seat belt without risking a lot of head movement, until a hand fastened the buckle for me.

Was it my imagination or was there more fumbling around down below than absolutely necessary?

Her fingernails were ragged under the paint. I risked a sideways glance at her ankles again. I'd never considered the possibility of a sexy ankle before that moment.

"The ride should smooth out soon, sir," she said sympathetically.

I could tell she was trying not to laugh. She had me where she wanted me: powerless and under her spell. Hers to abuse and discard. My misery retreated before an onslaught of surging hormones. I found a wry grin and tried it on. It felt okay so I looked into her face and said "Hi," before my tongue fled to its room, slammed the door and refused to come out again.

I earned a cold smile, which inspired me to attempt conversation. To forge into the breach, deploy the mains'l, split the face cards, turn into the slide and knock off a few epics before reality could wake up and fuck up my day.

"Ma'am, or please excuse me, is it *señorita?*"

Her body language announced a polite withdrawal so I rushed to delay her escape.

"I may live, thanks to you." No wedding ring on the finger, I noted. "Perhaps the magic of your smile is all one should ask of life." I raised my eyes to the ceiling and nodded wisely. "Yet, perhaps, this seeming need for moment is but only a light that shines on the way and illuminates so brightly the path. Perhaps a new path, and perhaps this path winds before us forever, to be travelled together, from this moment on, yet who is to say..." I allowed my voice to trail off. "Perhaps?"

I gazed at the ceiling, held my breath, and pondered the beauty and insight of the bullshit I'd just invented. With women, sometimes florid nonsense works. The killer clergyman on my left choked and sputtered a few words in Spanish that I didn't catch. Something about *cuentos de hadas pendejos*, a screwed-up fairy tale?

Her hand rested on my shoulder. A delicate trace of perfume, mixed with stale sweat, wafted as she leaned closer.

"*Señor*? You are poet?" She whispered the question.

I shrugged as I imagined a sensitive yet brilliant artist might shrug and shook my head in denial while locking my eyes onto hers. Her gaze widened, the tension grew, and she leaned closer yet. Her grip tightened on my shoulder and her lips practically brushed my ear.

"No," she murmured, "because there are no true gringo poets, are there? Your English, it rasps like monkey chatter."

She kneeled closer, with eyes only inches from mine, and I formulated a contingency plan that included the sad idea that I might sleep alone tonight.

"And then the lies, they flow like a river of shit, do they not? And you, *chi-chi cabron*, on your best day, are not half the man needed to get a hand inside my shirt."

I noticed she wasn't whispering anymore and that the plane had grown very quiet. She pulled away, long enough to check the aisle in both directions, and then leaned in again.

"*Comprende*, dickhead?"

I ignored poorly-smothered chortles from my seatmates and considered a response. I grabbed her forearm and pulled until her face descended and we were eye-to-eye.

"*Si, muy comprende, pica palos.*"

I inadvertently discovered a cure for air sickness and fear of flying. Rage. And she liked it; I could see it in her eyes. We had unfinished business. Some women want to be gently wooed and some want to be dominated. Some don't think they want to be dominated, but can't resist the pull. Even the killers in the neighboring seats were impressed. I pretended to sleep when she slipped her phone number in my shirt pocket. I was really sleeping when the movie started, but I didn't care because it wasn't one of Bunny's better ones.

I didn't wake until the plane banked hard and pointed its nose at the La Paz airport runway.

CHAPTER 4

Friday-Saturday, May 14-15, 1982

La Paz, Bolivia

Welcome to the Third World

The plane slewed so wildly that I couldn't believe it was under control. The pilot banked us into a narrow valley and we hurtled toward the ground like an owl diving at a mouse. Suddenly, I realized it was a very bad idea to go to Bolivia.

There was no real reason for traveling to Bolivia except, back on the farm, my beloved and gentle Alpacas were born there so I was sure it must be a good place. However, Ernesto Ché Guevara was killed there. Supposedly, Butch Cassidy and Sundance were killed there. In addition, it looked like Glen Wilson would be killed there too.

Seeking sympathy, I searched the cabin for Connie, but she ignored me while helping a *campesino* with his seat belt. She chattered in one of the Indian languages while gesturing at the No Smoking light flashing over his seat while he sucked his cigarette down to the last millimeter. The 737 bounced a couple of times and slewed eerily before solidly settling on the runway.

I'm not afraid of dying, but I'd prefer to slip away in bed next to an exhausted cheerleader instead of being ripped to pieces in a plane crash. However, I'd escaped again. The plane's nose pointed toward the ground as the pilot slammed on the brakes.

I couldn't wait to get out of the aircraft. I wanted to grab my suitcase and run out to kiss the dirty streets. With only a small amount of shoving and cussing, I was the first one at the door. I took the stairs of the jetway two at a time and hurried toward the terminal when I discovered that I couldn't breathe. My head throbbed and I felt like hurling every meal I'd ever eaten.

Was this it? I'd survived the maniacal pilot and his airplane of death to collapse from a heart attack on the tarmac?

Passengers walked by as I hunched over trying to get a lungful of air. I overheard someone say the word *saroche* which apparently described a gringo gasping his guts out and dying in enormous pain thousands of miles from home. I staggered through the customs inspection (which consisted of an amused teenager dressed in a baggy green uniform with an old carbine slung over his shoulder waving me through). A young man dressed in blue jeans, sandals, and a leather jacket tried to take my suitcase and I was almost too sick to put up a fight.

"Guide, señor? *Tener roster?*" he asked.

"Doctor," I replied.

He led me to the street where an ancient, muddy four-wheel drive truck waited. A few miles down the paved road we turned on a dirt trail and stopped at a cantina. Several ragged-looking men smoked pipes and looked thirsty. Inside, a young girl in a bright blue dress served hot, bitter tea. After a couple of cups I felt much better. My guide's name was

Francisco; I called him Cisco and he didn't seem to mind. With his fair English and my broken Spanish, we communicated. La Paz sits at an altitude of 12,000 feet and the air is thin. I should have laid off the gin on the airplane. I was startled when I found out the tea was made with coca leaves, *mate de coca*, but Cisco convinced me that it was the right medicine for *saroche*, or altitude sickness.

The *tener roster* was his four-wheel-drive truck. He was quite proud of it. It looked barely held together with baling wire and mud, but I wouldn't insult the man who just saved my life. I made life-long friends by buying *pisco sour*, a thick and nasty-looking purple drink (Cisco wouldn't let me drink any, not that I was tempted) for the old guys hanging around outside. After a couple of hours, Cisco staggered to the *tener* and drove me into the city. After several near-death experiences on the roadway, he dropped me off at the Residencial Rosario. I gave him twenty bucks and made a date for the next day.

The room was cold and I asked for extra blankets. I splashed water on my face from a basin, collapsed, and slept like a dead man for sixteen hours.

I woke slowly and for a few minutes couldn't figure out where I was. I heard Spanish though the walls, so, for a time, I operated on the theory that I was still in LA. The decor looked more like Tijuana but it seemed very cold for Mexico. I remembered bizarre dreams of wild dancing by masked people in colorful costumes. *Diablada*, devil dancing.

It occurred to me I was in South America. I laughed off that absurd thought, but it kept returning. I staggered to my feet. Through a small window, I could see an Indian woman squatting on the narrow street selling colorful knit hats. She was wearing 14 layers of dresses and had an odd

British-style bowler hat perched on her head. Bolivia. What the hell was I doing in Bolivia?

If I ever see those Alpacas again, I'll kick their fuzzy asses.

I pulled on my shoes (I still had no socks) and, clutching my suitcase, walked down a couple of flights of stairs to the hotel restaurant. *Mate de coca*, that's what I needed. And keep it coming, *muchas gracias*.

I noticed an older gentleman reading an English language newspaper, the Bolivian Times. He didn't want to talk to a wild-haired gringo with dirty ankles, but eventually stopped pretending that he didn't speak English and put the paper aside. He worked for International Telephone and Telegraph and was in town to sell microwave communication systems to the government.

I asked him about the coca tea and felt better when he told me that the Indians chewed coca leaves and drank the tea for several thousand years with no problems. The Spanish tried to ban it hundreds of years ago, but found they'd have to feed the silver miners more and dress them better to ward off the cold. It was cheaper to let the natives chew the coca leaves, so the conquistadors and the Catholic Church conveniently decided to make one exception and took over the coca business. When Mister IT&T concluded I would continue asking annoying questions, he popped the last of his toast and marmalade into his mouth, dropped a handful of Bolivianos on the table, and walked out.

I looked through his discarded Times, sipped bitter tea, and tried to decide what to do with my day. I didn't feel too bad as long as I didn't move too fast. I ordered starchy soup called *chairo* and tried to smoke a cigarette, but my lungs complained so much that I stubbed it out. The day stretched before me like a blank canvas. My stomach complained about the altitude, but I was ready to do what ever it was that came next.

While I pondered, I watched the people walk by. The native women were mostly short and round and wore elaborate dresses and odd hats, either bowlers or straw. The men were smaller and seemed to be drunk. There were plenty of people in western dress: high heels, nice dresses and men wearing suits and ties. Occasionally a cop or soldier would stroll by, look me over, make a mental note and carry on. It seemed, if I left them alone, they would leave me alone, at least I hoped so.

The vehicles were a mix of stake bed trucks, busses, vans, taxis and small sedans, most of which burned a lot of oil. I watched a huge woman set out low stools on the sidewalk. She lighted a small gas stove and cooked some kind of stir-fry. I suppose flies are added protein, but I didn't think I'd be patronizing her 'restaurant' any time soon. I felt cold, dizzy and sick, but wasn't in too bad of shape. I had $22,000 in my suitcase and it felt strange to be in Bolivia, but life can be funny, eh?

Midmorning, I was joined at my table by a short and wiry fellow who helped himself to my tea and cigarettes. He wore a nylon windbreaker that said Miami Dolphins and a baseball cap that said Ford. Like the IT&T guy, he was unimpressed with my dirty ankles and soiled clothes, but he was not too clean himself as his collar was dark with grime and his fingernails were broken and filthy. His English was good, considering.

"*Americano?*" he asked.

"Yes."

"*Negocio?*" Business?

"Tourist," I replied.

"My brother has a taxi, perhaps you'll have a tour?"

"Maybe later, I'm not feeling well."

"When did you arrive?"

"Yesterday."

"You'll feel better tomorrow."

"Thanks," I said, though I'm not sure why. Perhaps I thanked him for giving me hope.

"Political?"

"No, tourist."

"We can use your help to overthrow our imperialist oppressors."

"Who are *we*?"

"C-O-B, Bolivian Workers' Union."

I was ignorant of South American politics, but I knew there were more political organizations than people, so either the Alpacas were members or people belonged to more than one organization. I didn't care much.

"Tourist."

"Ah," he said, as if I had not already told him this. "Donation?"

"I'll take whatever you can give me."

This took a moment to sink in, then he gave me a thin smile.

"Humor is a luxury we can ill afford here in Bolivia. Only rich Yankees who steal our minerals and oil and punish us for growing the coca your people demand can laugh at times like these. Perhaps you will stop laughing if I open your stomach?"

He showed me a glimpse of his knife. It was rusty and I didn't want to die of tetanus. I pulled a handful of Bolivianos from my pocket and pushed them over. At the same time, I waved at a cop walking by. My new friend palmed the money and turned to see who I was looking at.

"See you around, gringo," he said as he slid my pack of cigarettes into his shirt pocket.

The cop eyed him and me. I shrugged and returned my attention to my tea and the next time I looked both the cop and my revolutionary friend were gone. I didn't have anywhere to go, but I was tired of sitting at the cantina, so after visiting the toilet (perhaps I should start a business importing toilet seats, as, outside my hotel, I had not seen one yet) and paying the bill, I wandered up the street. The sidewalks were steep in places and I was breathless after a block or so. I sat on a bench and immediately a woman and her son brushed dirt off my shoes and applied something that looked a little like polish.

I searched my memory and came up with what I think is the Spanish word for socks, *calcetin*. This word, combined with pointing at my bare ankles and offering two American dollars resulted in an eloquent speech by mom to the kid and his running off at full speed. He came back with two pairs, one a hideous argyle-style and the other a very nice hand-made pair woven from gray wool. I waved off their chewing gum and necklaces and eventually they wandered off so I could enjoy the warm socks by myself. I needed a nap, so I gathered my strength and made the three-block journey back to my hotel. Barely.

When I woke, the sun was a pale ghost hovering over the rooftops. The wind had picked up. I felt only 80% dead, so I decided I needed nightlife. A nice dinner, beer and perhaps a lady to help ward off the chill if I could find one that didn't look too much like Humpty-Dumpty. The lady at the reception desk hailed me a taxi who took me to place called *Tetecos*. I froze in the cab because the temperature dropped like a rock after sunset.

45

I liked the look of the bar. There was a charming mix of locals and tourists so I felt safe. I was warm and the drinks, in funny metal bowls, kept coming. I chewed on leaves being passed around, and panpipe music swirled in my head like audio fantasies. I'm not saying this to make excuses; I was high and this was one of the best evenings of my life. I don't remember everything clearly. I danced with a cute Spanish-looking lady and her college girlfriends. I bought drinks for the house once, twice, or three times. I did not keep count. I remember the cold night, stairs, a strange room, and having sex with two girls for an hour before my soul exploded through my manhood and I was absorbed by the night.

I woke to rapping at the door amplified, in my head, to an earth-shattering pounding. I still had green leaf in my mouth; a disgusting wad I couldn't completely spit out. The room was filled with bright light that speared my brain like a screwdriver. I was nude. No matter how many times I said *Go Away!* the monster hammering at the door would not leave.

I sat up and found most of my clothes. I was happy to find my new woolen socks. I pulled them on along with my shorts and pants, then answered the door. I was in a cheap room I did not recognize and I talked to an irate lady who didn't understand my English or broken Spanish. She clearly wanted money, so I looked through my clothes. I had a few American dollars and a wad of Bolivianos in a shirt pocket; once I handed these over, she gave me a dirty look, but left me alone. At that point I realized how much trouble I was in. In my search for money, I did not find a wallet, a watch, a passport, visa, or, worst of all, my hotel key. A search of the floor under the bed, the bedding, the drawers and the small bathroom resulted in a cache consisting of one partial package of Bolivian cigarettes, a book of *Tetecos* matches, a lady's costume jewelry earring, and beer bottles. One of the beer bottles had a few swallows in it, which I chugged. I felt marginally better.

I staggered downstairs and gingerly tapped the bell on the reception desk. An old man came out. I asked him for *aspirina*. He handed me green leaves and a pinch of baking soda. *Was this their answer to every ailment?* At that time, I hadn't figured what the leaves were, but I wasn't getting aspirin, so I chewed the leaves and they didn't make things worse.

I walked outside and noticed the difference immediately. I was invisible. The day before I could not walk ten steps without someone trying to sell me hats, soda pop, chewing gum, or goat flanks on a stick. No longer did I look like a customer. My eyes were bloodshot, my clothes were dirty, and I staggered from wall to wall blending into the background filth.

I found my way back to my hotel with a feeling of doom hovering around my head. The receptionist looked at me like I was dog shit on a sandal, but I managed to get on the elevator before she shooed me away. My room was being cleaned and was completely empty. The thieves took my suitcase and even all my toiletries, everything. I was six thousand miles from home, hell, I didn't even have a home. I had no money, no papers, and no hope. I was at the bottom and even today, I'm not sure why I didn't just jump out the window.

Ken Coffman

CHAPTER 5

Sunday, May 16, 1982

The Bottom of the Bottom

On the street, amid short, brown men, I wandered from place to place with my eyes on the ground as if hoping no one would register my insignificance. I'd been broke before, but there was always someone I could call or a temp job I could take for quick cash. Here, I could not even make eye-contact with the passing crowd.

As the day passed, I observed the mechanics of a few things. For example, if a guy hovered behind the fat lady's street restaurant, she'd hand back a few scraps left over from an order. It wasn't much and she'd run you off if you abused the situation, but a guy could get by.

I began to see a few folks I recognized, like the cab driver that brought me in from the airport, the soldier/cops on the beat, and even the COB activist who'd hit me up for cash over breakfast (was it really only yesterday? It seemed like a lifetime ago). I noticed the COB guy was cozy with one of the cops and went out of his way to avoid the rest. I didn't know what it meant, but it was interesting and I had nothing else to do, so I followed him. At one stop, I overheard his name: Carlo. He picked things up from one place and delivered them to another. It wasn't dope. It appeared to be notes, brochures or letters. I must not have been a good shadow because I got caught.

"Papers? *Papel*? *Pasaporte*? *Visado*?"

I turned and found Carlo's *policia* friend with his hand out. It occurred to me that, instead of tailing a Bolivian revolutionary, I should have stopped by the U.S. Embassy to see if they would help me.

Oops.

"I have been robbed, so I do not have papers and I do not have money."

He patted my pockets to be sure, but eventually believed me. A few dollars would have satisfied him; the penalty for vagrancy could be settled on the spot. He consulted with Carlo and they made a decision. My problem with finding a place to sleep was solved. I was going to the San Pedro jail.

I laughed when they checked me in. Though they produced a canvas bag for my personal items, there was nothing to take and the bag was filed away empty. I still had to sign a property log.

Being in a La Paz jail is not bad as you can imagine, it's worse. I shared a cell with an unconscious man who reeked of alcohol and vomit. His breathing was ragged and intermittent. He didn't stir when I took his woolen sweater. I almost felt guilty, but it was damn cold; the walls were concrete and stone and they sucked the heat from my bones.

We had a window, for which I was thankful. Through rusty bars I looked out into an alley. The alley was shared with a bar or restaurant, because it hosted a constant parade of inebriated men pissing against the wall. For myself, I pissed into a pipe that poured out into the alley. I was not sure what I was supposed to do if I needed to take a dump, but I was highly suspicious of a reeking bucket in the corner. They brought food for us and I helped myself to the drunk's portion. Added together, it was almost enough. The meal was a tin plate of greasy stew. When I asked, the server said it was *plato tipico*, which was not helpful, because everything she brought was called *plato tipico*, regardless of what it looked like. Perhaps it means leftovers in Aymara, I don't know.

The guards thought I was a very funny man. I know because each time I asked for a lawyer or a phone to call the embassy, they laughed. I always asked and they always laughed. I'd been in the cell for a day when my roomie woke up. He vomited into the pipe. Silly me, I thought the place could not smell worse. The fellow spoke fragments of English, which I appreciated. We didn't get much chance to get to know each other because as soon as he realized where he was (he was so out-of-it, this took a while) he shouted for a guard. They argued in a language I didn't understand, but the end result was his discharge. When I talked to the guard, he said "Law 1008" and pushed me back in the cell. Later, that same guard came out and unlocked the cell door. He didn't say a word, just unlocked the chain and left. This was odd and it took me a while to gather the courage to venture out.

I thought the jail consisted of my cell housed in a crappy part of town, but it turned out that this part of town *was* the jail, the whole city block. I'd seen kids and women wandering around and there were the usual street vendors; the place looked like many other rundown neighborhoods. I was not paying attention when I was checked in or I would have noticed the inmates were literally running the prison.

As soon as I left my cell, a fellow named Fernando gave me a tour.

The place was highly segregated. The area where the drug lords were housed looked great. These guys had everything to outfit a good hotel: apartments with real doors, televisions, refrigerators, mammas and children, and squat, ugly fucks who made sure only the right people climbed the stairs. At the other end of the spectrum were drug addicts and child molesters, they slept on threadbare blankets laid on the cobblestones.

Kids were allowed out to go to school, otherwise, they were all over the place. I was introduced to the boss and they made sure I knew he was one-not-to-be-fucked-with. They showed no curiosity about me, apparently they knew everything they needed to know. My brain could not process what I saw. This prison had open access to drugs, alcohol, whores, food, clothing and everything else if you had money, which I didn't. Some people made leather sandals and carved Incan-looking figures. I could make a very little bit of money doing that but it looked like hard work, which is not my style.

After my tour, I found an out-of-the-way spot and settled down to watch. Fernando was in charge of tourists who came for a look at the prison. His guided tour was much like the one he gave me, but more colorful. The place had a hierarchy and a rhythm. The only thing I saw that troubled me was a new inmate beaten with a chain and thrown down a flight of stairs. Fernando would only say the guy was a *carbon y garcon*. I guess they don't like child molesters here. The guy, sobbing and bleeding, crawled into a corner and no one paid him any further attention.

I asked Fernando what it would cost to break out of this place and he laughed. He said my bail was set at $200 because no one gave a shit about me. I was a long way from $200, but it seemed achievable. After more *plato tipico* for dinner (Fernando made sure I noticed him writing in a notebook, I accumulated a tab that would have to be paid someday), I snatched a filthy blanket from an unconscious doper who had two.

I did an inventory. I had shoes, lovely, warm Bolivian socks, grimy American clothes (including briefs that were a third-world peril all by themselves), and my wits.

Would this be enough?

My overheated mind worked at the possibilities as I drifted into sleep.

CHAPTER 6

Monday, May 17, 1982

Nowhere To Go But Up

I traded my American shoes for twenty Bolivianos and a pair of sandals, so I had a small stake. The currency inflation was so outrageous that it took a big pile of Bolivianos to buy anything, and the pile would be noticeably bigger each day. This was scary, but there was nothing I could do about it. I needed to start somewhere.

After buying an incomplete deck of American playing cards and three packs of bubblegum, I convinced kids to play 'find the Queen'. From my days as a carny, I knew the point was to randomize the cards so the odds the rubes saw, regardless of where they thought the Queen might hide, was always precisely one-to-three. It took time and I nearly tapped out a few times, but eventually I reliably worked the odds to my favor and accumulated a large stash of bubblegum in a canvas bag.

Slowly, I began playing for small amounts of money. I would set up my box at 9:00 at night and close down at 11:00. Eventually, men lined up and were ready to play when I opened. Regardless of the sad lessons of history,

53

men, spellbound by the payout, could not resist my doubling their money 33% of the time. Stubbornly, they thought they could beat me. Business was steady. As long as I didn't play too long each day, they'd come back the next. I had competition of course, people who wanted to emulate my success, but I'd make little jokes, make a big production of the payouts, and give a free try now and then, so I developed a loyal clientele and my imitators eventually gave up.

Slowly, my situation improved. I bought back my shoes (they looked funny on the *campesino* with short pants and no socks). I acquired a knife and a suitcase. The pleasure of the suitcase surprised me. I now had a place to store my stuff and it made me feel better, I don't know why.

The boss of my section was a cheerful *mestizo* named Joaquin Zenteno. Predictably we called him Joe. He was a stocky man about five-foot-seven. Missing several teeth, his grin was a story unto itself. I paid Joe fifteen percent of my take and got an upgrade in living condition. I slept on a cot in a room with several other men. With blankets and a pillow, I was in heaven. In addition, Joe didn't kill me, so it was a fair deal.

There was competition for control of the regions of the prison and occasionally I was harassed by a squinty-eyed doper; an unpleasant political named Epifanio Verezain. Epifanio thought he should run gambling on the ground floor where I worked. Trouble brewed. Epifanio and Joe would exchange words and Epifanio would back down, but he'd be back the next day.

The dopers in this prison were generally low-level middlemen short on cash to bribe their way out of trouble. They dipped into their product, skimmed too much of the bosses money, diddled the wrong girl, or had some other sad tale to tell. Some of the guys in the upper-floor apartments still ran their business from jail and had plenty of cash to show off. They could get out, but found it safer and more convenient to stay in. I'd been involved with dope when I was in Vietnam, so I knew the ins and outs. You could make a lot of money in a short time, but you always relied on others to carry the dope or the money, and eventually one would succumb to greed or get turned by the cops, and this caused trouble. Trouble I grew tired of dealing with. Plus, many customers died and I had trouble being cynical enough to take their money and their lives.

The politicals constantly lectured or complained about one damn thing or another. Usually, they were obsessed with historical oppression by the Spanish Catholics, the European upper class, or the evil *Nort Americanos*. They spewed endless, tedious, Marxist rants.

I know Ernesto Ché Guevara was murdered in Bolivia by the army in 1967, please excuse me if I don't give a shit. I have a game to run.

Things slowly improved. I could afford a haircut and better food. I was shocked after finding out the leaves I'd been chewing were coca. I was not a big fan of narcotics. *I'm high on life, baby.* However, coca in this concentration had been used for thousands of years and there was no particular hazard. We *Nort Americanos* created our problems by concentrating this shit into cocaine and crack. When something becomes illegal, you condense the product so it weighs less and is easier to transport. If you're smuggling a pound of something, you might as well smuggle a pound worth $100,000 instead of a few dollars.

Who cares if this new product is deadly poison to the consumer?

That's not the starving farmer's problem and it's not the *narco-trafficante's* problem either. If you're dumb enough to use it, too bad for you.

I collected all the money I needed to get out, but decided to stay in until I had a plan.

Eventually, the turf war became a problem. One night, Epifanio came up after I shut down my game. His friends had beat up Joe. He shoved Joe against the wall by my table and stood, looking at me. The message was clear, Epifanio was the new boss and I would pay him instead. I counted out fifteen percent, but Epifanio gestured that he wanted more. I counted out another five percent, but Epifanio pushed me against the wall and held out his hand.

Then he made a mistake. He slapped me. I pulled my knife out of my belt and jammed it, upward, into the center of his diaphragm. The blade was about seven inches long and it easily tore a large hole in his heart. A cheap knife, the blade broke off when his body spasmed. Epifanio tottered on his feet for a few seconds and then fell over backwards. His friends looked at me and at Epifanio's quivering body, then quietly wandered away. Joe gathered the money, counted it, and handed me back my five percent. He stood staring for a minute as if he'd never seen me before.

"Steel waters run dip, *amigo*," he said respectfully in a thick Bolivian accent.

He gathered a crew and hauled Epifanio's body off. I expected repercussion from the guards, but nothing happened. Apparently, they accepted the story that he accidentally fell on his knife while cutting up potatoes.

That knife thrust was no accident, I was educated as an Army Ranger and almost made it through the whole training regimen until I had a problem with a Captain that ended when I was forced to beat the crap out of him. The result was

30 days in the Army brig and a transfer to infantry. It took hard conniving on my part to get my rifleman role changed to a safer back-line logistics assignment in Saigon. From my Ranger stint at Fort Lewis, I knew about knives and where to place a lethal blow. I also knew about other weapons, including Rocket-Powered Grenades, shaped charges, and hand-to-hand combat of various styles. These skills were handy from time-to-time. I'd already killed a few people and I suppose it's psychopathic to not care too much.

We're all tiny spokes in the big wheel.

Besides, I tried to kill only the most deserving.

I bought another knife and noticed other prisoners treated me with more respect and deference. Otherwise, my business was the same and I gathered strength and saved money. About the time I decided to buy my way out and grab a taxi to the embassy to see what I could do to get new papers, I received a visitor.

Just before dinner, the rhythm of the place changed. Mommas herded children to their rooms and corners of the courtyards. Things got very quiet. I noticed a small European man dressed in western business clothes (light-colored suit, tie, and trenchcoat) and a Tyrolian hat walking around with four mean-looking bodyguards. I had not seen a lot of guns beyond the old Argentine rifles the guards carried and the M-1 Garands the cops slung their shoulders. These bodyguards had holsters and carried large revolvers.

I sat on a five-gallon bucket eating *anticuchoes* (beef heart on a stick), drinking *pisco sour* and enjoying life. As the man and his entourage came through the compound, there was far too much gesturing in my direction. Soon these five men stood in front of me and looked me over.

I took an instant dislike to him. He had a superior manner for which I've never had tolerance. In the military, you're supposed to respect the rank, not the man. I could never do that; if you're an idiot, I don't care what hardware you carry on your shoulders.

At five-foot-seven and balding, he was a weasel of a man with a hatchet face. His eyes flicked like a caged cat. He spoke clear English with a slight accent. He was about 70 but seemed younger. This was unusual because life can be hard in Bolivia and most people age rapidly. He pulled over another bucket and sat. He looked at me; weighing and measuring. I felt like a supermarket cantaloupe being molested by an old woman on a low budget. With a finger gesture, the bodyguards lifted me, patted me down, extracted my new knife from my belt and plunked me back down on the bucket. This took about three milliseconds.

"My name is Klaus Hansen. Now you will tell me your name."

The guy was cold, like a robot. He had a European accent. I placed him as originally from either Germany or Austria.

"I'm Wilson, glad-to-meecha." I held out my hand to shake. He looked at it until I pulled it back.

"Why are you here?"

"My wallet was stolen. I had no money, so they brought me here."

"No, why are you in Bolivia?"

"Tourist." I said.

I didn't see the command, but I was lifted, held against the wall, and slapped a few times by a guard with a huge wen on his nose. Apparently, telling this man what he wanted to hear was more important than the truth. They plunked me back on my bucket. My nose bled. I dabbed at it with my shirtsleeve.

"Why are you in Bolivia?"

58

"Tourist."

Lift, press, slap, plunk. Now both nostrils streamed. One of the bodyguards pulled a sweatsock filled with damp sand from his pocket. I got the message. If I didn't produce suitable answers, there would be real pain. I had the feeling they had experience with beating answers out of the helpless.

"Why are you in Bolivia?"

"Go fuck yourself."

Why do I do these things?

I was angry of course, but I could have spun a bullshit tale that would satisfy this asshole and save my skull a fracture or two. Unfortunately, the Glen Wilson road is not always the easy road. The sweatsock started an arc toward my head, but Hansen stopped it by gesturing with a finger. He reached in his jacket and pulled out my wallet and passport. He flipped through the pages.

"Glen Wilson of Medford, Oregon."

He tapped my license against his teeth and made a decision. One of his goons opened my suitcase and packed in two large bundles wrapped in newspaper. Hansen handed me my passport, wallet and a three-by-five card with notes scribbled on it.

"You will deliver these packages (he pointed at the suitcase) to this man (he pointed at the card). The man will give you eighty thousand dollars and you will come back here and give me that money in three days. My phone number is on the card. You will call me when you get back. For this, I will pay you five-thousand dollars."

It was not exactly a question, but he sat there and looked at me expectantly.

I shrugged and said "Okay."

With that, Hansen slipped my license into the wallet and dropped it on the ground. He and his men got up. Wen-face patted me on the cheek, pointed to his sweatsock, and said *"Chaucito"* which I translated to something like: *My blackjack will enjoy breaking your face later, little man.* Cute. By the time I'd come up with a suitable reply, they were gone. For the record, I was going to call him a *cretino malnacido rata de al cantarillo* which translates to something like an idiotic sewer-rat bastard. I memorized it in case I might use it later.

Hansen poisoned the atmosphere in the jail, so I didn't do much business that night. Besides, I was distracted and fluffed the card movements; it wasn't a good night for making money. I needed to decide what to do. I could dump the dope and run. Or, I could follow instructions. The card had phone number and said Miami. The smart thing would be to leave Bolivia and not come back. I had my passport and money.

Unfortunately, the smart way is not always the Glen Wilson way. I owed something to Hansen and his crew. My karma was skewed and I needed to deliver unto their wickedness to get back in balance.

The next morning, I did not even pay my fine. I stood by the front gate until a group of tourists came for their tour. Then I slipped out. The guards looked me over, but did not say anything. This could have been related to the Hansen visit or perhaps I could have walked out at any time, I don't know.

I stood on the street and looked back at the San Pedro prison. I felt a loss. The place was easy and once I had a job and money, it was comfortable. Once accustomed to the squalor and the prison caste system, it was an easy ride. I'd been in jails on three continents and this was the oddest I would ever see and the only one I could imagine coming back to willingly. Through a dirty window covered with corroded iron bars, I caught a glimpse of Joe. He waved and I waved back.

I lifted my suitcase, hitched up my pants, and walked through the city. I would spend my last night in Bolivia someplace where the shower had hot water that was actually hot.

CHAPTER 7

Monday, June 14, 1982

The Last Night of My First Visit to Bolivia

I looked and smelled like a Bolivian sewer rat. If you've caught a whiff of the river that flows under La Paz, you'd be impressed with how bad that can be. However, I had money, so I rented a room in the *Presidente*. I sent what was left of my western clothing to the laundry and took a long shower. I wore three pounds of dirt and it felt good to wash the filth away. I talked the lady sweeping the hallway, Dona Bella, into bringing me *saltenas*, *cervesas*, and cigars. I sat on my small balcony wrapped in blankets smoking a cigar while planning strategy for returning to the USA.

I could dump the coke and head for LA, but I'd already decided not to take the easy road. This decision was made when I was ten. My business with Señor Hansen was unfinished. Besides, why risk my life to steal 80 grand when I could risk my life and steal more?

I unwrapped the dope. It numbed my gums, so I knew it was real. After working through language difficulties resolved with a stack of Bolivianos, Dona agreed to bring one-kilo bags of sugar from the kitchen. I carefully wrapped the sugar bags in newspaper so they matched the packaging of the coke and carefully packed them in my suitcase.

My work for the day was done, so I set out to find dinner. I thought about going back to Tetecos; to see if I could find my old friends, but decided to save that for later. As I exited the hotel and tried to decide which direction to go, a small Spanish-looking fellow offered me a cigarillo. I was happy to accept and he lit me up. He told me his name was Pedro.

"*Nort Americano?*" He asked.

"*Si, yanqui,*" I replied.

I was curious about his game, so I talked with him. I'd seen many scams on the streets of Saigon and run a few when I needed money. Pedro was a fast talker skimming over the weather, football (soccer) and little jokes about *Presidenté* Reagan. A fellow dressed in police-brown stopped and flashed a tattered card.

Pedro grabbed the card and pretended to inspect it closely, and then nodded and said, "Yes, sir, yes sir," before handing it back.

I didn't get an opportunity to take a look at the 'official' identification. Probably a Bolivian library card if such a thing existed. Pedro produced papers and the 'cop' examined them in great detail, and then looked at me expectantly. I pulled out my wallet and handed over my Oregon voter's registration card. He looked at us angrily and told us that we would have to accompany him to the *officina*. A taxi pulled up. It was one I'd been warned about. *Never get on a Bolivian taxi that does not have a phone number emblazoned on the side.* The 'cop' herded us into this outlaw taxi. These guys were slick.

In the taxi, while the 'cop' riffled through my wallet, I shoved my palm into the back of the driver's neck. He cracked his nose on the steering wheel and the taxi slammed into a parked car. I smashed the 'cop's' nose with my elbow and landed a quick blow to Pedro's Adam's apple. This took about three seconds. I grabbed their wallets, the rest of Pedros' *cigarillos*, and was out of the taxi in an instant.

Briskly, I walked down the avenue a few blocks. That was as far as I could go, as I was still not used to the thin air and those steep streets. As I walked I extracted papers and cash before discarding their wallets in the trash on the sidewalk. Finding a cantina, I caught my breath and enjoyed *masaco* (stringy beef with plantains) and a few *cervezas* purchased with the scammers' money.

Afterward, I read a discarded English language newspaper and enjoyed more of Pedro's tobacco. For some reason, a nice meal bought with stolen money tastes the best. Like taking a dump on government time. Fewer things in life are sweeter.

Glen Wilson is back on the street. Crooks and loose ladies pay heed.

Back in the United States of America

The next morning I roamed the hotel hallways until I found a couple that met my needs. They looked religious and straight. I overheard them talking about traveling to Miami the next day. He was about 40 with a tight belly indicating an inflamed liver. She was younger, a bit stocky with hennaed hair and elaborate eye makeup. I liked the way her breasts rebelled against the restraint of her woolen vest. They called to me for liberation.

It cost me twenty US dollars, but the desk clerk allowed me access to their bags while arguing with them about a mysterious entry on their bill. It took two minutes to pack the coke in one of their suitcases and jot down their Fort Lauderdale address.

While waiting for a taxi to collect them in front of the hotel, they were targeted for the birdshit scam. I could it coming, so I positioned myself at the edge of the building. The way this works is: something that looks like pigeon shit is dribbled on your shoulder. A helpful person points this out and helps you clean it off. While you're distracted, your bag disappears. It takes about five seconds.

The man with their bag walked quickly but unhurriedly toward me. As he reached my corner I caught him in the chest with a roundhouse swing of my suitcase. He went down like a bag of rocks. I liberated their camera bag and left the thief writhing on the cobblestones. He'd have broken ribs to deal with, but nothing serious.

Mrs. Tourist, named Ellie Brown, was grateful to have her bag back. Things happened so quickly, she didn't even realize it was missing. Mr. Tourist, Roger Brown, looked at me sourly. Mrs. Brown was so grateful that she offered me a ride to the airport in their taxi, which I found ironic. Ellie spent the time in the cab pressing her substantial hips into mine more than I thought could be caused by the twisting and turning of the death-defying cab ride.

Roger looked out the window and refused to meet my eye. The international airport is in El Alto, a slum about 1000 feet higher than the metropolitan La Paz. La Paz is dirty, but El Alto is beyond dirty.

I bought a round-trip ticket with cash. The customs inspector read a folded newspaper and didn't look up as he stamped our papers. Our LAB DC-9 was only an hour late taking off and seemed to linger a long time on the runway before struggling into the thin air. We banked to the north and I bade farewell to my first visit to Bolivia. I was seated several seats behind the Browns and occasionally Ellie turned to catch my eye. Unless I'm mistaken, an invitation was offered.

Interesting.

I leaned my seat back and caught fitful sleep. I was mostly unconscious until the plane hit the runway in Miami. It felt good to be back in the USA.

As I picked up my suitcase from the carousel, I watched the Browns pack their luggage onto a baggage cart. They breezed through customs, but the inspector wanted to have a chat with me.

How did I know this would happen?

I just did. The little room off to the side was straight out of the 60's, all linoleum, flickering fluorescent lights and cheap, metal folding chairs. A customs officer, his supervisor and a DEA agent looked over my plane ticket, my passport stamps, and my customs declaration.

"You're sure you have nothing to declare?"

I motioned for them to hand me back the form and I slowly added four cigarillos to the list, accounting for the remainder of Pedro's pack. They examined this revision carefully. I took the form back and crossed out the four and wrote three. Then I lighted one. They didn't like this. Rougher than necessary, they patted me down and threw my pocket change and chewing gum on the table. I had a few hundred dollars in my wallet, but they didn't bother with it.

"Do you mind if we open your bag?"

"I'd rather you didn't," I said slowly as smoke drifted from my mouth.

They smirked, opened my bag anyway and sorted through my stuff. They passed knowing glances while removing the newspaper-wrapped packets.

"What's this?" Mr. DEA asked with eyes dancing.

I slowly took back the customs form and wrote in 'four pounds of granulated sugar'. They unwrapped the newspaper and looked at the sugar bags. With a pocket knife the DEA guy slit open the bags. He poured the sugar on the table. He took a taste.

"Sugar," I said.

They didn't like this. Conferencing in the corner, they considered their options. They didn't come prepared to plant coke on me, which took advanced planning. They dumped my suitcase on the table and sorted through my underwear and toiletries. They broke up my cigarillos and looked for anything inserted. They squeezed out my toothpaste and emptied my can of shaving cream. After an hour of this, the DEA guy snorted and left.

"Okay Wilson, you can take off."

I slowly threw my stuff back in the suitcase and left the mess of shaving cream and sugar on the table for them to clean up. I walked out of the terminal into the blazing sunlight of Miami. The air was thick and humid. I waved for a cab, gave the driver the Brown's address and settled in the back seat for a nap.

Ellie

I paid the driver and stood on the sidewalk in front of the Brown's place in a lower-middle class neighborhood. They lived in a stucco rambler with green rocks in place of grass. An old Taurus was parked on their oil-splattered driveway. The drapes were pulled tight and newspapers were strewn across the porch. I wondered why the place hadn't been burgled, but I saw neighbors peeking through their curtains.

Neighborhood watch. A lot of retirees don't have anything else to do. I knocked on the door and Roger answered. I could see my packages on their dinette table; they'd found the stash. Ellie sat at the table snorting a line; her nose was frosted. Roger looked resigned. He was clearly a fellow who had seen trouble and did not like it.

"So, it's you. I told Ellie someone would come." He gestured for me to enter. "Please don't hurt us," he said. "We're LDS missionaries. We do good work and we don't want any of your problems."

Ellie came up behind Roger with a golf club. It looked like an old three wood. She took a three-quarter swing and hit Roger on the back of the head. He fell like a sack of potatoes.

Perhaps Ellie's commitment to Mormonism was less than rock-solid?

"Don't stand there, help me tape him up," she said, proffering a roll of duct tape. I did her bidding. Her reddish hair was loose and she wore a fluffy pink bathrobe showing freckles on her substantial (and interesting) cleavage swelling beneath Mormon underwear.

"I don't want you to get the wrong idea about me," she said, while sipping from a can of diet Pepsi. "I love the church and the Lord, but sometimes I long for the carefree days of my youth. When I met Roger, he had a Harley and he took me away from Podunk Hell, Idaho. We had good times, but more of those good times would kill us, I know that. Jesus saved us from that life. Praise Jesus. What we're doing here is wrong, very wrong. I'm weak and it's wrong for you to take advantage of that. You're a sinner."

I wasn't in tune with her yet, but I thought it might be safer if she wasn't clutching the golf club, so I eased it out of her grasp and tossed it into the living room. She had a touch of madness in her eyes I'd not noticed before, probably liberated by the coke. She was jittery and on the edge of hysteria.

"That's great coke," she said. "Uncut. Beautiful." She seemed to notice me standing there again. "I've forgotten your name..."

"Wilson."

"Okay Wilson, you're going to fuck me like I haven't been fucked for a long time. I know this. It's wrong, but you give me no choice, I have to bend to your will or you'll kill me with the golf club."

I thought of reminding her that *she* was the one who whacked her husband, but I didn't bother. She shrugged off her robe and peeled off white garmies. I could see pubic hair curling from under her panties. She was supposed to wear her panties *over* her Mormon garmies, but I did not mention it. She took the trouble to dye her private hair too. I appreciate that sort of attention to detail by a woman. She took my hands and placed them on her breasts. They were warm and heavy. She could stand to lose thirty pounds, but she wasn't grotesque yet. Not at all. This might have been part of the point. In another decade she'd be matronly and sloppy. Even a less-than-fussy man like me might not want her. But for today, she'd do fine. More than fine. She closed her eyes eased her head back.

"Please don't kill me, I'll do whatever you want," she whispered.

"I'm not going to kill you," I said while massaging her breasts.

"Shut up," she replied, "and tear my panties off."

Who am I to argue?

She leaned back on the floor and spread her legs over her husband. This seemed more than passing strange and not especially comfortable because my legs ended up bent backwards, but if that's what the lady desired.... She wanted it rough so I spanked her ass and bit her nipples. She came twice before I let myself go. I went to their bathroom. The toilet seat was covered with lime-green carpeting. From a framed picture, Jesus watched me take a much-needed piss. When I came out, Ellie worked on patching up the coke bags with duct tape; she stuffed them into a Safeway grocery bag. She was still naked. I put my arms around her and kissed the back of her neck. Weeping, she turned and pushed the grocery bag into my hands.

"You're going to steal our car," she said. I shrugged. She handed me the keys. "We won't report it missing until tonight. I suppose you'll want Roger's passport?"

I nodded.

Why not?

She walked with me to the front door.

"Wait," she said a desperate edge in her voice.

I turned and looked at her.

"You have to bind me up," she said, holding out the duct tape.

I taped her up and gave her a kiss on the forehead as I ran a finger around a nipple. She moaned and thrust her hips against me.

"By the door there is a book. Take that book with you," she said through clenched lips.

The book was The Book of Mormon. I have nothing in particular against the LDS folks, they are just as normal (and as screwed up) as everyone else. I opened the book at random and read.

For they shall not lead away captive the daughters
of my people because of their tenderness, save I

*shall visit them with a sore curse, even unto
destruction; for they shall not commit whoredoms,
like unto them of old, saith the Lord of Hosts.*

Too heavy.

I tucked the book into Roger's arms. "He'll need it more than me."

I ground the starter for a while before their shitty Taurus would start. It passed a burp of blue smoke; this thing would need engine work soon. As I drove off, I pondered.

Was it just me?

Weird things happened. I saw one of the neighbors writing in a notebook.

Were they making a note of their neighbor's license plate?

I waggled my fingers.

Parked at a stop sign, I fished Hansen's card from my wallet. My next stop was in Miami. It was time to trade the coke for eighty big ones. I found salsa on an AM radio station and, whistling along, made my way south.

CHAPTER 8

Tuesday, June 15, 1982

Becky

I checked into The Rest Inn on the Dania highway. The room was stifling, but the noisy window unit air conditioner soon cooled the place. I drove to the Rainbo Café and ate a massive plate of chicken-fried steak with French fries. I left the Brown's car on the street with the keys in the ignition and walked back to the hotel. In that neighborhood, the car would sit no more than a half-hour before someone would take the bait.

By the time I arrived back at the room I was sweating. My body was used to the bone-chilling cold of Bolivia. The next step was to deliver the coke to a man named Enrique Del Castillo. I looked up his address in the phone book to make sure I knew where I was going. His address was in North Miami Beach.

While looking through the phone book, I accidentally stumbled on the escort service section where Becky Peeks caught my eye. Though I'd just enjoyed the creamy thighs of Mrs. Brown, I felt a spiritual connection with this girl. I don't know which I was most interested in: classy and sophisticated companionship, her skills as erotic masseuse, lingerie model and private dancer, that she was a 22-year-old working her way through college, her adventurous attitude, or the line drawing that emphasized glorious 36C assets. I could afford to pay a hundred-bucks-an-hour for sophisticated companionship.

I called and left a message and she called back twenty minutes later. She was unimpressed with The Rest Inn, but agreed to stop by. I walked down the street to the Circle-K and bought a half-rack of Coors and a big bag of Cheetos. Room 216 was now party headquarters. When Becky knocked on the door, I was ready. I swept the door open with a grand flourish.

I should have known. Becky was decades beyond being any kind of college student. She had frizzy brown hair, garish eye makeup, black net stockings with snags, and wore a Madonna-style corset, leather belt, and a short skirt.

"So much for truth in advertising," I said.

I left her in the doorway and sat on the bed.

"So? You don't look like the playboy businessman you said you were," she replied defiantly. "The Rest Inn, fer Christ's sake," she said caustically.

She had a point. I tossed a can of beer that she snagged out of the air. After entering, she shut the door and sat in the only chair in the room, an old nagahyde-covered thing scarred with cigarette burns.

"Okay Becky, what now?" I asked. "I'm sure as hell not paying you a hundred bucks an hour."

"Alright, big spender. Fifty an hour with a two-hour minimum."

I thought of something. "Do you have a car?"

"Yes."

"Is it a Taurus?"

"No, it's a Delta-88."

"Are you available by the day?"

"Sure. I'd have to make a few calls, but I can get free. Five hundred a day."

"Three hundred."

"Cash in advance and you fill the tank."

"Done. Did you bring exotic massage oils?"

"No, but I brought Jergen's hand lotion." She fished in her handbag and pulled out the tube.

"Okay," I said. I pulled money from my wallet and tossed it to her, then took a pull off my beer and loosened my belt. "You're on the clock baby, so get to work."

Enrique

I bought Becky breakfast at the Rainbo. She polished off a large helping of biscuits covered with sausage gravy. A girl works up a big appetite with exotic massaging. Afterward, we drove around until we found Enrique's address. The place was a bar in a run-down Cuban neighborhood.

"What kind of business do you have here? I know this place, it's not safe."

"Don't you worry your pretty little stretch marks over it, Becky. Keep the air conditioner running, I'll be back in a flash."

The bar had low ceilings. The lighting was dim and I was blind after coming from blinding noontime sunshine. Carrying the cocaine in the Coors box, I stood in the doorway until I could get my bearings. The bartender read a Wall Street Journal and smoked a pipe.

"Enrique?" I asked.

The bartender pointed to a group playing Foosball in the back. I watched them play for a minute; they were way too good at it. Dressed in sport jackets over wife-beater T-shirts, their wrists were marked with prison-style tattoos. In current fashion, they wore elaborate necklaces decorated little silver coke spoons.

"Enrique?"

"What about it?"

The speaker had an effeminate feathery strand of hair snaking down his back.

"I have a package to deliver from Señor Hansen."

That got his attention. He stopped playing and looked me up and down. He took the Coors box, placed it on a table and gestured for his partners to frisk me. This was done with unnecessary roughness, particularly where my *cojones* were concerned, but I said nothing. Enrique sat at the table and opened the box. He noted the Bolivian newspaper as he unwrapped the packages. After dipping his spoon into one of the bags, he took a snort. He nodded and they took the packages to the back room. Not wanting to let the dope out of my sight, I followed them.

After weaving around stacked cases of beer, we entered a small office. Enrique sat behind a desk and stared at me. I didn't have anything better to do so I stared back.

"Hansen?" he asked.

I nodded. "Hansen."

"You're late. I expected you yesterday."

"The delay was unavoidable."

"And you're here to pick up fifty?"

"Nope," I said. "One hundred."

Enrique laughed. "Why don't I save the money by cutting open your belly and feeding you to the sharks in Biscayne Bay?"

"Because Señor Hansen would be upset with you."

He spent too long considering the merit of my argument, then nodded. He swiveled in his chair and dialed the combination into a large antique safe. He pulled out bundles of cash and stacked them on his desk. Eight bundles.

"Eighty," he said. I nodded and packed the money into my Coors box. "See you next week, *mulo?*"

Mulo. Mule. "Is that the way it works?" Enrique nodded. I put the box under my arm. "Until then, I guess."

In her Oldsmobile, Becky painted her toenails and listened to the radio. I had her stop at 7-Eleven where I tore a page out of the phone book. We spent an hour looking over private mailbox places. I found one I liked called The Mail Stop. Inside, I had a pleasant conversation with the owner, a brown wisp of a man named Efrain. I rented a box using Roger Brown's ID.

Back in the car, Becky buffed her fingernails with an emery board.

"Take me to Miami International," I told her.

On the way, while stopped at a traffic light, a bum with a damp cloth smeared bugs and dust on Becky's windshield. He was white and roughly my size. I put my head out the window and asked him if he wanted to make two hundred bucks. He jumped in the back while Becky gave me a withering look. The guy smelled like a rupture in a Caribbean rum factory. I passed him a hundred dollar bill.

"I want you to fly to Bolivia and back."

"Is that by San Diego?" he asked.

I nodded.

Sure it is, pal.

At the airport departure gate, I gave Becky a peck on the cheek and a C-note for a tip. She gave me a card with her pager number on it.

"Call me when you're back in town," she said.

"Sure, baby," I replied.

I led the bum into the terminal and looked for an out-of-the-way bathroom. He was older than I first thought and was not very bright. I trimmed his hair and beard with scissors from my shaving kit and mopped at his armpits with wet paper towels. He still stank, but didn't make my eyes water so much. I dowsed him with Old Spice and dressed him in my clothes. If you didn't look closely, he'd pass for me. I got a boarding pass from the Lloyd counter and led him to the departure gate. I put the boarding pass and passport into his pocket.

"You're Glen Wilson, got it?" I told him.

I don't think he *did* get it, but I thought my plan might work anyway.

I went to the Lloyd ticket counter and loitered until the clerk that served me earlier went on break. I gave the new clerk Roger Brown's passport and bought a round-trip ticket.

My plan was in motion. I was headed back to La Paz as Roger Brown. I had eighty thousand dollars packed in my suitcase and access to a private mailbox. I had a clueless bum flying as Glen Wilson.

Why?

I wasn't sure but it felt right. Layer upon layer. I napped until the boarding call and watched my bum to make sure he got on the plane. I almost felt sorry for him. He had a one-way ticket to a foreign country he knew nothing about.

Glen Wilson works in mysterious ways.

CHAPTER 9

Wednesday, June 16, 1982

Back to La Paz

I walked off the plane. My Roger Brown passport got me through customs without any problem. Airport security watched for someone and I had an idea who. I stood near the front entrance and waved off kids selling chewing gum and carved figurines. My bum was hustled into a corner where unformed security folks screamed and waved weapons at him. They didn't believe he didn't have luggage and tore at his pockets in their search. I'm sorry, but guys like him are expendable. The money I gave him may have been enough to buy his way out of trouble, but I wasn't hanging around long enough to find out.

I hailed a cab. The driver suggested I try the *Residencial Rosario*. Not wanting to go back to the *Presidente*, I agreed. At the hotel restaurant, I slurped warm tortilla soup and enjoyed a couple of *cervesas* before going to my room and sleeping for a solid fourteen hours.

In the morning I ate banana-filbert pancakes and sipped strong coffee. The thin air teased a headache in the back of my head. Otherwise, I felt great. From the lobby I called the number Hansen gave me and the man on the phone said he'd send someone to get me. While sitting in the lobby, I tried with limited success to read a discarded Spanish-language newspaper. The country was in turmoil. Military and civilian governments jockeyed for control. This had been going on for several hundred years as far as I could tell. The driver found me and we went uphill from the business district on *Calle Yamacocha* to a white stucco building on the hillside overlooking La Paz. The view through the haze was interesting. I looked down on jets streaming in and out of the airport.

Señor Hansen came into the sitting room and gestured for me to sit.

Have I mentioned that I don't like this guy?

I opened my suitcase and stacked bundles of cash on his desk. With a nod of his head, he gestured for his assistant to take the money. We sat and looked at each other for five minutes before the assistant came back and placed an adding machine tape in front of him. Hansen studied the numbers.

"You're a few hundred dollars short," he said.

"I had expenses," I answered.

"Expenses come out of your end."

"Fifty-fifty."

Hansen looked as if I suggested something obscene.

"No."

Responding to another head gesture, the assistant left, and then came back with a small stack of money that he handed to me. I leafed through the bills, it was a few dollars over four thousand.

Hansen opened his desk drawer and handed over my passport.

"You appear to have resourcefulness," he said. "Who was the unusual man at the airport who held your passport?"

"My passport and plane ticket were stolen in Miami," I said.

"Stolen?" Hansen said skeptically.

"Stolen," I replied.

"We will give you four kilos this time."

"I'm done with all that."

"You will deliver four kilos to Enrique and you will pick up one-hundred-and-fifty thousand dollars. Of that, I will let you keep twenty thousand."

"I'm not doing this."

"And we'll split expenses 50-50 this time," he said with a thin-lipped smile.

I wanted to grab his big floppy ears and smash his face on the desk.

"No."

"And when you come back, we will do a deal that will make you one million dollars."

I stood up.

"Deliver the dope to my room," I said.

I held out my hand to shake on the deal. He hesitated, but gave me a limp handshake. Our relationship was making progress. His driver took me to my hotel and I strolled to the Witches Market on *Calle La Gasca*. I did not buy candles, sweaters, soft drinks, fruit, or dried llama fetuses, but I did find a sturdy box and strapping tape that I purchased and hauled back to the hotel.

When the coke was delivered, I packed it in the box and sealed it up carefully. I took a taxi to the DHL office, filled out the customs forms, and shipped it to the mailbox, care of Roger Brown in Miami. I was exhausted from walking the steep streets and I felt slightly sick. Better than the last visit, but ill just the same. I was so tired and queasy that I almost decided to stay in my room and sleep.

Instead, I hailed a taxi from the Rosario lobby and told him to take me to *Tetecos*. It wasn't far, but I did not feel like walking. The driver dropped me off on *Sagárnaga* about 50 meters from the front door. Standing in the doorway, I scanned the crowd. It was early but there were a fair number of tourists, military-looking men in fatigues, and a knot of locals dressed in western clothes dancing to the Pina Colada song performed on pan flute, guitar, and conga drums.

I tried to get comfortable on a reed mat and ordered *saltena* and a lukewarm Pacena's *cervesa*, which I nursed as I watched the crowd ebb and flow. I would avoid the powerful drinks in bowls this time. I felt *tranquilo*. Mainly I watched pretty Argentine girls dance in fashionable miniskirts. I tried to figure out which of them played a part in my earlier debacle in this club. I bought coca leaves and baking soda; soon my mouth was numb and my brain raced as I worked the soggy mass between my lip and gum. The world became brighter and more pleasant.

As the evening wore on, I saw how things worked. The girls would bring bowl after bowl of liquor to their target, then they would stumble out together. An hour later the girls would come back and sort through wads of money and loot. Watches and cameras were handed to little brown boys who ran off at full speed. The girls kept some of the cash, but most of it went to a hard little man wearing tight trousers stuffed into black leather boots.

He had a pock-marked face and sat erectly. I overheard him called the Colonel. I recognized a couple of the girls, but it could have been my imagination. Everyone had a good time singing and drinking and dancing. Approached by ladies several times, I waved them off. I was not ready. A few hours after midnight, I laid my head on the table among the empty beer bottles and pretended to pass out.

Isabel was one of the prettier ones. She massaged my shoulders and tried to get me to drink an oily bowl of *Chicha de Manín* (peanut liquor) that I accidentally spilled on the concrete floor. She had bobbed hair with dyed blond streaks. She wore a short knit skirt over fetching black leotards.

She said she was from Brazil and I told her I was from New York City.

Fair enough.

I invited her to my room and she insisted on seeing my room key. She showed it to the Colonel and he nodded. Though I had gone easy on the alcohol; the coca, beer and altitude made me feel disconnected. My limbs seemed to belong to someone else. On the street, she supported me, but I refused to get into a cab. She didn't like this, but the hotel was only few blocks downhill. Draped around each other, we slowly made our way.

The glacial elevator carried us to my floor and Isabel got the door unlocked. I sat on the edge of the bed and she pulled off my shoes and lowered my pants. Disconnected from my body, I drifted around the room and watched from near the ceiling.

Under brighter lights, Isabel was older than I thought, at least 30. I looked pathetic with my pants around my ankles and my shrunken penis laying on my thigh like something dead. Isabel chewed coca leaf paste and rubbed the spitty mixture on my dick. From the effect of chewing the stuff, I didn't think this would do anything, but instead of more numbness, I felt the familiar, welcome tickle. It was a miracle. A reincarnation.

Her breasts, once released from her blouse, were larger than advertised; an attractively solid, doughy perfection in my hands. Her skin was salty and sweet at the same time. She was either an accomplished actress or I woke her hot Latina blood. She moaned and shivered for a lusty eternity. It was so good that I floated down from the ceiling to get closer to myself.

After I came (and came and came), I almost made a mistake. I almost fell asleep. The void settled like a soft blanket. There are inflection points in your life where things can go in alternate directions. I could see the path. I would wake up in an empty room both broke and broken and it would be back to Mamma's kitchen for hand outs. But, close as it was, that's not the path I took.

I groggily sat up and tugged my wallet and watch from Isabel's hands. With tousled hair, she sat and looked at me with her blouse hanging off her shoulders. There was a soft tapping at the door. I got up and looked for a weapon. All I could find was a shoe. I gave Isabel a stern look and stood behind the door. She opened the door and the Colonel came in. While he sized up the situation I slammed him in the head with my Buster Brown Oxford.

This stunned him long enough for me to tie his hands and feet with neckties. I searched Isabel's beaded handbag, but did not find anything useful, just a wad of money and a nice silver lighter that I put in my pocket. I jerked my head at the door. She needed no convincing; she was up and out with a quick flash of sooty eyes. I enjoyed the sight of her wriggling bottom and saggy black stockings as she trotted down the hallway.

I splashed water on the Colonel. He sputtered and wriggled as I searched his pockets. He had military ID and a huge wad of American dollars, Bolivianos and Argentine pesos. I relieved him of a nasty blackjack; a short piece of teak with an iron weight in one end and a stout leather strap on the other. I gave him a sample tap with it on his kneecap. My grasp of Spanish is poor, but I caught the drift of his invective. *Chigara de madre* and that sort of thing. Uninventive.

What was more interesting was his litany of names. I assumed these were people who would be my mortal enemies if I didn't immediately take well-deserved medicine from this important Colonel Osvaldo Dorado. Pedro Fiebelkorn, *Generale* Vildoso, Roberto Suarez, Alvaro de Castro, Klaus Hansen, Pierluigi Pagliai, Emilio Carbone, and Celso Torrelio were names I sort of recognized, but the Colonel recited a whole phone book.

Now I had an angry Colonel for an enemy and ten hours to kill before my Lloyd flight took me from Bolivia again. When I grew tired of the Colonel repeating himself, I hit him in the back of the neck with the blackjack and he was quiet. Still breathing, but blessedly quiet.

I packed my suitcase with the four kilos of *Unagro* S.A. sugar wrapped in newspaper. I thought about napping, but I figured there was a good chance that Isabel would return with reinforcements, so I got the reception desk to call for a cab and I went to the airport eight hours early. I found a semi-quiet corner, tilted my hat and slept with one eye open for a few hours.

You don't know much about me because I haven't been fully open. Sure, you know I abandoned my wife and made a few trips to Bolivia for some reason. Let me explain. I'd seen the movie about Butch Cassidy and the Sundance Kid and liked the scene at the end where the Bolivian soldiers overwhelmed the two anti-heroes. Also, I'd followed the escalating drug wars in the newspapers, so I was not completely ignorant of Bolivian politics and South American current events in general. The people I talked to that were active in the drug business told me that things would heat up in South America and that a lot of money could be made in this new frontier. I craved action after hiding out in Oregon for so many years. So you see, my selection of Bolivia was not completely random.

I had to decide if I would grab Hansen's $150K and disappear. That might be the smart thing to do. However, I had not forgotten the beating I took in the San Pedro Prison and I could not forget the insulting little traps Hansen set for me. Every time he tried to trip me up, my karma got more out of balance. And a million-dollar payoff should be considered. There would be risk associated with money like that, but I could handle it.

Was Glen Wilson a guy who gets exploited and ravaged by an old Nazi?

I was curious about that.

I was the first in line for the flight to Miami. I'd gotten good at sleeping on these long journeys and the next thing I knew we were on the ground in Miami.

CHAPTER 10

Thursday, June 17, 1982

Miami

Again, I was pulled from the line at customs and led to the examination room. I knew the way. Inside, I found the same mismatched pair of DEA and Customs officers. This time I noted their nametags: the DEA guy was Morales and the Customs guy was Bartholde. I put my suitcase on the table and sat on it. In a loud and insistent voice I told them that I wanted to see their supervisors.

"Do we have your permission to search your bag, sir?"

"Yes, but only when your supervisors are in attendance."

"Do we need to restrain you?"

"I want to see your supervisors."

The DEA guy tried to push me off my bag, but I kept hollering. Before long, the Customs supervisor, Garcia, poked his head in the door to see what was going on.

"These assholes are violating my civil liberties. I demand the DEA shift supervisor be in attendance when my bag is searched. This is an outrage."

"We will cuff you if you don't cooperate," Morales said. "We have a right to search your luggage."

"I know. You can search my suitcase when the DEA supervisor joins us."

"Shit," Garcia said. "Get Stephens."

"But, Boss," Bartholde sputtered.

"Just do it."

Bartholde gave me withering look as he left the room. Fifteen minutes later, he came back with a large black man in tow. I knew Stephens, in fact I worked for him in 'Nam. Master Sergeant Steve Stephens. There was a flash of recognition in his eyes, but he did not comment. He knew me well, so I suppose it goes without saying he didn't like me much. Sink or swim, I was on my own.

So it goes.

"What's the situation?" Stephens rumbled.

"This guy wants supervisors present during the search of his bag," Garcia said.

"Wait," I said, "before we look at my stuff, please check the pockets of your men."

"Now wait a minute," Morales said.

"I will cooperate fully as soon as you look in their pockets," I said, looking sternly at Stephens.

Stephens was an asshole, but, unless Miami had corrupted him, he was a straight-shooter. He was honest after Vietnam, so I didn't think Miami had a chance. But, how could I be sure?

"This is preposterous," Morales said.

"Humor him, then we can get on with our day," Stephens said.

He looked questioningly at Garcia. Garcia shrugged and nodded. They turned out Bartholde's pockets and found only keys and chewing gum.

When they turned to Morales and he said "Alright, already," and tossed a packet onto the table.

It was a half-kilo wrapped in a Spanish-language newspaper.

"Would you excuse us please, Officer Morales?"

Unhappiness was written on his face as he left the room.

"Did you know anything about this?" Garcia asked Bartholde.

Bartholde did not answer; he stared at the corner and would not meet anyone's eye.

"Shit," Garcia said. "Now can we look in your suitcase?"

I hopped off the table and gestured that they were welcome to it. It took fifteen seconds for them to find the eight pounds of sugar. Garcia lined up the packets neatly on the table.

"What's this?" Stephens asked.

"Granulated sugar," I replied.

Stephens looked at me sourly. He motioned for Bartholde to cut open the packages. He tasted a sample from each. "Did you claim this on your customs form?" he asked.

I produced the form and handed it to him. He glanced at the paperwork.

"Okay, Wilson," Stephens said. "Get the fuck out of here. The next time you stir up a ruckus on my shift, I'm going to plant on you myself, do you read me? Fly through Atlanta or Dallas or LA, not Miami."

I loaded the sugar in my bag and closed the latches.

"Sure, Sarge." I replied.

I wasn't exactly sure what the story was. I was being tested, probably by Hansen, to see if I was capable of handling a big job. Either that or they were screwing with me. Mules were caught when they got complacent and ran the same scheme over and over. You could disguise yourself as a priest or fill crutches with coke once. I planned to use a different approach for each load.

The best way to bring in a shipment is via diplomatic pouch, but that took connections I did not have.

I rented a minivan at the National counter. My first stop was at a La Quinta where I rented a room and called Becky's pager. She called back and told me she could join me in an hour. When I told her to take a shower first, she cussed and hung up. I sprawled on the bed, smoked a cigar, and waited for the complete massaging to start.

When Becky arrived, she was squeaky clean; her hair was slightly damp. She hadn't bothered with heavy make-up after her shower, which suited me. After she relieved me of built-up tensions, we watched TV and sipped beer the desk clerk sent up. All-in-all, it was a perfectly pleasant evening except Becky took the remote and insisted that we pick a show and watch it all the way through without clicking around. I fell asleep anyway, so it didn't bother me.

Women, what can you say?

Friday, June 18, 1982

Miami

I had lurid dreams where I floated and looked at the world from high in the sky. In Vietnam, I sensed realities buried in realities; as if the game we thought we played was merely a smokescreen. I had the odd feeling the drug trade was more complex than it appeared.

Why should it be?

No reason, but my mind works at combinations and permutations until the formula is factored. It's always

simple, just follow vortex of money and power. Once you
know the players and the rewards, everything falls into place
like a cosmic jigsaw puzzle.

I poked Becky until she roused. We had breakfast at a
Denny's. I needed to collect my package at the Mail Stop.
We drove back to the room and picked up Becky's Delta-88.
I had a good rapport with the Mail Stop owner, Efrain,
facilitated by a hundred dollar bill. Becky would open the
lockbox and turn in the slip to collect the package. Efrain
would substitute an innocent, abandoned package he had
stashed in the back. The DEA, watching the lockbox from an
RV parked across the street, would converge. They would
grab Becky in the parking lot or follow her and see where
she took the package. She looked like a courier, so they
decided to follow her. While they were busy on a tour of
Miami Beach, I slipped in and picked up the real package.

It went smoothly. I drove around scouting for a good
place to make the exchange with Enrique. Five hours later, a
worn-out Becky appeared at the room. By that time, she was
hot, frazzled and grumpy. Her package was filled with
canisters of Kiwi shoe polish, an errant shipment from
Philadelphia. The DEA guys were unhappy, but they cut her
loose.

From the motel room, I called Enrique at the bar. I
could hear the billiard balls cracking in the background.

"Allo?"

"Hello Enrique. I have another package for you from
Señor Hansen."

"I don't do business over the phone. Bring the package
here." He said business like 'bees-nest'.

"We'll do things differently this time. I want you to
send someone to make an exchange."

"No, you come here."

"No."

He was silent. With the phone at my ear, I watched Becky fix her make-up and fluff her hair.

"Okay. Where?"

There must be a serious problem with the supply chain, otherwise he not agree to my plan. I would not be comfortable until I figured this out. I explained when and where I wanted the drop to take place.

"Enrique?"

"Si."

"I am giving you my personal assurance that the package is complete and untouched. You will hand over one-hundred and fifty thousand dollars. No games. This is me and you."

I listened to dead air for part of an eternity.

"Okay," said Enrique. Then he hung up.

I left Becky in the room and drove to Eagle Arms and Collectables where I bought a pair of binoculars and a Marlin semi-automatic .22 rifle. I convinced the clerk (by peeling off more cash, of course) to sight-in a 10X scope for me. This was too much scope for the rifle and the clerk tried to get me to buy something heavier like a 7.62, 30-30, or at least a .223. I didn't convince him I knew what I was doing, but he soon gave up his argument.

Back at the mall, after the construction crew left for the night, I set myself up on the top floor of a parking garage 200 yards away. 200 yards is a long way for a .22, but I was loaded up with solid (not hollow point) ammo so the shells would not tumble. I sat and watched the parking lot until dusk. Becky pulled under a floodlight and parked. Through the binoculars, I watched her buff her fingernails for 45 minutes.

A shiny Suburban cruised the parking lot, and then parked 30 feet away. The windows were tinted, so I could not see inside. It was riding low on its springs, so I figured there were at least three or four big guys inside. After a minute, one of Enrique's crew came out with a nylon sport bag. Becky came out with our grocery bag. I watched her carefully; I was surprised at how cool she appeared. They made an exchange and drove out from opposite sides of the parking lot. Smooth.

I was back at the motel room in fifteen minutes. Becky appeared ten minutes later after driving a wide loop around town to make sure she was not followed. She tossed the bag on the bed and turned on the TV with the remote. I opened the bag, which was filled with paperback books. This was okay, because the bag Becky handed off was filled with the bags of sugar. I walked out on the street to call Enrique from a pay phone.

"Hey Enrique."

"Did someone tell you to play games with me? I'll slice off your face and feed it to my Dobermans."

"Herr Hansen will not be happy to hear you're trying to cheat him. He might take it personally."

"Let's do this deal, alright?"

"That works for me. Same place, same time tomorrow?"

"Why don't you make the drop yourself this time?"

"I'll think about it. Make sure to send the money this time."

There was a click and the line was dead. I strolled back to the room.

Becky examined the split ends in her hair. "If I have to do this again, the price goes up."

"Hey, I'm on a low budget. I can pay a hundred more, but that's about it."

Becky fluffed up the pillows and leaned back on the bed. She kicked off her Keds.

"I have a feeling about you, Wilson," she said. "You won't let them hurt me?"

"Stick with me and everything will be fine," I promised. Beer cooled in our ice bucket. I tossed her one. She turned up the volume on the Movie of the Week.

"Is Mork and Mindy on?" I asked.

"No, that's on Thursdays," she replied. "Shush, I'm watching this." We fell asleep in front of the TV like an old married couple.

Saturday, June 19, 1982

Miami

I don't like repeating things, but I was too lazy to find a different place for the drop. Besides, the setup was perfect. I had a good view of the approaches and it would be difficult for anyone to sneak up behind me. The setting was isolated so I could fire and still get away. Part of the reason I picked the .22 was for its relative quiet.

Through the scope, I watched Becky work on her eyes with an eyebrow pencil and eyelash curler. The Suburban parked at the same place. The same guy came out with another sports bag. Becky came out with her grocery bag.

Looking into the lens, I had a sense of hyper-reality. In sharp contrast, I could see butterflies and their shadows. I glimpsed something shiny in the courier's hand. I didn't hesitate before aiming carefully and squeezing off a round.

A large hunting knife skittered across the pavement. He dropped the bag to cup his injured hand. Firing rapidly, I punctured the SUV tires and scanned the scene. Becky dropped the grocery bag and grabbed the sports bag. She was perfection in motion; she didn't run, quickly she slid into the Delta-88 and reversed out of the parking lot.

One of the windows in the Suburban eased down and I emptied the chamber of the .22 into it. This took fifteen seconds and by that time Becky had accelerated to the street. I discarded the .22 and hit the road myself. The entire exchange took about a minute.

I figured Becky would want something stronger than beer, so I stopped at a package store and bought a fifth of Johnny Walker and a quart of ginger ale. I fixed her a tall cold drink with lots of ice and handed it to her as she walked in the door. She tossed the bag on the bed and flopped on our easy chair. I watched her carefully to read her reaction; she was calm and collected. I was surprised. My hands had a little quiver and there was a hole in the pit of my stomach. She was made of stainless steel. My respect for her grew.

"Did you peek?"

She shook her head and shrugged her shoulders as if she didn't care.

"Care to wager?"

"No," she said. "Just open it."

I slid open the zipper and pulled out bundles of hundred dollar bills. I quickly flipped through them and counted them out. One hundred and fifty grand, exactly. I tossed her one of the bundles. Five thousand dollars. She slipped the packet in her handbag and drained her drink.

"Weren't you scared out there?" I asked.

"I knew you'd watch over me," she replied.

I felt like a loyal watchdog receiving a pat on the head. Men are simple and obvious. I wanted to marry this girl.

"Marry me and take a honeymoon trip to Bolivia?"

"Nope," she said, "I don't do South America."

And that was that.

Sunday, June 20, 1982

Miami

The next morning, I spent a couple of hours making phone calls. I started with the DEA main office and got the answering service. They are a government agency, so, of course, I got jerked around, but eventually I left the motel phone number with someone who contacted Steve Stephens. Grumpy, he called about 11:00. In all the time I'd known him, he was always grumpy, so I was unsurprised.

"Wilson?"

"Yeah, Sarge. How are you?"

"It's Sunday. It's the only day I have off with my family. This better be good."

"I wanted to chat. It's been a while."

"Right. That crap you pulled at the airport was cute. What do you want?"

"I'm getting a weird vibe. Something is going on in the coke business. I'm trying to figure things out."

"Everything you touch is weird. I don't know why I'm talking to you. My kids will be late for church."

"Just give me hint."

"Damn you, Wilson. I can't say much because I don't know much. We've lost a few undercover cops. The CIA pukes swarm around like horseflies on a nag. They help us bust some shipments, but the overall traffic increases."

"The CIA? What are they doing?"

"What else? Saving the world from the evil of global Communism. Glen, I meant what I said about playing your games in Dallas. Stay the hell out of my airport. Okay?"

"Sure, Sarge," I said to a dead phone. Steve had hung up.

CIA. I'd run into these guys in Vietnam. They were always running some convoluted scam in the name of fighting commies. I'd see them when they came from up-country looking for ways to ship stuff back to the States. Usually black tar heroin, but sometimes they'd ship an ARVN General and his family. These guys could justify anything in their fight against the Reds.

The library in Miami was open on Sundays, so I left Becky in the room and spent the afternoon giving myself a headache poring over microfiche. There were many recent articles about Congress trying to shut down funding for the Nicaraguan Contras. I'm as cynical as anyone, but I couldn't quite accept the CIA running drugs in exchange for money to fund anti-communist militias in South America.

If the CIA ran a coke route, then I could see why the Columbian families would have trouble getting their product through. The CIA shipments would slide in and competing shipments would get burned to the DEA. This was the sort of twisted game they liked to play.

I thought of one of the helicopter pilots I knew in Saigon. He knew the CIA guys. I searched through phone books until I found a listing near Baton Rouge. Emile Carter. He was a screw-up. Drunk, he'd crashed a Huey, but blamed it on mechanical failure. No one liked flying with him.

"Emile? This is Glen Wilson. Long time, no chat."

"Glen. From Saigon? What have you been up to, my brother?"

"A little of this and a little of that. I'm in Miami now with a marching powder importation business."

"No shit? Me too. What a business, eh?"

"What can you tell me about the CIA?"

"The Cocaine Importation Agency? I can't tell you anything. My lips are sealed."

"Remember Sergeant Stephens? He's with the DEA now. He's pissed that his undercover guys are getting burned."

"That prick? Doesn't surprise me. Still playing it by the book. The DEA is warned where they shouldn't be snooping. If they can't be smart, they are going to get fucked. Look, Glen, it's great hearing from you, but I can't talk about this stuff."

"Can you help me catch a private ride to Bolivia?"

"Bolivia? No, but you can get a ride to Barranquilla. That's in Columbia. Go talk to Bekins over at Southern Air Transport. It will cost you a few bucks, but you'll get there. Take care, Glen. Look me up if you make it to Baton Rouge and I'll buy you a beer. Bye-bye."

I sat and looked at the handset.

Layers on layers, that's the way the world's built.

I drove to the Miami airport and found the Southern Air Transport office in the air cargo area. The office was closed but a group of mechanics worked on one of their aircraft. It looked like an old Lockheed C130 we had in Vietnam, a Hercules, but it must have been a L382 or some other civilian version. The mechs directed me to a flightline coffee shop and told me to look for Fat Barry.

He wasn't hard to spot; a mountain of a man chomping a Chiliburger and guzzling from a can of Mister Pibb.

"Barry?" I asked.

He nodded and belched. "Excuse me," he said.

"I'm looking for a ride to Columbia. My old friend Emile said you might help me out."

"Emile Carter? Crash?"

"Yeah," I said. "Crash Carter. We served in 'Nam together."

"Who are you? Fed? Local? Wait," he said. He wiped his mouth with a greasy napkin. "Sorry, I don't need to know. I'm rolling deadhead on Tuesday, show up about nine-o'clock and I'll take care of you. One thousand?"

"Sounds about right," I replied.

"Cash, of course."

Of course.

When I got back to the room, Becky was gone. I thought about calling her because I liked her company, but I didn't. I stared at the walls while sipping the last of the Coors and worked things through in my head. Congress cuts off funding for anti-communist Contras. Nothing matters more than fighting Communism in our hemisphere. Collateral damage is painful, but we're at war and there will *always* be casualties.

It's the price of freedom.

I slept and dreamed of layers built on layers.

Monday, June 21, 1982

Miami

I ate grits and bacon at a Shoney's. Back at the Eagle gun shop I bought a used .45 automatic and a box of shells. Since I was not flying commercial back to Bolivia, I thought I'd try taking a handgun and see what happened. The clerk remembered me and asked how the .22 worked out. I told him I didn't know because it had been stolen from of my car.

"Welcome to Miami," he said.

I sat in the car and tried to decide what to do with my day. I thought about having a chat with Enrique. I could introduce him to the butt of my new .45, but I decided to save that pleasure for later. I also thought about visiting my Mormon girlfriend Ellie Brown, but decided against that too. I wasted the afternoon in Dania getting drunk and losing almost a thousand dollars betting on the pari-mutuel Jai-Alai.

CHAPTER 11

Tuesday, June 22, 1982

Miami

I'm not exactly sure how I got back to my room, but I woke with a splitting headache. My pockets were stuffed with losing Jai-Alai tickets. Fortunately, my gun and the drug money were safely tucked away in the back of the rented van.

With a throbbing skull, I packed my suitcase. Breakfast was of a handful of aspirin tablets and coffee followed by a cigarette for dessert. I dropped off the rental van and took a taxi to the Southern Air Transport terminal. Each step sent a pulse of pain directly up my brainstem, so I didn't move very quickly. Bekins, wearing a flight jacket and baseball cap, looked me over as if I was deranged. I handed over cash and he handed me foam earplugs and an old flight jacket decorated with Canadian maple leaf patches.

I'd ridden in cargo planes before, but assumed this plane would be outfit with a passenger compartment. It wasn't. Jump seats were bolted to the outer wall and there was just enough room for my legs between the wall of the aircraft and crates strapped to the deck. I tried to guess at the content of the crates, but gave up. The markings gave no hints.

I dozed through the engines spooling up, but woke when the Hercules bounced on the runway and eased into the air. The noise was ear-shattering; deafening even with earplugs. Within half an hour, I was freezing. Bekins brought out hot chocolate laced with brandy, which helped. The flight lasted five hours, but I was convinced my watch had stopped. Given the strength, I would have wrestled open a hatch and jumped into the eternal sea... Anything to put an end to this torture.

South America

We landed in Barranquilla. The air was hot and thick. It was like breathing through a damp, scalding towel. I staggered down the cargo platform and shrugged off the jacket. The aircraft was parked at the cargo terminal. Unforgiving sunlight broiled my eyeballs. There were soldiers around, but they paid me no attention. Two kids sat on boxes around a metal cart protected by a ragged canvas umbrella. I bought an Orangine and a pair of sunglasses from a skinny little girl dressed in a t-shirt and shorts.

Overhead, the sky was a washed-out pale blue decorated with drifting clouds going nowhere. Bekins chatted with an army officer who waved me over. The officer asked for my *passaporte*. I'd inserted a pair of twenties inside. After glancing at my picture, he smoothly pocketed the bills, and then jerked his head to get rid of me.

Bekins gestured for the return of his jacket and pointed toward a DC-3 parked a hundred meters away.

The old goonybird looked like a wreck; rusty with oil streaks dripping from the engine cowlings. They were the most reliable aircraft ever built and I'd logged many miles on them, but this one looked like it was built in 1836, though I knew that the first ones were built in 1936. The pilot waved at me impatiently. I lugged my suitcase up the gangway and handed over $500 in cash.

I'd only been on the ground for a half an hour, but my shirt was soaked-through with sweat. At least this plane had seats. I found a spot near the back. The passengers were a mixed bag: dark-skinned business types wearing suits and ties, a few nuns, and a *peon* with a rooster in a cage. Cockfighter? As I walked to my seat I was scanned by a blue-eyed man wearing a pink Guayabera shirt. He had thinning, sandy hair and a scar over his right eye. CIA. He worked on a New York Times crossword on a folded-up hunk of newsprint.

I settled in my seat and watched the scenery as the plane bored through air like a weevil. The Caribbean looked blue and inviting and I could see surf caressing the beach. It looked like a great place to vacation. I hoped I'd never see it again, but that could have been my bad mood. My head ached and my stomach churned orange soda.

The passengers passed around a greasy bag of tamales. I wasn't hungry, but I gnawed one anyway. The man with the chicken walked around the cabin with a plastic bucket full of Carta Blanca beers. I proffered a dollar and he handed me two ice-cold long-necked bottles. I washed down three more aspirin with the heavenly brew and immediately felt better about life. The CIA guy lighted a cigar and filled the cabin with blue smoke. The plane turned to the east and soon drifted over miles and miles of deep-green jungle. My seat wouldn't recline, so I couldn't sleep. I drifted in a waking hallucination.

A few hours into the flight, Mr. CIA walked down the aisle and sat in the seat across from me. He offered a Cuban cigar, which I took. He lit me up with a kitchen match and we smoked in silence. He offered his hand.

"Felix Gonzalez," he said.

He didn't look Latino and spoke with a flat drawl born in Oklahoma or the Texas panhandle. He looked as if he was only a generation removed from a failed dust-bowl farm.

"Glen Wilson," I replied, shaking his hand firmly.

"I know," he said. "Fat Barry works for me."

We smoked and I practiced making ghostly smoke rings.

"I don't suppose you'd tell me what you're carrying in your suitcase?" he asked idly.

"Cash, an old Colt 45, and a couple pairs of dirty underwear," I replied.

He laughed. "That's funny," he said, "because that's pretty much what I carry too, except my underwear is clean. Listen, Wilson, are you looking for a job?"

"Not really. Who's hiring?"

"Uncle Sugar."

"The last time I worked for him, he paid one-hundred-and-eighty-two bucks a month for the privilege of getting my dick shot off by gooks in Southeast Asia."

"You'd still run the risk of getting your dick shot off, but the pay is a little better. Plus, you get good benefits and a retirement plan."

"I'll pass."

"We can use good men like you, Wilson. If we don't put a stop to it, the Commies will take over the whole of

South America. We can't allow that to happen. Not in our back yard."

"Viva revolution," I said.

Gonzalez laughed. "Yankee go home." he said. He handed me a business card. "Change your mind? Leave a message at this number."

I slipped the card into my shirt pocket. After a while, he spoke again.

"Have you figured out who the old Nazi is?"

"The old man? Is he someone?"

Gonzalez chuckled. He walked up the aisle to his seat, and then returned with a thin folder that he tossed on my lap.

"You'll find this interesting," he said. He also handed me a sticker that said 'Diplomatic'. "Put that on your suitcase. When we get to La Paz, follow me through customs and I'll make sure you get through without a problem. Until then, happy reading."

He gave me a two-finger salute and walked back to his seat. He slid a Panama hat over his eyes and immediately began snoring. The folder was a dossier. Much of it was redacted with opaque black ink, but I got the gist.

Hansen was a Gestapo officer stationed in occupied-France during WW2. He was responsible for a few dozen deaths directly, for the torture of hundreds more, and indirectly responsible for the deaths of thousands of Jews sent to the camps across the border in Germany. All-in-all, not a nice man. Gonzalez was right; I found the reading interesting, particularly the heavily edited parts that thinly-obscured the fact that Hansen worked for U.S. intelligence after the war. The fight against Communism makes strange bedfellows. When they couldn't protect him anymore, they paved the way for him to quietly relocate to Bolivia. Anything to avoid the public embarrassment of having a war criminal, twice sentenced to death in absentia, appear on the U.S. payroll. War is hell.

The plane's engines labored as we gained altitude to clear the Andes rising before us. The air grew colder and thinner. I stubbed out the cigar and wished for the jacket back. I dozed and dreamed of dogs tearing flesh from screaming women and children. For some reason, I watched and didn't do anything. It wasn't really a nightmare because I wasn't troubled by the carnage. It didn't seem real; more like something seen on TV. I slept.

Gonzalez took back the folder and tucked it in his briefcase. On the ground, I followed him over the tarmac and he led me into the terminal and through a hallway passage I'd never noticed before. He spoke quickly in Spanish to a clerk and we were waved through. No stamps, no luggage inspection, no airport tax, and no bribes. It took two minutes.

We walked to the exit. I was immediately confronted by a man in an olive drab shirt insisting on seeing my papers. I was groggy and in no mood for his scam, so I handled him the way I dealt with muggers in Saigon. After dropping my suitcase, I hit him in the nose as hard as I could. His face exploded in blood as he went down hard. Real troops walked toward us caressing their M-1s. Gonzalez shook his head with exasperation and pushed me into a cab.

"You owe me one, asshole. *Vamanos*", he said to the cab driver.

It was late and the lights of La Paz spread before the taxi like an overflowing bowl of fireflies. It was deadly cold, but I was mellow and felt good. I asked the cabbie to take me to the Residencial Rosario. I wasn't in the mood for chasing around town, so I checked in and looked for a hooker at a bar down the street. I had my choice between a plump bleached-blonde in a leather miniskirt, a cute brown-eyed 14-year-old and a dark-skinned and mean-looking drunk with smudged lipstick and skewed eyes that didn't align. From charity or perverseness, I picked the latter. Rosa had a thin mustache and disturbing wens on her face. I could not resist her charm.

On the way back to the hotel, we were approached by a group of four young men. I had my eye on them, but a fifth teenager popped from behind a van and slipped a cord around my neck and began choking me. I could feel the hands of the others tearing through my clothes. I was proud of my whore, she shouted and pounded on the back of the kid strangling me.

I wouldn't be conscious for long, but I managed to cock the .45 and jam it under the chin of one of my attackers. That got their attention. The cord loosened and they scattered. I gasped for air and sat on the dirty pavers that lined the street. I checked my pockets. They got my cigarettes and lighter, but my wallet and passport were still zipped in an inside pocket. I had the cord, a meter-long colorful piece of rope. I figured I could use it as a belt. Once I caught my breath, Rosa supported me and we staggered to the hotel. The clerk scowled at us as we tripped in, but didn't say anything before turning away and pretending to do something important behind the counter.

From the room, peering between big buildings of the La Paz business district, we could see snow-capped Illimani glowing far off in the moonlight. Magical. The skin on my neck was abraded and painful, but there was no bloodshed. Rosa flipped off the lights and produced a reefer. I took a few tentative puffs, but worried about the weed being doctored so I didn't inhale much. The room was illuminated by the moon and the lights of the city leaking through the window. Rosa let me undress her slowly and I was surprised at her taut and lithe body. Her breasts were small and her nipples pointed uphill in the cool air.

She liked me. I could tell because she almost forgot to get the money up front. She wanted fifty U.S. dollars, but I talked her down to twenty. I let her tease me for a while, but when I couldn't resist, I emptied myself into her. I was dead-tired, but determined to stay awake until she was gone. She put herself back together in the bathroom while I smoked a cigar and stared out over the city. She gave me a kiss on the cheek and left. I finished my cigar, locked the door and propped a chair under the knob. Finally I felt safe and released myself into a dreamless sleep.

Wednesday, June 23, 1982

La Paz

My sense of well-being stretched into the next morning. The window was open a crack and I felt harmony with rattling diesel trucks idling by and children arguing on the street while walking to school. I thought about Klaus Hansen. I already figured he was a Nazi because of his age, attitude and accent. That generation of Deutschlander did not end up in South America by accident. I would steal his money and leave him in as much trouble as I could. I decided this when his thugs beat me in the San Pedro Prison. The additional information was interesting, but didn't change my plan.

I called Hansen from the lobby phone and he said he'd send his driver. I sipped strong coffee and ate a sweet roll until I spotted Alvaro parked outside. I tossed my suitcase in the back seat. Alvaro and I grunted at each other in greeting. In Hansen's office we went through the same routine. The assistant took the cash in the back and returned with an adding machine tape. Hansen scowled at the sum. I had not counted the money, but I knew the expenses for this trip were higher this time.

"Unavoidable business expenses," I said.

Hansen wanted to snap his fingers and have me beaten to a bloody pulp, but he must have sensed I was armed this time. It's hard to fake confidence that comes with a loaded .45 stuffed in the back of your pants. He tapped his fingers and flicked his eyes between me and the adding machine tape. Then he whispered to his assistant who disappeared. When his assistant came back, he carried a bundle of bills.

"I believe our agreement was to split the expenses this time?" Hansen said.

He attempted a grin, but the result was hideous; a humorless grimace through clenched teeth. I scanned the money. It was light by four-thousand dollars.

"We had excessive business expenses on our side too," he said. "Would you mind telling me how you arrived in the Alto? You didn't fly on LAB this time."

I sat and flipped through the dollars. I wasn't volunteering any information.

"As you wish, Mister Brown or Mister Wilson, whichever you prefer." He stood and walked to the window that looked over the city. "Things in Bolivia are changing. I am old and my wife is sick. My son died recently in a tragic accident. The Generals have political problems, more than usual, I sense. No longer can I do business in Argentina. The cocaine pipeline is broken. Only the Ochoa family gets shipments through. It's time for me to retire, but I need one last profitable run. It's difficult to fathom, but after all I have done for Bolivia, my retirement is unassured. I have access to product, but I don't have a secure method of getting it into the United States. This leads me to my proposal. For a one-million dollar fee, I want you to arrange a ten-ton shipment of paste."

He turned and leaned against the windowsill. He stared at me with cold eyes for a moment before walking to his desk and pulling out a sheaf of Polaroid photographs. One-by-one he glanced at them before flipping them onto the floor before me. Picture after picture of men and women hanging by their wrists. Slaughterhouse photos. I didn't want to look, but they were sickly compelling. So much pain. God should be ashamed. I should put a bullet in Hansen's forehead and rid the world of this monster. But that would be too easy on him. Plus, I didn't have my million dollars yet.

"One week," he said.

I looked at him.

"One week," he repeated. He pulled a typed piece of paper from his desk and tossed it on the scatter of photographs. I leaned over and picked it up. It was an itinerary; a list of names and addresses. Cochabamba and Miami.

"I will need more cash."

He reached into his desk drawer and tossed me a bundle of bills.

"Fifty thousand. This is an advance on your payment."

He did business like a record company. I slipped the bills into my suitcase.

"Do you have suggestions about how I do this?"

"I can tell you that our shipments through Santa Cruz have failed. Perhaps a cargo flight to Bogotá, then onto Miami."

Okay, that was a route I would not take.

I would take no advice from this old Nazi fuck. I stood and stepped on his precious pictures.

"Until we meet again," I said.

"You have one week to return with the money," he replied. "Or else."

He didn't need to add the 'or else'. That was redundant. I decided to go to Cochabamba without delay. I wasn't sure where it was, though I thought I'd seen it on a map somewhere. Outside, I told the driver to take me to the airport. I'd heard that you could catch a ride on a military plane so I told the driver to take me to the *Transportes Aereos Militares* terminal.

He took the toll road to the airport and I watched El Alto street vendors through the car window. Ten thousand pounds of cocaine paste...

How would I pull this off?

Perhaps it would be enough to doom Hansen if this much dope simply disappeared. That didn't seem sure enough, and I wanted the money, so I would get this load to the states. Somehow.

I loitered around the TAM terminal smoking cigars and shooing off street kids for a few hours before I was able to arrange a flight. They didn't check my papers, but they walked a drug-sniffing dog around my suitcase several times. I got the last seat in an old Fokker F-27. The young soldiers on this flight looked at me suspiciously, but I didn't bother them and they didn't bother me. The flight was spectacular, though we flew too close to the rugged mountains for my comfort. The air was smooth and we were in the air for two hours, then I found myself standing on the jetway of the Cochabamba's Jorge Wilsterman Aeropuerto wondering what to do next.

Cochabamba

Cochabamba had an arid climate; sparse trees dotted endless brown, rolling hills. Mountains towered in the west. The airport was more modern than I expected and the runway was recently paved. The stucco terminal was decorated with colorful tile floors.

In the arrival area, I was surrounded by taxi drivers and kids selling trinkets. Not as bad as La Paz, but bad just the same. Deciding to seek out a partner, I looked over the *camiones*, minibuses, and taxi drivers for a candidate. I wanted someone who spoke English. Smart enough to help me, but not so smart that he'd steal from me. I peered into a taxi and made eye contact with a little girl about three-years-old. She had a round brown face, a rough pageboy haircut, and wore a shirt that was both backwards and inside-out.

She gnawed a pear and decorated the taxi window with the pulp. The driver was about 25 and wore a Chicago Bulls jersey, Nike tennis shoes, and a straw cowboy hat. The other drivers were unhappy that I picked him, but I glared at them until they backed off. The driver said his name was Ricardo Rojas and that the little girl was his sister's kid. Her name was Duanna, but everyone called her Doofy.

First, I wanted to check into a room. Rickie suggested the American Hotel and I liked the sound of it. Maybe I'd be able to get a hamburger and hot water from a tap. Things spoiled *Americanos* enjoy after forking over a hard-earned twenty-dollar bill for a night's lodging.

Rickie took off to drop the kid. When he came back, I met him in the café where we enjoyed Cochabamba *chicha*. I showed him Herr Hansen's instructions and we talked about things in general. Klaus Hansen had a house in Cochabamba and was well-known, but not well-liked. Cochabamba was a larger and more cosmopolitan city than I expected since I'd barely heard of it a day earlier. It had 400,000 people, a fair amount of industry and tall buildings in the business area. There were too many Spanish-style churches and statues of Christ hanging around for my taste, but what the hell.

We brainstormed ideas. How to move ten tons of material from Bolivia to the U.S.A.? There weren't many suitable options; air cargo was too obvious, the trains didn't connect anywhere helpful, and there were no reliable truck routes leading to acceptable exit points.

What to do?

We agreed I would pay Rickie $100-a-day plus expenses. We set a time to meet in the morning and I sat at the table getting drunk while thinking about my problem. Every time I came up with a halfway decent plan some fatal flaw would jump out at me.

I was tempted take my chances: box the stuff up and simply hire DHL to ship it. Most dope passes across the borders without problem. I could call the contents pineapples and ship it to my attention at the Days Inn. However, for this kind of money, I didn't want to take unnecessary risks.

Late in the evening, a band assembled. Soon, Andean pipe music beamed into my brain. I picked up my drink and retired to my room so the music could pour through the walls and keep me awake there instead.

When morning came, I still did not have a plan. Hoping for inspiration, I asked Rickie to drive me around. We passed one of hundreds of street vendors and a zoomorphic pot caught my eye. I made Rickie back up for a closer look. The pottery design didn't look Bolivian; it was Peruvian or Chilean. The vendor, a crone wearing a shawl, spoke no English and very little Spanish. I could not understand a word of her Aymara, so Rickie translated. She said the pot was old and very rare. She wanted $100 U.S. for it. The pot was shaped like a duck and looked like it would hold a kilo. The workmanship was very good.

I lifted a tarp. Predictably, we found fifty more very-rare, one-of-a-kind pots. Immediately the price dropped to ten bucks. With Rickie translating, I told her I'd buy a thousand for five dollars apiece. She screeched and squealed as if I stabbed her with a hot poker. We walked back to the car twice before she agreed. I paid for what she had and we filled the back of Rickie's truck. He asked what I was going to do with them and I couldn't answer because I was not sure. It would be a bad idea to fill them with coca paste and ship them. My subconscious brewed a plan and I did not argue or hurry the process.

We covered the city in concentric circles. Rickie asked if he could stop at his brother-in-law's lumber mill. There, they chatted and shared a *cervesa* while I walked around and looked at the planer, the ripsaws, routers, stacks of lumber, the gluing operation, and the short, dark-skinned men sweating over the machinery. They made beautiful doors with hardwood veneers of Bolivian Rosewood. They filled the inside chambers with closed-cell foam. It occurred to me that each thick door would hold about twenty pounds of paste. I wondered if they would fool drug-sniffing dogs once they were glued and sealed. It seemed possible. Rosewood is aromatic and dense.

After many more *cervesas* and a couple of hours of conversation, we struck a deal. Rickie's brother-in-law agreed to assemble a crew to build 500 doors stuffed with coca paste. This would cost me almost $9000, which took a big chunk from my budget. I still had no idea how I would get 500 heavy doors to the United States, but I had faith. I'd think of something.

Over dinner, I chatted with a French couple at an adjoining table about their trek around Bolivia. They mentioned the world's largest salt flat was a couple hundred kilometers southwest. I decided to fill my pottery with this salt. What I would do with 1,000 clay ducks filled with salt, I did not know, but the idea felt right, so I was determined to execute it.

Worried about running out of money, I went to bed early before I could think up other expensive ideas.

CHAPTER 12

Friday, June 25, 1982

Cochabamba

Rickie drove me to the central plaza to meet Hansen's contact and arrange the paste delivery. In a busy government building, I knocked on door 12. The nameplate said Colonel Eladio Ascensio. Colonel Ascensio wore a peaked hat with a shiny bill. His chest was covered with a fruit salad of ribbons and impressive medals. After looking both ways down the hall, he closed the door behind me. He topped off a cup of espresso with brandy from an ornate bottle, but didn't offer me any. I showed him Hansen's letter. He read it twice, then took off his reading glasses and stared at me coldly.

"Did you bring me a package from Herr Hansen?" he asked.

"Nein," I replied flippantly.

Package? What package? Did this prick expect to be paid for something?

He cursed under his breath.

I then made a mistake by pulling a wad of cash from my pocket, peeling off a hundred dollar bill, and tossing it on his desk. He stared like it was something dead. I couldn't tell if it wasn't enough or if this was not the way he did business.

He slipped the bill into his shirt pocket and picked up the phone and barked instructions. Thirty seconds later, the door flew open and three young troops filed in. They handcuffed me and hauled me out of the building. Rickie, goggle-eyed, leaned against his minivan as they dragged me down the front steps.

I caught his eye and shouted to him to follow my instructions, and that I would be back soon. I hoped this was true. The troops stuffed me in the back of a black Land Rover and pulled into traffic.

Would they take me to the dope? Would they take me into the wild and leave me with a bullet in the back of my head?

I didn't know. The cuffs were tight and my arms hurt. After an hour of this torture, a bullet would be a relief.

We drove out of the city to the northeast. The road changed from pavement to gravel and then to a kidney-wracking expanse of ruts and potholes. It was dusk before we stopped the first time. We were waved down by a group of men dressed in black, carrying AK-47s. They wore natty berets, but no nametags or military insignia. Somebody's private army, I guessed. After a few minutes of conversation and passing out a few packs of cigarettes, we drove into the pitch-blackness. I couldn't say how long. Many hours.

The troops shared a bag of *saltenas* and passed around a gallon jug of water, but I got nothing.

Assholes.

They stopped to piss, but I was supposed to piss my pants, I guess. It appeared they would not uncuff me for anything. Finally, the truck stopped at a camp. Under floodlights, it looked like a plantation. The trees of the surrounding jungle were thick and the air was damp and warm. They dragged me out of the cab and rapped on the door. After a few minutes a short, fat man dressed in a satin robe came to the door. He was unhappy at being roused at such a late hour. I didn't catch a last name but the troops called him Jorgé and treated him with familiar respect, like he was a mafia don or something.

Jorgé ordered them to tie me to a post in a barn with his horses. They cuffed my hands around a vertical roof support. Then, at least I could unzip my fly and relieve my complaining bladder. I pissed for a half hour and it felt like heaven itself. Afterward, I squatted in the mud. By laying down and extending my leg, I snagged a plastic bucket and pulled it to me. Sitting on this bucket helped take strain off my knees and I could sleep. Somehow I made it to morning feeling pretty good, though my ass ached from being planted on that damned bucket all night.

Saturday, June 25, 1982

Las Yungas

I shared the barn with snorting horses and chickens that stirred before any noticeable sign of daylight. This made me grumpy. When the light streamed through cracks in the wallboards, a kid of about 10 came in with a basket and collected eggs. He nodded when I asked for *agua*, but didn't come back. I had plenty of time to get to know my barn-mates: the horses in stalls and rats that hid in the hay.

I played with a large scary-looking beetle when the barn doors flew open and morning light blinded me. Jorgé came in with oats in a bucket. He was accompanied by Felix, the CIA guy. Felix glanced at me, but gave no sign of recognition. Apparently, a gringo handcuffed in a barn is no big deal in Bolivia.

I listened to their conversation as they fed the horses, but all they talked about were thoroughbreds and race tracks. An hour later a *campesino* brought me a plastic cup of water and bowl of lamb soup; he told me it was *thimbu*. When I asked what was in it, he didn't exactly answer my question, but I was too hungry to care. A few hours later, as I tried to get beetles named Felix and Jorgé to fight to the death, the *campesino* came back and unlocked the handcuffs. He wandered off and left me rubbing my wrists and wondering what I was supposed to do.

I walked into the yard and was amazed by the view. Snow-capped mountains hovered in the distance. Sharply delineated hills scalloped the land between. Wisps of cloud slid over the green landscape. It was not what I imagined in the barn. I was staring across the valley when Felix come from the main house and motioned for me to get in his old Toyota Land Cruiser.

"You had a comfortable night, I assume," Felix said.

"Fuck you." I replied.

He grinned at me. I wanted to slap him, but squelched the impulse. We drove downhill on the dirt road for a half hour before he spoke again.

"What were you doing out there?"

"I don't know what happened," I told him. "I was arranging to pick up a load for the Commandante when they grabbed me and hauled me up here."

"Hansen is about done in Bolivia," Felix commented.

"Thanks for the warning."

"Ever seen a coca farm?"

"No," I replied.

He made a sharp turn up a rutted donkey trail and we bounced over potholes and scraped by underbrush. After parking on the edge of a clearing, we looked down on a rustic farm scene. Around a tumble-down building, green leaves dried in the sun on tarps spread on the ground. The whole farm was an acre or two.

"That's it?" I asked.

"Yes, most farms are a few acres, that's all. The *cocaleros* make a few dollars per kilo of leaves. It's not much, but it's a lot more than they can make growing oranges. Plus, dry leaves are easier to transport than pineapples or the other crops the U.S. government wants them to grow. Thousands of farms just like these are the basis for the drug trade. Close this one and twenty others pop up elsewhere."

"Doesn't make much sense, does it?"

"No, but so what?"

He slammed the Toyota into gear and we rejoined the main road. I was glad it was dark when we came up the night before. The road was in bad shape; washed out in places and covered in landslide rocks in others. Several times the edge of the road fell away for a thousand feet. I wasn't a nervous rider, but this scared me, especially the way Felix drove.

"How do you plan to get your load out of South America?"

"I'll fill Indian pottery with paste and ship them via airfreight."

"The old Indian handicraft export ploy. A tried and true classic. That will probably work." He scribbled a phone number on a piece of newspaper. "We can help with the transport," he said.

"Thanks," I replied. "What about picking up my load?"

Ken Coffman

"Try the Colonel again. I talked Jorgé into doing one final deal for that prick Hansen."

The road slowly improved. We stopped at a checkpoint and Felix chatted up the troops and, from a cart made from the rusty pickup bed of an old Datsun, bought cold bottles of Coca-Cola and greasy potatoes he called *papa rellena*. The afternoon temperature rose and my mood improved.

I felt nearly normal when Felix dropped me off at my hotel. In my room I pooped a two-day load and brushed moss off my teeth. The electrical Frankenstein shower spit out hot water for a shower and I washed off filth accumulated over the last few days. After cleaning up, I felt nearly human. I asked the desk clerk to call a taxi. Soon I climbed, two-at-a-time, up the stairs at Colonel Ascensio's building.

Cochabamba

The Colonel was not happier to see me. He stared with a cold hatred, but summoned a Corporal Mandepora to assist me. We jumped into a stake bed truck and drove to the outskirts of town. The paste, filling hundreds of clear plastic bags, was stored in a concrete-block shack with a roof made of Phillips Petroleum signs. No one paid attention to us as we loaded the bags into the truck. We drove the load to the lumber mill. I was pleased to see Rickie supervising and the workers busy stuffing plastic bags of salt into the pottery. The finishing of my beautiful doors was well under way.

Rickie was glad to see me; he kissed both of my cheeks like a European. The crew helped us unload the paste; what took two hours to load was off the truck in twenty minutes. Corporal Mandepora didn't say a word

120

before heaving himself into his truck and driving away in a cloud of dust.

I looked over the operation. In a day or two, the pottery would be filled with bags of salt and the doors would be stuffed with cocaine paste and sealed. I helped by stuffing and gluing doors until dinnertime. Rickie insisted I join him for a supper at his sister's place.

Rickie's sister, Louise, was married to an expat Brit named David. They lived in a small two-story house with a wide porch and cascades of flowers in colorful window boxes. Doofy had three bothers that ran in and out of the house screaming at the top of their lungs. I was disappointed that Doofy wore her blouse buttoned properly, but she redeemed herself by wearing mismatched shoes splayed out on the wrong feet. Happy to see me, she gave me a dead gecko and a sticky kiss that tasted of grape soda.

David, reading a week-old copy of the London Sun, shared his chair with two fat cats that napped in the mayhem. Louise sprinkled chopped peppers into a cubed beef and sausage goulash she called *pique a lo macho*. David was keenly interested in news of the world and asked me in three different ways whether I thought Ronald Reagan would start World War Three with the Russians. He was disappointed that I didn't know or care anything about World War Three or world football matches. That didn't leave us much else to talk about, so I sat quietly with my dead lizard and watched the boys sword fight with broom handles.

I don't know many normal people. My family was fragmented, scattered and mostly hostile. It was refreshing to see a family like this. They shouted at each other over the clamor and the kids got a hug after a swat on the butt when they went too far with their language or let a galloping dog in the house.

Ken Coffman

Everyone settled for supper. David mixed a high-octane tropical punch that went right to my head. The *pique a lo macho* was delicious, though I'd be farting smoke rings for a couple of days. After dinner, we sat in front of the TV and watched an episode of Alf dubbed with a squeaky Spanish voice. Louise passed around a bowl of homemade fruit sorbet, which Doofy insisted on feeding me with a not-quite-clean plastic shovel.

The scene nearly restored my faith in our fellow man. I imagined finding a woman like Louise, having nine kids like Doofy and eating like a pig until I was fat as a king. I don't deserve such a life. In the car, I felt empty when Rickie pulled away from the curb and I caught my last glimpse of a dozing Doofy sagging in her mother's arms like a broken doll.

At the hotel, I stared through a window at rooftops and the distant mountains. I felt empty. Alone. Forgotten. Bereft. If I fell over dead, who would care? Obsessively, I cleaned my gun and even polished the cartridges. I counted my money. I lost count, then counted it again. It was enough, I hoped.

I have a black spell on occasion and know better than to take it too seriously. Life would look better in the morning. I sipped a cold Pepsi, which settled my boiling stomach. Eventually, I slept.

Sunday - Wednesday, June 26-30, 1982

Cochabamba

Over a leisurely breakfast of *huevos paila*, which the menu said was served in Mexican style (heavily laced with

Jalapenos which I painstakingly picked out), I studied maps and finalized my plan. It seemed impossible to get my load into the USA, but it needed to be done, so I had to figure it out.

After church, Rickie picked me up and we went to the lumber mill. The pottery was ready. I supervised while the crew built wooden crates. We loaded the pots into crates, stuffed in straw for padding, mounted the crates on home-made pallets and used a forklift to load the pallets on the stake bed truck whose springs creaked and complained under the load. They stenciled FRAGILE and *QUEBRANTABLE* all over for whatever good it would do.

Rickie called the number Felix gave me and we drove the truck to a warehouse near the airport. We filled out twenty forms and paid three hundred dollars in various taxes, tariffs and fees including some that ended up in the shipping supervisor's shirt pocket. And that was that. The pallets were stashed in a corner and we drove away. It was too easy. I doubted I'd ever see them again.

We went back to the lumber mill and worked on gluing and loading doors until well after dark. Rickie invited me to his sister's for another dinner, but I felt bloated from the prior dinner. I wanted to shower glue out of my hair, drink a few beers and get some sleep.

The next few days were a blur of billowing sawdust, gluing, binding bundles and wrapping everything securely with plastic. I explained my scheme to Rickie who described it as impossible. However, after days of hard work and evenings of endless *pisco sours*, Rickie relented... Perhaps I was not so crazy and my method was worth a try.

By Wednesday morning, we were ready to roll. The stake bed truck was loaded and covered with a tarp. Rickie's brother insisted that we drink a toast of *chicha*, a Bolivian corn liquor, which tasted like kerosene, but I would not argue with the tradition.

The crew at the lumber mill was dirty and tired. I passed out twenty-dollar bonuses and they pounded me on the back and grinned at me with gap-toothed smiles. I was in a good mood when we left Cochabamba. This mood lasted until we drove on what must be one of the worst roads in the world.

How we got by minibuses and *camiones* to navigate to La Paz on the tenuous ribbon of road, I do not know. My firmest memory is hanging my head out of the truck window and vomiting my guts into a sheer drop-off. My breakfast did not touch anything before hitting rocks 300 meters below. I lived and died so many times that I lost count.

I was very happy to reach the relative flat of the Alto. The whole way, Rickie and the laborer laughed at me. If they weren't my best friends in the entire world, I would poke out their eyes and spit in the empty sockets. We spent the night in a hostel near the airport. I was shaky the next morning. We were up early and on the road because I wanted to travel west to arrive at Charana by nightfall.

The plan? The closest seaport was the Pacific port of Arica, which, due to a quirk of history, was in Chile. The plan was to find a freighter to take our load of doors to North America. Sound crazy? Make your own plan and leave me alone, this was the best I could come up with.

The drive to Charana was long and dull compared to the death road east of La Paz. As bad as that road was, Rickie assured me that the road north to the Cordillera was worse. I vowed to never find out if he was right. After studying the map, I was not looking forward to the road that descended into Peru. I should have been more worried about crossing the border.

Steel Waters

We were stuck in the freezing town of Charana for three hours while various people looked at our paperwork, my passport, and the load in the truck and then repeated the process with various permutations. Rickie screamed, chatted, cajoled, and sweet-talked our way across this border, otherwise, we'd still be there. The fees and services charges were obscene.

All for the privilege of killing ourselves on switchbacks that descend 12,000 feet toward the Pacific Ocean. Part of the problem was that we were headed to Arica. If we were going to the Peruvian port of Ilo, things would have been easier. I had no reason to pick one port over the other, but by the time we were done screwing around, I wanted nothing more to do with Peru.

I don't want to say anything about the road, as I do not wish to relive the memory. At one point, we exchanged a flat bald tire for an inflated bald tire with the help of people from busses headed in both directions that could not get around us. I was past caring, I sat on a rock and froze my ass while watching clouds drift below my feet.

I could not see the bottom of this canyon. It was thousands of feet away. I could have been back at the farm in Oregon eating bacon sandwiches and watching the horizon for changes in the weather, but I needed more adventure. I wanted to see more of the world. So, I flipped peanut husks into an endless void while listening to twelve men debate in three languages about how to change a truck tire.

Once the tire was fixed, we argued about who would back up (there were more vehicles trying to go down than up, but it's traditional for the downhill vehicles to back up). That took another half hour to sort out while I enjoyed my nervous breakdown. On that road, I died many times and each time came back to life with the road disappearing

125

around a blind corner wrapped around a gut-wrenching drop-off. Part of me is still there, careening around a corner and hanging off the edge of an endless cliff.

Regardless of my bitching, we made it to the Chilean border and crossed without the huge hassle experienced in Charana. The air was as thick as a milkshake but the temperature was pleasantly spring-like. I was alive. Pissed off, headachy, congested, nauseous, shaky, sweat-soaked and insane, but alive. In Arica, we found rooms at Casona Azul and I fell into bed where I dreamed of falling and smashing on rocks over-and-over until morning.

CHAPTER 13

Thursday, July 1, 1982

Arica, Chile

Slowly, my mind allowed consciousness to intrude. I had an odd, clueless feeling: where am I? I could hear the surf's white noise and the sound of wind caressing palm fronds outside my window.

Arica. In spite of the road of horror to get here, it seemed like a great place. The town was modern. Most of its streets were paved; there were a few tall buildings downtown and it was not as dirty and crowded as La Paz. I heard English spoken on the street by tourists carrying backpacks and Nikons. Despite being on the coast and nestled against the Andes rising from the east like the biggest wall in the world, the climate was arid. Brown hills rolled away to the north and south.

The specialty of the hotel restaurant was breakfast steak with fried eggs called *lomo a lo pobre*. After stuffing myself, drinking a quart of strong coffee and smoking the last of my American cigarettes, I felt almost human. Better than human. As if I'd been tested and passed with a better-than-average grade.

I checked the load on the truck. The tarp was in place and the straps were secure. Another miracle. This may seem funny, but I bonded with these lovely doors. They were well-constructed and the vivid wood grain was striking. We'd been through the back door of hell together. Now, this was personal. I would see the doors on U.S. soil or die trying. I felt the same way about the pottery ducks. The feeling is hard to explain.

I walked to the ocean and idled along the beach. Early in the day, the wind was cold, but I felt like I was on vacation. Teenagers tried to surf, but the gentle waves were tame and uncooperative. For an outrageous five U.S. dollars, I bought a pack of Camels from an Indian woman bearing twenty layers of clothing and one silver tooth. Highway robbery, but they tasted good and the old woman threw in a matchbook with a naked woman on the cover. A picture of a naked woman is always worth something.

I walked to the harbor, such as it was, to look at a bobbing, motley collection of sailboats, some rundown and listing, but others freshly painted and colorful. Through a porthole, I glimpsed a woman getting dressed. I don't know if she noticed my gaping eyes, but she took her time while fluffing her hair and wiggling her breasts more than seemed necessary. My sense of well-being was boundless: it stretched from sea to sky.

The industrial part of the harbor hosted a hundred fishing boats, a single, derelict-looking ferry and a few freighters with Chinese and Japanese markings. As I loitered, a rusty freighter, pressed by a straining tugboat, eased up to a dock. The Birkle. The crew was South American, but I did not recognize the flags they flew. It was not large or prosperous, but had a crane. If the ship was going in the right direction, I assumed I could make a deal with the skipper.

Captain Lomax was German, but he had enough English to get us through the negotiation. He wore a white beard stained with chewing tobacco. He had bandy legs and deep-set blue eyes. His ship was running a milk route up the Pacific coast with stops in Peru, Panama, Mexico, and Vancouver, British Columbia. Perfect. We coordinated radio frequencies and I bought a passage for my doors to the coast off Coos Bay, Oregon. I would pick up my load in international waters. This arrangement cost me five thousand dollars in cash, half of which I paid in advance, which seemed reasonable.

I walked back to the room and pounded on Rickie's door. Within an hour we had the truck alongside the Birkle. The crane lifted the doors onboard. I watched as they tied my load to the deck. They didn't do as good a job as I would, but the creates seemed sufficiently secured.

All the sudden, I was done. I had nothing to do and nowhere to go. I bought Rickie and his assistant lunch at Mayacuya and we repetitively toasted our good fortune. I should stay away from tequila, but this was a special occasion. Back at the hotel, I paid them and added extra dollars for their trouble. I gave Rickie my .45 to hold for me; he stashed it in a toolbox.

He was a good and reliable friend and I wondered if I'd ever see him again as they started the old truck and weaved down the street. They disappeared. I'm not a sentimental man, but between our parting and the tequila, I confess to being misty-eyed as they drove away. Feeling sorry for myself, I sat on the patio and watched clouds drift overhead while downing shot after shot of tequila until the sun died in the west. Then, I staggered to my room to vomit endless bitter dregs of booze and bile. After drinking draught after draught of cold tapwater, I passed out.

Friday-Saturday, July 2-3, 1982

Arica, Chile to Miami

The next morning, I felt better than I had any right to. The gastric purge before sleeping saved me. Still, my mouth tasted like a latrine and my head throbbed. It felt as if it was swollen to twice its normal size. It looked okay in the mirror except for whiskers, gray skin and bloodshot eyes. I didn't like myself much.

Why drink so much when I felt so good?

It was like pissing in a vase full of roses. Ugly. I regained my humanity by drinking coffee and smoking Camels in the restaurant. Slowly, my world transitioned from black and white to color. Arica was pleasant. It would be difficult to sustain a bad mood in such a lovely place. I tried, but the cool breeze and clean air were irresistible.

The airport was called *Aeropuerto Chacalluta.* I booked a flight from Arica to Santiago with a connection to Dallas/Fort Worth on a 737 flown by *Linea Aerea Nacional* Chile. I could have flown through La Paz, but I was done with Bolivia for now. To annoy me, they sprayed the cabin with nasty chemicals. To kill mosquitoes, they said. I read old People magazines, the only English magazines on the flight. We changed planes in Santiago and I breezed through customs. They looked in my suitcase, but I was clean and worried about nothing. Inspectors somehow sense this; mainly I was waved through, though there were a few half-hearted searches of my dirty underwear.

Generally I sleep well on long flights, but this time my mind raced. I struck up a conversation with a newlywed young lady, but could not charm her away from her new husband. The problem might have been my odor; I had not showered for days. I wasn't serious about picking her up, just trying to pass the time. She dug a board from her carry-on bag and we played cribbage. At a penny a point, she cleaned out the change in my pocket.

Soon enough we were on the ground in Dallas. The customs officers were unfriendly and I had to explain the route described by the stamps in my passport several times before they waved me through. I took a taxi to the nearest Hilton, raided the minibar for a dinner of Macadamia nuts and Heineken, and lay in bed for hours before sleep swept over me.

On waking, it took several minutes to remember where I was, then a few minutes more to remember why. I was happy to be back in the USA, but it was hard to get my body moving.

Maybe I'm getting too old for running around the world like a lunatic.

The weather was fine, not too hot yet. I had watery oatmeal and weak coffee in the Hilton coffee shop and read the Dallas Morning News to catch up on things. After booking an American Airlines shuttle to Miami, I arrived early in the evening. By this time, I was plenty sick of airplanes and airports. I wanted to sit in one place and let the earth rotate under my feet for a change. After sleepwalking to the Holiday Inn, I checked in. Minibar. Television. Sleep.

Sunday, July 3, 1982

Miami

I took a taxi to the Budget truck rental office and leased a step van. I argued with the clerk about my Oregon driver's license and lack of a commercial license rating, but after I bought all the insurance they could dream up, I was on my way. The difference between this extortion and the bribes necessary to get around in South America is subtle. At Miami International, I drove around until I found the DHL bonded storage area.

Was I surprised there were more cars with official license plates than seemed reasonable for a quiet Sunday morning? No, I was not. I passed from counter to counter, signing form after form, and paying fee after fee before finding myself on the loading dock. A forklift pulled into the staging area and stopped. The operator jumped off and ran back into the warehouse. Then the cops converged.

I was handcuffed and slammed against my truck. There were at least 15 agents, including DEA, local cops and FBI. In the crowd, there were a few faces I recognized including Sergeant Stephens and CIA Agent Felix Gonzalez. Press was present and photoflashes intermittently illuminated the warehouse like lightning strokes. Stephens wandered over.

"Wilson," he said.

"Steve," I replied, "any chance of getting these cuffs loosened up?"

"Nah. I told you to run your dope through Dallas or LA. Anywhere but here."

"I'm an honest businessman. You're making a mistake."

"You're the one making a mistake. Why did you think you could run this load through my backyard?"

"Maybe I thought I had protection." I nodded toward Felix, who nonchalantly smoked a cigar while leaning against a pillar. "Can I ask you something, Steve?"

"Sure."

"Why are Ochoa's shipments the only ones getting through?"

Steve looked troubled. "I don't know," he admitted.

A K-9 officer brought in a drug-sniffing German Shepherd. He padded around the crates, sniffing without much interest, no matter how many times they tried to get him excited about my pottery. They cut the restraining straps and opened the crates. At this point, Felix sensed something and vaporized. Slick. The officers pried open crates. There was high-fiving bustle and photoflashing when the first of the plastic bags were retrieved.

"You've done it to yourself this time, Wilson," Stephens said.

"It's salt. Did you know the world's largest salt flat is in Bolivia?"

"What?"

Stephens gave me a curious look before walking over and grabbing one of the plastic bags. He slit it and sniffed. After tasting the content, he made a sour face. They scattered pottery ducks and checked several of the bags. In the process, they broke a couple of ducks.

"Hey asshole, careful with those. They're valuable artifacts."

The officer turned and deliberately dropped one. It shattered like a china bomb. A newsie snapped a photo.

Stephens walked back over. "What's the story, Wilson?"

"I'm importing salt."

"Salt?"

"Salt."

"Is your import paperwork in order?"

"Yes."

"I don't understand. Help me out."

"Sure," I said while turning so he could get at my cuffs.

Stephens spoke sharply to the nearest officer.

"Uncuff this asshole."

I rubbed life into my wrists.

"Get those shitbirds away from my inventory," I politely suggested.

"Alright, clear out, there's nothing here." The cops wandered off. The newsies packed their gear and laughed among themselves. One caught my eye and pointed to a duck. I nodded that he could take it.

"Wilson's Bolivian salt is great on poultry."

Stephens looked at me expectantly.

"Speak," he said.

"What happened to Felix?"

Stephens looked around and shrugged.

"How sure are you that you play for the same team?" I asked.

"I don't know about his game. Are you planning more shipments?"

"I'm trying the seasoning business. If this batch sells, it might be the start of something big. How about helping me clean up the mess?"

Stephens was a good sport. He found a push broom and after sweeping up shards, helped me patch the crates so they mostly held together. We rebanded them. When the forklift operator showed his face, he loaded the pallets into my van.

This was as far ahead as I had thought. I figured protection promised by Felix would be worthless. I considered abandoning my ducks, but the idea did not feel right.

What to do?

I drove to my favorite Days Inn and grabbed a room. While nursing a Coors Light, I read the Miami Herald. While looking at an ad that offered a cremation/ urn special for $495, an idea hit me.

I called funeral homes and crematoriums until I got a call back from a guy who called himself the Body Baron of Miami. He said he'd take a look at my pottery, so I jumped in the truck and drove to his place.

The front was tastefully landscaped and the inside was all plush shag rug and expensive wallpaper. He was a plump black man in a double-breasted suit. He shook my hand with soft, pudgy fingers, told me to call him BB and asked me to drive the truck around back. The scene was different once I pulled in through the chain link gate. The back was filthy and I caught glimpses of bodies stacked like cordwood. I won't tell you how much the place smelled like a greasy BBQ joint.

I broke open a crate and showed BB my ducks. My idea was to use them as inexpensive urns for holding cremated remains. They were frivolous, but well-made and I figured BB could sell his clients on their value. He agreed. He offered $25 each. We settled at $35 in cash with disposing of the bags of salt his problem.

For obvious reasons I did not want to take a check from this character. I did not ask him why he had $35,000 in cash in his safe and he did not offer an explanation.

Apparently, business in the southern Florida bone yard was good.

I did a quick figuring and determined I'd made almost twenty grand on the deal once expenses were tallied. So, I was in a good mood when I returned the truck and got my deposit back. I called Becky to see if she'd give me a ride, but she hung up on me.

Returning to the rental desk, I signed for a monstrous Ford Crown Victoria. I picked up a bucket of Kentucky Fried Chicken, beer from a Circle-K and settled in my hotel room to watch a soft porn channel on cable TV.

Life can be grand.

CHAPTER 14

Sunday, July 4, 1982

Miami

I turned in the rental car and caught the shuttle to the airport. I'd forgotten the day was a holiday, which meant the airport was a ripe, stinking human zoo. I couldn't get the nonstop flight I wanted, so I was stuck with a Delta itinerary through Atlanta, changing planes in Dallas/Fort Worth, then on to Portland, Oregon with a connection in Seattle.

You may visualize hell as sulfur and flame, but to me, hell is an eternal, boring expanse of crowded concourses and surly ticketing agents. Let's not forget exhausted staggering from plane-to-plane and stomach-churning flights through midsummer thunderstorms. I could afford a First Class ticket, so that helped. The dirty look from a deadheading off-duty pilot forced to give up his freebie First Class seat and move to the coach compartment slightly improved my sullen mood.

Portland, Oregon

It was dark in Portland when, at last, my plane landed. The coolness of the air was welcome, but I could do without the drizzle.

Dear God. Can't we have the evergreens and clean air without all the damn rain?

Did I mention I was half-drunk and bone-tired? I caught a random hotel's airport shuttle, checked into a room, and collapsed.

I felt more human the next day after gobbling biscuits drowned in sausage gravy and drinking coffee until my nerves jangled.

I planned to rent a truck, but decided to buy one instead. After taking a taxi to a used truck lot on old 99, I looked over the inventory. The owner was a beefy old guy in overalls. He had a plastic smile that slipped a little when talking about money. He shook my hand with an odd precision. I felt measured as he weighed the content of my wallet and character. He certainly noticed there wasn't any way for me to leave except in one of his trucks. His mind worked at how much that was worth.

"My name's Harry, but every one calls me George." The lot was called George's Great Used Trucks. "No sense in throwing away a perfectly good sign, is there?" he asked.

Can't argue with that logic.

"I'm looking for something good for five-thousand miles that can haul a couple of tons. No Mexican tune-ups and no sawdust in the tranny."

He looked at me intently.

"How about no-smoke additive in the oil pan or sealant in the radiator?" he asked.

"None of that either."

"I have a '78 Custom Cab." He waved at a big purple truck with tandem wheels and tinted windows.

"I'm on a low budget."

George deflated. "Do you care how it looks?"

"As long as it's reliable, I don't care."

"Well, I have a '55 Dodge 300. It's not much to look at but the engine was rebuilt by a wrench-jockey who actually knew what he was doing. If you can stand rust, then she's your best bet for the money."

"How much?"

He looked at my shoes. I looked at them too. They were suede desert boots that had seen better days. Somehow they told him the right number was one-thousand and they were right. I looked over the old truck. The tires were okay and the oil puddled underneath was spotty, not a flood. It started immediately and idled smoothly.

"I'll come back and shove it up your ass if it dies on me."

"That's not the warranty I had in mind. I'll deliver another truck and help you with your load if it dies within five thousand miles. How's that suit you?"

I laughed. We were far enough from the city that I actually trusted this old fossil. I forget what name I gave him for the title: Jones or Smith or O'Malley. Half an hour later, our transaction was complete and I was on the road. I decided to call the lumbering beast Lindy in tribute to my wife. Lindy had an AM tube radio, a CB, and one functional windshield wiper (fortunately, on the driver's side). I was upset with the stupid 55 MPH speed limit on I-5, but soon realized, the way this thing was geared, even floored, 60 was the best she would do anyway.

On the CB radio, I listened to truckers tell each other where Smokeys were cherry-picking. The State Patrol liked to protect and serve the public by hiding in foliage between the north and southbound lanes and tagging out-of-staters. All's fair in business and war.

Salem and Eugene were soon left behind. I passed through the farm country of central-western Oregon. Lindy was a thirsty old gal, getting about eight-miles-per-gallon at an outrageous buck a gallon. More highway robbery.

I cut over at Roseburg and followed the Umpqua River toward the Pacific. By this time it got dark. Rain poured as if from buckets. This was the country Ken Kesey wrote about in *Sometimes a Great Notion*, so I had a romantic attachment to the soggy landscape. I'm not sure where my mind was as Lindy and I crawled down a two-lane road in mist lighted by the faint, rosy glow of the sun from the west. It was dark when I pulled into Coos Bay and I could barely keep my eyes open. On Highway 101, I found the Lazy J hotel, checked in and fell unconscious on the bed.

Coos Bay, Oregon

I woke and looked around the room. I couldn't remember where I was. Cochabamba, Miami, Portland? I opened the curtains and looked into the wet parking lot. I smelled salt in the air. The long trip flooded my mind. Oregon. I'd made it.

Do you wonder why I traveled all the way across the country to Coos Bay? For one thing, it's the largest deepwater port between San Francisco and Vancouver, BC. For another, it's isolated enough that I felt there was a good chance I could quietly get my shipment ashore with minimum hassle. And thirdly, I had a friend in the area that would help.

The last time I saw Dwayne, he was being loaded on a medivac helicopter for transport to a shipboard hospital. He'd taken a bad infection from a punji stick wound in his calf and was half crazy with fever. We were both from southern Oregon, so we had something in common. I'd see him when he came in from the field. We played a lot of poker when he was in town.

Dwayne was a photographer and he shot stark black and white photos when he wasn't too drunk to focus the lens. I had some of his pictures stored in a box under Linda's bed. In particular, photos showing a piglet tangled in concertina wire and a dead kid clutching a Winnie the Pooh blanket came to mind. The guy was a genius with a weird sense of humor. His head was full of loose screws, quite unlike the finely-tuned machinery of my brain.

I found a listing for his dad in the phone book. The address was northeast of the waterlogged hamlet of North Bend. I found the mailbox and drove up a rutty, quarter-mile, muddy trail before parking in front of his rundown, doublewide trailer. A fallen tree had crushed a corner of the trailer before sliding off and smashing an old Rambler station wagon. A cat skulked in shadow with a blue jay wing in its mouth. The place looked abandoned except for a trickle of gray smoke seeping around a rusted-out chimney. I parked, walked up mossy stairs, and pounded on the door. Within a minute, a clumsy fat man, dressed in a filthy terrycloth bathrobe, opened the door and waved a sawed-off shotgun in my face.

"No trespassing. Bugger off. Not buying nothing," the man said.

Under whiskers, folds of blubber and grime I saw signs of my old friend. The flat back-country twang of his voice was familiar though now roughed-up by intervening years of whiskey and tobacco. He spotted the six-pack of Hamm's I carried and lowered the gun.

"Oh, you brought beer."

He shambled into the darkness of the trailer leaving the door open for me to follow. Inside, the place was a mess of moldering old clothes and heaps of empty tin cans. Apparently, Dwayne lived on chili and canned pears. I moved damp clothes and cleared a spot on the couch. Dwayne laid the shotgun across his lap and reached for a beer. He drained it in one long gulp and reached for another. When that one was gone, he peered at me with piggy eyes under shaggy brows.

"Do I know you?" he asked.

"Glen Wilson, Summer '67, Saigon."

"Wilson," he said contemplatively. "Yes, I remember."

He made an inquiring gesture at the beer and I nodded. Slowing down, he only sucked down half in the first draught.

"Sorry about the gun. I'm expecting the Marshall to evict me any day. Back taxes. How private is your property if you gotta pay the governor every year for the privilege of staying on it? Leeches. You're just in time. I'm going to kill myself if I can find the shells for this thing. You can help me look."

I opened a beer and gazed around the room. It smelled of rot and despair. Some of Dwayne's photographs hung on the walls but they had varying degrees of water damage.

"What the hell happened to you?" I asked.

"My parents died in the seventies. The lumber mill closed and there ain't no work. My back hurts and the world turned into a giant shit hole. That's what happened. As soon as I remember where the shells are, I'm going to stamp paid on my final invoice. I'm going to slam the book shut. I'm…"

"I get it, Dwayne."

"I'm going to close the door and turn out the lights."

This upset me. Suicide was too easy. The coward's way out. Surely there was always some enemy worthy of one final charge.

"Soldier!" Dwayne looked at me suspiciously. "You're going to help me with one final mission. I have a shipment off the coast on a South American ship. We're going to find a boat and unload on the open sea. Then we're going to transfer that load onto my truck. Then I'm going to drive off. If you still want to blow your head off, you can do it then, but not before."

The room was silent except for intermittent dripping from the kitchen sink. Dwayne finished his beer and crushed the can. He tossed it onto a pile. I sipped mine and waited for him to respond. He looked pointedly at the two beers sitting beside me on the old couch. I tossed them to him and he stared at them as if they were his last friends on earth. They probably were. He sighed.

"Alright, one last mission. What's on the boat?"

"Hardwood doors from Bolivia."

"Check. Why are you unloading in the ocean? Why not bring them into port?"

"I don't want an inspector looking at them too closely."

"Ah, well. I know a guy. Got money?" I nodded yes. He popped the top on a beer. "Then let's do this the easy way," he said. "Do you know where the ship is exactly?"

"Nope."

"Marine radio?"

Again, I nodded.

Dwayne assembled an outfit from clothes scattered around the living room. I was pleased when he went down the hall to a back bedroom to put them on. He came out wearing a jeans-jacket and canvas painter's pants that were covered with, well, paint. He drained his beer and grabbed the last one to go.

"I'm ready," he said.

His breathing was ragged. The effort of dressing, leaving the trailer and climbing in the cab of my truck left him gasping and out of breath. He gave me rough directions, then dozed off as I traveled south on 101. We drove toward Bandon and turned off on a gravel road. When the neat little ranch-style house came into view I was impressed with the rats-nest of antennas that erupted from a shop along side. I pounded on Dwayne's shoulder to rouse him. He wiped slobber from his face with a dirty hand. After stumbling out of the cab, he banged on the shop door. A nearly-blind, stooped old man came out.

"Who is it?" he asked, blinking filmy eyes.

"Mert, it's Dwayne and my friend Glen Wilson."

Mert was about eighty and wore a plaid shirt, polyester pants, and running shoes.

"I heard you was dead," he said.

"Not quite yet," Dwayne replied. "How's your marine radio working?"

Mert cackled. "One-hundred watt linear. On a clear day I can talk to God and I have the QSL to prove it."

He waved us in. He wrinkled his nose as Dwayne went by. "Fall in a pig pit?"

I shook Mert's gnarled hand and walked over to admire his display of QSL cards. He had a collection from as far away as Burma. Dwayne flopped into an over-stuffed chair, pulled the last beer from his jacket pocket and gulped from it.

"This is a nice selection of cards," I said.

"Damn tootin'," Mert said, "once I caught skip and transmitted all the way around the world and ended up talking to myself. Had to send myself a card, it's up there somewheres. You want to talk to a ship?"

I fished the paper with the frequency out of my wallet.

I read him the numbers. "One-fifty-six-point-three-seven-five."

"Humph. Must be runnin' dope, nobody uses that frequency around here. Mississippi River drawbridge operators use that channel to jawbone to each other."

"I have a load of hardwood doors on a ship from Bolivia."

"Right-o. Crates stuffed with wacky-tabacki. I'm no fool, young man." He shuffled to his operator's chair and sat down to twist dials. A lot of his equipment was powered by vacuum tubes. They glowed with dim orange light.

"What's the ship's name?"

"The Birkle."

"And the Captain?"

"Lomax."

"And you are…?"

"Wilson."

"Got it." Into the microphone, he said, "Birkle, this is Wilson at Bandon Station. Come back, over."

We sat and looked at each other for a few minutes until the speakers crackled.

"This is Birkle, over." The voice was scratchy but intelligible.

"Please advise ETA Coos Bay, over."

"July 6, twelve-hundred local, over."

Dwayne roused. "Tell them to dock in port. Stamper Terminal, Coos Bay."

"Are you sure?" I asked him.

"Do it," Dwayne said.

I shrugged.

"Advise dock at Stamper Terminal, Coos Bay to offload Wilson cargo, over."

There was a delay of a minute or so.

"Say again, over."

This time I recognized Lomax's German accent. Mert repeated the message. Dwayne told him to relay tugboat instructions, which Mert dutifully repeated. There was another slight delay.

"Confirmed. Out."

I turned to Dwayne. "You're sure about this?"

"They owe me a favor."

"What about the port authorities?"

"They can't even get out of their own way without stepping on their dicks."

I shook Mert's hand. "Thanks," I said.

"Wacky tobacki," he said.

I herded Dwayne out the door and he hauled himself into the cab.

"Shall we go to the terminal and get things lined up?"

"Sure, but I'll need a drink first."

"Work first, then drink."

"You always were an asshole, Wilson. Drive on," he said.

I pointed the truck north and we drove to the docks. The Knutson and Jones terminals were well-maintained, but we drove by them and stopped at a tumble-down set of buildings with faded lettering: Stamper. I walked around the building to the water. The pilings were rotted and the moorings were corroded and decrepit. It looked like I could simply kick the rusty moorings off the dock.

I watched the oily river flow by while Dwayne talked to a miniscule woman with frizzed-out hair and tight pants tucked into cowboy boots. I walked over. The closer I got, the older she looked. Her hair was dyed a weird brownish color that reminded me of rusty steel wool. She wore garish eye makeup and a ring on each finger. Her skin was leathery from too much sun and she must have been 65. She looked me over.

"You're a strapping young buck," she said. She made me nervous. "Call me Claire. What's your cargo?"

"I'm importing hardwood doors from Bolivia."

A puzzled look crossed her face. "We have lots of hardwood around here, curly maple and oak..."

"These are exotic woods from the Amazon rain forest. Rosewood."

She looked unconvinced, but shrugged.

"I can whip up paperwork, but it will cost you."

"How much?" I asked.

"Two thousand for the import fee, three thousand for the tugs, and another six hundred for the tariff, two-fifty for the port fee. With expedite fees and my commission, let's call it an even seven-thousand."

Seven thousand or attempt a risky off-load on the open sea into a boat I did not have.

"Done," I said.

We walked to her office. A Rigid Tool calendar from 1978 hung on the wall beside photographs from better, happier days. Claire stood beside me and looked at the photographs.

"I buried two good men. I loved them and then planted them. I don't suppose you'd take me to the senior dance at the Elk's Club tonight?"

I shook my head and gave her the cash. She scribbled on a receipt. I looked at it. It had been a long time since I'd done a transaction that involved a receipt. If I filed taxes, I could deduct it.

Like that would ever happen.

Dwayne hovered, shifting from foot-to-foot like he had to pee. I handed him a twenty and he hustled down the street to a bar called the Rusty Anchor. He moved fast for a fat man. Claire and I watched him go.

"That's sad a waste of a man," she said. "Do you know what happened to him?"

"I lost track of him after 'Nam. He wasn't operating on all cylinders then either. But, let's not blame everything on that war."

"Once I get your cargo paperwork set up, I have spare time. Care to have a drink with me?"

I looked at her. She was an antique, but still trim. She'd waxed her upper lip, her fingernails were carefully painted and her beauty shop dye job was fresh. Even at her age, a man could do worse. I was tempted, but the image of waking up next to her in the morning was too vivid. It was not her fault, but I couldn't see this working out. Somewhere, there had to be a man closer to her generation. She could stuff him with oysters and pull a few strokes out of him.

"Thanks for the offer, but I'll have a beer with Dwayne and make sure he gets home."

"You change your mind later..."

"Then I'll give you a call."

It wasn't that intense of a day, but I felt like I'd earned a couple of beers. I walked across the street and pulled up a stool next to Dwayne. From the change on the bar, I could see he'd already sucked down a few boilermakers. The bar was dim. A couple of guys played pool and a pair of drunks stared morosely into their drinks. One man watched a Red Sox game on a fuzzy black and white TV. I ordered a schooner of Rainier.

"South American doors, huh?"

"Yep."

That was all we said during the three hours we were there. When we walked out, the sun was faint and barely visible on the horizon. It was drizzly, which was no surprise; it was almost always damp and cold on this part of the Oregon coast. The rain was slightly warmer in the summer, which was the main difference between the seasons.

I helped Dwayne into the truck and drove him home. Once there, I guided him to his bedroom. It was a horror show. Damp clothes covered every horizontal surface. There were heaps of pulpy science fiction books in piles everywhere. I worked off his shoes and threw a blanket over him. He snored before I got out of the room. I looked around his living room. Even the mouse rustling up dinner in a pile of cans looked sad. I searched through cupboards and cabinets until I found an old box of 12 gauge shotgun shells hidden behind a wad of carefully-folded aluminum foil.

It was dark when I left Dwayne's place. My mood was dark. I stopped at the A&W on 101 and ate a couple of teen burgers with root beer and felt generally better about life. With a belly full of greasy beef I read the newspaper in my room until about eight o'clock, then fell asleep in my chair.

I woke with a headache. The morning weather was more of the same; windy and cool with episodes of pouring rain. I bought sausage muffins and coffee at McDonald's and drove back to Dwayne's place. I didn't bother to knock this time. After walking in, I planted myself on the same couch. Dwayne, bleary-eyed and tousled, sat on his overstuffed chair caressing his shotgun. I tossed him a couple of mashed sandwiches and passed over a coffee. He wasn't happy about the coffee, but he said nothing. The man craved a beer with his breakfast like a daffodil craves the sun.

He finished the sandwiches and wiped his hands on a flannel shirt. Then he pulled that shirt on over his grimy t-shirt. I'm not a fastidious man, but stuff like that grossed me out. We climbed into the truck and made a silent trek into town.

At Stampers, we found Claire feeding split wood into a pot-bellied stove. Like all old people, she liked the room stifling. Outside, a longshore crew idled on the dock smoking and taking turns spitting into the river. Claire handed us mismatched mugs of coffee and we waited for the Birkle to drift into view. About one o'clock the guiding tugboat, with the Birkle looming over it, appeared like a ghost from the fog. Lines were tossed and secured.

Lomax stomped down the gangplank and let me know what he thought about the change of plans. Apparently he didn't care if I capsized while trying to offload in heavy seas as long I didn't interfere with his precious schedule. I slipped him five hundred dollars and he stopped bitching and started supervising the crew manning the ship-board crane. Within a half an hour, my doors were strapped to my truck as the Birkle pushed away from the dock. I waved at Lomax. He made a rude gesture and spat a wad over the side.

I signed the harbormaster's papers. The customs inspector wandered over and wanted to look at one of the doors. Dwayne and I disassembled a bundle so he could inspect it. Through a mysterious telepathic process, he let it be known that it would be all right if we slipped a couple of them onto the bed of his pickup. The rain beaded on the rosewood finish and I was reminded how beautiful they were. While the inspector chatted with Claire, we put a pair of doors in his truck and covered them with a tarp. He came back and I signed his paperwork and that was it. My doors were on U.S. soil and Dwayne and I were on the road.

To celebrate, we picked up a case of beer at a general store and I took Dwayne home. The truck was sluggish with the weight of the doors. A stream of cars passed us as we trundled up Highway 101. At his place, I followed him in. He headed straight for his chair and settled his ass on the saggy cushions. He reached over and picked up his shotgun, laid it across his lap, and drank a beer.

"I found a shotgun shell," he commented.

I was not surprised because I'd left one on the bathroom sink. As screwed up as he was, he could hardly miss it when he took a piss.

"So this is it then," I said, saluting him with my beer. "Thanks for your help. You've completed your mission and life still sucks, so I guess you might as well get it over with."

I could see hurt in Dwayne's bleary eyes.

Was he expecting sympathy?

"Screw you, Wilson," he said sadly.

He carefully placed his beer on the filthy carpet and settled the muzzle of the gun under his chin. "I leave you to this sweet cesspool."

He stole that line from George Sanders, but I didn't mention the plagiarism. He braced himself, closed his eyes, and pulled the trigger. The click was loud in the room. It took a few seconds for Dwayne's eyes to flutter open. He lowered the gun and looked at it.

"Wow," I said. I leaned over and plucked the gun from his hands. He picked up his beer and took a long swallow. I broke the gun open and extracted the shell. I showed him the base. There was a clear indent where the firing pin had struck home.

"That's really weird."

I loaded the chamber and aimed at the back window. I fired and the room filled with thunder and acrid smoke. Dwayne had a dazed look on his face. I popped the top on a beer and handed it to him. We sat and looked at each other. It took a minute for him to begin shaking. After putting his beer between his legs and dropping his face into his hands, he sobbed.

"That was intense," I said. "What are the odds?"

The odds were good since I'd carefully pried the primer from the shell in the chamber and switched it with a live round after showing him the supposed misfire.

"That was a message," he said with tears streaming down his face.

I threw him a dirty towel and he wiped his jowls.

"Yes, it was," I said.

CHAPTER 15

Thursday, July 8, 1982

Coos Bay, Oregon to Miami, Florida

The next morning was a rerun. I brought sausage muffins and coffee for breakfast. We sat and looked at each other without speaking. I couldn't tell where Dwayne's mind was, but his eyes were clearer and his shoulders less slumped. I was not sure how much sleep he'd gotten, but I'd slept like a lamb and felt good.

"So?" he finally asked.

"God wants us to burn this damn place to the ground and hit the road."

While looking around at the squalor of his home, his brain worked at the idea. Finally, he shrugged his massive shoulders.

"Okay," he said.

He decided beer was the only thing worth saving. After gathering an armful of cans, he stood by the front door looking back at me. I grabbed some of his photographs from the wall. When he saw me do this, he sheepishly walked back into his parent's back bedroom and took down a framed photo. The way he held it against his body, I could not tell what it was. I unhooked the propane tank from his barbeque and twisted open the valve. After rolling the hissing canister into the middle of his living room, I lit a road flare and carefully handed it to him. He looked at it for a moment, and then tossed it through the window I'd blasted with the shotgun.

I pulled him away to safety, but even from fifty feet, we had trouble staying on our feet when the trailer blew. It was too wet to burn, so fifteen minutes later the open flames died. Steam rose from the eviscerated trailer. We climbed in the truck and drove off. Almost immediately, Dwayne needed to piss and I decided to top off the fuel tank. We pulled into a Gulf station. Dwayne ran to the toilet while I tended the diesel pump.

"Hey, Mister."

I turned. The man speaking was about thirty and wore overalls, a wool shirt and a baseball cap. The logo on his hat matched the logo on his truck, Nielsen Construction. He held out a hand for a shake. His palms were calloused and he wrung blood from my hand with a crushing grip.

"Steve Nielsen."

"Wilson," I replied. "Pleased."

I turned to watch my money disappear into my fuel tank. Steve did not go away. He tapped me on the shoulder.

"Look, Mister, I heard you have hardwood doors."

I turned back to him. He shifted from foot like a timid schoolboy. "I'm building a custom house for the Mayor. I could really use some of your doors. I'll give you a couple-hundred each."

"Sorry Steve, the doors are spoken for."

The pump clicked off. The damn truck would drain me dry. The meter read almost ten bucks.

"I'll make it worth your while. I need five doors and I'll give you twenty-five hundred in cash."

"They're not for sale. Have a nice day, Steve."

"The mayor's wife saw the doors and she likes them. She's driving us crazy; she doesn't like anything. Except your damn doors, those she likes. Please, Mister, name your price so I can get back to work."

I thought of the crew in Bolivia working long days and how the vivid wood grain looked in bright sunlight. The doors were works of art.

"Alright Steve, if you have cash, I'll sell you five doors for a grand apiece."

A stormy look crossed his face. "That's highway robbery, you prick."

"If you don't want them, then buzz off and leave me be."

Dwayne came out as we eased the last door into the back of Steve's truck. Steve grumbled, but I had the dough in my pocket and he had his doors. He cussed under his breath as he pulled away. Dwayne watched as I arranged the plastic tarp around the remaining doors.

"What was that about?"

"The customs agent bragged about the doors, so we made a sale."

"Okay. We need beer for the road. Give me cash and I'll get it."

"I'll do it, I need to pay for the fuel anyway."

Dwayne heaved himself into the cab while I walked in to pay the bill. I bought pepperoni sticks, potato chips and a case of beer and handed them to Dwayne through his window. I started the truck as Dwayne inventoried my purchases.

"Light beer?" he complained. I'd purchased Olympia Gold. "This stuff is worse than drinking tapwater. Let me get real beer."

"This will hold us until the next stop."

He popped open a can and stared at me suspiciously as if thinking I was up to something. We were nearly to Roseburg before he asked where we were headed.

"Miami," I told him.

"Humph," he grunted.

He tossed an empty can out the window, and then popped open another, sipped, and glared out the window at the sodden evergreens that crowded the highway.

We stopped for dinner in Grants Pass. Dwayne wanted whiskey, chicken-fried steak and French fries. I told the waitress to bring him a diet Pepsi and a chef's salad instead. When she left our table, Dwayne growled.

"You're not my nursemaid. Let me have real food."

"Don't you get it? The shotgun shell? God has a mission for you. He wants you lean and mean, soldier."

He stubbornly refused to touch his diet drink, but sipped water with his salad. He chewed with a petulant expression, like a snot-nosed kid forced to eat spinach. There *was* spinach in his salad, but he ate around it. In the parking lot, he grabbed my shoulder and turned me around.

"I see what you're doing."

"Me?"

I shrugged off his hand. His features twisted and he took a swing. He was slug-slow and I easily slipped under the blow. I grabbed his arm, twisted it behind his back and rode him into the gravel of the parking lot.

"Don't do that again," I hissed into his ear while pressing his face into the crushed rock.

He was on the verge of tears.

"Get off me, Wilson, you asshole."

"If you don't want to come to Miami, just say the word. You can hitchhike back home. Oops, we blew up your home didn't we? You got nowhere else to go."

"Damn your black soul."

I let him up and brushed debris off his clothes before turning and walking toward the truck.

"You coming?" I said over my shoulder.

He stood for a few moments, and then shuffled over. He sat in the cab and cradled a light beer in his lap as if it was unworthy of opening. We merged onto I-5.

"At least let me drink real beer."

"When you have money, buy what you want," I said. "Until then, you'll drink what I buy."

"I hate you, bastard."

"Of course, but it will be more interesting when you hate me more than you hate yourself," I replied.

Glumly, he stared through the windshield and did not speak.

We spent the night at a Motel 6 in Medford. I toyed with the idea of checking on Linda. She was only a few miles up the highway, but I discarded the idea. There was no sense in courting unneeded trouble. I kicked Dwayne's bed.

"Good news, Dwayne. I'll let you order whatever you want for breakfast."

He sat up and rubbed his eyes. "Omelet? Browns? Sausage? Extra toast?"

"Absolutely, breakfast is whatever you want. After our walk."

"Walk? What walk? What are you talking about?"

"We'll take a stimulating walk before breakfast."

He groaned and flopped back in bed. I poked and prodded him until he got up and got dressed. The weather was typical for this time of year, cool in the morning, but it would be hot in the afternoon. Dwayne walked almost a mile, but I had to let him stop every few hundred yards to catch his breath. He sweated and wheezed when we got back to Denny's where he flopped in the booth. I ordered a big meal and he looked at me like I was crazy.

"I'm going to be sick," he said.

I made him eat a little oatmeal, but that was all he could manage.

Back in the truck, I had an idea. We stopped at Copeland's Lumberyard. I talked to the manager and sold him a pair of doors for five hundred dollars apiece. I made up a sign: Exotic hardwood doors on the cheap. I taped it on the side of the truck. None of the people I talked to thought $500 was cheap, but a large percentage of those who looked at the pretty doors bought them.

I'd sold ten doors by the time we reached Sacramento. If the lumberyard manager wouldn't cut a deal, I'd loiter nearby until making a sale to prove a point. We stopped at rest stops because Dwayne needed to pee every hour or so. At each stop, I'd refuse to move until we sold a door or two. I watched for construction company trucks, they were an easy sell.

The weather was hot; Dwayne sweated buckets in our overheated cab. The only air conditioning was searing desert air pouring in the windows. I held him captive; we stayed away from bars and he didn't have money to spend at a package store. He reluctantly drank the cheapest and most watery beer I could find.

His mood was surly, but his eyes cleared and his bitching grew more eloquent. He called me a bellicose pedagogue just before we hit Reno. I'm not sure where the insult came from, but I took it as a sign his brain was starting to work as he dried out. He could walk a mile without stopping, but his face would be flushed and he'd pant and be too nauseous to eat a big breakfast. He'd be starving by lunchtime, so I'd let him have a fatty meal, but all he was allowed at dinner were salads and diet sodas.

As the fat melted off, I bought him new clothes. When we pulled into Denver, he wasn't skinny by any measure, but his skin had more tone and he'd started combing his hair and using deodorant. For that, I will be forever grateful. He'd come a long way from the wreck I'd found in Coos Bay.

We rolled slowly across Kansas when he started asking intelligent questions.

"What's the deal with the doors?" he asked after crumpling a beer can and tossing it out the window.

"What do you mean?"

"You're a prick and you've always been a prick. There must be some angle. For one thing, they're heavier than they should be."

"They're solid rosewood. Of course they're heavy."

"Bullsnot. They have hollow cores. I think they're stuffed with something. Not something light like Mary Jane. I suspect cocaine or heroin."

"You should rein in that overheated brain."

"Alright, be that way. At least tell me what my cut is."

"Cut?"

"That's right, you cheap son-of-a-bitch. You're making a shit-load of money selling doors and I want to know what's in it for me."

"God didn't save your life so you could horn in on my business."

Ken Coffman

"That's another thing. I don't think that was any fucking miracle. You doctored a shotgun shell."

"The good lord works in mysterious ways, my friend."

"There's nothing mysterious about you being a conniving, manipulative shit-bird."

"Okay, here's the deal. I need your help in Miami. If we live, I'll cut you in for half the profits."

"Oh shit," he said resentfully. "It's not even your dope we're running. I should have guessed."

I pulled the truck onto the shoulder. Cornfields stretched endlessly to the horizon.

"If you want to quit now, then hop out and that will be it."

He thought about the situation. He was broke and the intense temperature in the cab was rising. He could probably hitch a ride, but if he didn't, he'd die of heat stroke in a few hours.

And where would he go?

"Just drive, cocksucker," he finally said.

We blew a radiator hose outside Salina just after we turned south on I-35. We hitched a ride back to town. Dwayne followed me around while I bought a new hose and tools. At a quickie mart, I filled plastic milk bottles with water to replenish the radiator. He asked for ten bucks to buy cold sodas. I gave him the money.

Through the window, I watched him stand by the beer cooler staring at the alluring array of cold bottles. The pull was hard and I was proud of him when he turned his back on the alcohol and pulled out a cold case of Tab instead. We sat in the shade of the front porch and waited for someone to offer us a ride back to the truck.

"Didn't they have Diet Pepsi? I hate Tab, it tastes like chemical toilet fluid."

160

"Shut up, Wilson. If you don't want it, don't drink it."

I was pleased. He was becoming a real pain in the ass.

I weaned him off beer and we walked two miles each morning. Stronger now, he could eat a decent breakfast afterward. We traded driving duty so our arms hanging out the windows would burn evenly. Tedium weighed on us as we made slow progress across the United States. As loaded as it was, the truck could only do 50 MPH on flat parts of the highway and a lot less on upgrades. At one point, we were passed by Volkswagen bus. That was a sad day. Sometimes it felt like we were not moving at all, but time passed and mileage glacially accumulated.

By this time, Dwayne actually talked to me. He caught up on current affairs from news on the radio and newspapers. It was as if he'd been on the moon. He insisted we detour by a bookstore so he could get reading material. I trusted him with fifty bucks and he came back with a bag full of Stephen King and Ross Thomas novels. I was happy as long as they shut him up for a while.

"What are we going to do when we get to Miami if you sell all the doors and the dope is gone?"

"Excuse me?" I asked innocently.

"You know what I'm talking about. For five hundred bucks a shot, you're selling gangster dope hidden in hardwood doors. What's the dope in each door really worth? Twenty thousand? Twenty-five? We'll get to Miami where someone expects a big delivery. We'll have nothing left. Someone will be really pissed off."

"With the brainpower between us, we'll think of something."

"That's fucking outstanding, Wilson. We'll think of something. That's it? I don't need this shit." He pulled out the shotgun. "Why not kill ourselves now and save a lot of pain and aggravation?"

I tossed him shells. He looked at them, then stowed the gun back under the seat.

"You're a piece of work, aren't you, Wilson? I didn't like you in 'Nam and I don't like you now. If I had any sense, I'd take my cut now and bid your sorry ass adieu."

"I can't argue with your logic," I replied.

I couldn't help but grin. He was absolutely right, but we both knew he was tied to me for the duration. He stared out the window at the flat landscape.

"Pull over, I gotta piss."

"What a surprise. How did a big guy like you end up with a school girl's bladder?"

"Shut up and find a place to pull over," he said tonelessly.

Dwayne drove through a summer thunderstorm when he figured out my plan. Minding my own business, I peacefully read *Yellow-Dog Contract* when he slapped the book out of my hands. His eyes were wild in the reflected lightning and headlights of oncoming traffic.

"I don't know why I didn't figure this out earlier. I must be stupid. You're taking down the dealers. Jesus-fucking-Christ with a peg leg, you're denser than I thought."

I retrieved the paperback from the floorboard and began reading again. After fifteen minutes of muttering under his breath, he asked the question I'd been waiting for.

"Alright Wilson, if I'm getting half the profits, how much will that be?"

I didn't bother looking up from my book.

"About three million in cash."

"Oh," he said.

I hadn't noticed that he'd slowed down, but he hit the pedal and we slowly eased back up to 50 MPH.

"We'd better get there and get it done," he said.

When we hit Gulfport, Mississippi, we were both sick of Motel 6's and Denny's restaurants, but we briskly walked three miles every morning and Dwayne lost thirty pounds. His skin tanned nicely. He'd taken up the chewing gum habit, which drove me nuts, but as long as he stayed off booze, I didn't say much about it. The Gulf air was so humid it was like breathing raw steam.

Filled with sexual frustration and ready for action, we picked up two girls hitchhiking to Mobile. They insisted they weren't professionals, but five hundred dollars quickly disappeared into their handbags. They made us upgrade to Howard Johnson's for the two nights they spent with us. I asked my girl to marry me, but she laughed.

I watched Dwayne, but he didn't show any sign of craving a drink himself. I suppose he thought only about how three million tax-free dollars improved a man's outlook. After the girls dropped us for minor league baseball players driving a Cadillac convertible to their next game in Huntsville, we spent a few days in Pensacola resting, collecting our thoughts and reading novels in a Jacuzzi.

At a garage sale, Dwayne found free weights and spent hours in the hotel room glaring at me while lifting them and working up a sweat. He began looking like the man I knew in Vietnam so many years ago. I was proud of him, but he was a bitchy slut. Part of the point I'm sure, but his constant gum chomping drove me to distraction.

Near dusk, we sat on a beach watching breakers lap the shore while girls in microscopic bathing suits played volleyball.

"Tell me what we're up against," Dwayne asked soberly.

I decided to answer his question.

"We deliver cocaine paste to an unsavory subhuman named Enrique. He pays us eight million in cash."

"Who owns the paste we've been giving away?"

"A creepy Bolivian Nazi."

Dwayne sighed.

"Assuming we live to see the money, we'll have enemies on both sides."

"Don't forget the competition-hating CIA and the DEA who occasionally slips a leash and makes a bust."

"Great. Isn't there an easier way?"

"Not that I know of."

"How do we pull this off?"

"We slide through with the Nazis if we get the DEA to bust the Columbians."

"Will you get me killed?"

"As far as I'm concerned, you died when you pulled the trigger on that shotgun back in Coos Bay."

Dwayne bit his lip and stared into the emerald water of the Gulf. The way he blinked, he might have been fighting off tears.

"So, that's where we are?"

"Yes," I replied.

"Wilson, when this is over, I don't want to see you again."

"I read you," I said. I held my hand out to shake on the deal, but he slapped it away. After he took off for a lonely walk down the beach, I went back to the hotel coffee shop for a big plate of liver and onions.

We followed Highway 10 to Jacksonville where I sold the last of the doors, save one, to a building contractor building a housing development on artificial canals near Gainesville. The remaining door, forlornly lying alone in the back of the truck, had been damaged along the way. A corner was smashed and, like my soul, it had a large gash across it. Dwayne did not speak to me, but I didn't mind because I was sick of his banter. We took our time driving down the coast on I-95. We stopped when we felt like it and spent a day in Titusville trying to seduce Australian girls backpacking across Florida during their winter vacation. We did not succeed, but it was fun, though expensive.

The next day, we made it to Delray Beach and checked into the Rest Inn. I left Dwayne and drove the truck to visit the Body Baron. I hung around while he ran a wake and final viewing. I watched his workers smoke cigarettes in the back lot while on break. I did not want to think about the source of black clouds erupting from the furnace, like clockwork, every twenty minutes. Apparently, business was good.

BB, dressed in a fine black tuxedo, came out and glanced without curiosity at my old truck and its Oregon license plates. I explained that I wanted my ceramic ducks back and the help of his crew to load them on the truck. He shrugged. He'd sold fifty or so, but was willing to sell me the remainder for a small markup over what he originally paid. His idea of a small markup was three thousand bucks. I got the feeling the Body Baron wouldn't take a dump unless there was profit in it for him.

He sent a couple of his Cubans to help with the ducks. They didn't speak English, but I showed them how I wanted them stacked and secured. I removed plastic bags from some of the ducks and emptied the salt on the parking lot. I got the crew to tear apart the last door and stuff coke paste in the empty ducks. I tipped them fifty bucks each, then drove over to a Big 5 store where I bought a pair of large duffel bags.

From a payphone, I called Stephens' pager number. When he called back I arranged to meet him at a nearby Dunkin Donuts. He didn't look happy to see me considering I offered him a career-making bust. He got a Styrofoam cup of coffee and sat across the table looking at me.

"You're still carrying around those stupid ceramic ducks."

"Yes, but I don't think they're stupid."

"Right. What do you have for me?"

"I will set up Enrique's goons. You can use them to burn Enrique and you can use Enrique to burn his bosses. All packaged and tied with a bow."

"How much coke?"

"Somewhere around twenty pounds."

"And we get the money too?"

"Of course."

"Should be a couple million or so."

Why was he so suspicious? Beyond a few minor betrayals, what did I do to lose his trust?

"Yes."

"What's your angle?"

"Excuse me?"

"You never do anything unless there is something in it for you. What's the deal this time? You think you'll get the money? You're trying to screw me? You're trying to take your enemies off the street? What is it?"

"I feel like I owe you one."

Stephens stared at me from under furrowed brows as if trying to bore into my brain.

"I don't like the sound of that. You owe me nothing. Never did and never will."

I try to spread joy in the world and no one appreciates it. Don't we have enough cynicism in the world? Can't we give peace a chance?

I tried to look innocent.

Not one of my specialties if you believe my ex-wife. Which you shouldn't.

"I'm not saying I'm on board, but how would this work?" Stephens asked.

"I set up an exchange. You wire my courier and give him a panic button. He presses the button and you swoop in, arrest the bad guys, and claim the dope, the money, and all the credit. What could go wrong?"

He stood. "I'll get back to you after I think about it." He walked to the door. "How is the Bolivian salt business going for you?"

"Great," I replied.

Stephens gave me a hard look as he left the donut shop.

I drove to the bar to see if Enrique was around. I grabbed one of the duffel bags and took it with me. I didn't ask for him, just bellied up to the bar and ordered a frosty mug of Pearl. It took five minutes for the word of my presence to spread to the back. Enrique stormed up, grabbed my shoulder and spun me around. He was accompanied by one of his goons with a hand wrapped in a large bandage. I gave him a look that indicated I'd shoot him again if I had to.

"Where the fuck have you been? We've been waiting for weeks for our shipment."

"I had to take a circuitous route. Aren't you happy I finally made it? Do Cubans understand the concept of 'better late than never'?"

"We've been waiting. Where's my shipment?" he demanded.

He so wanted to slice me into fish food.

"I have the coke if you have the money. Eight million, right?"

He thought about the situation. The distribution channel must be really fouled up; it was clear he desperately needed this shipment. The CIA and Ochoa brothers were really screwing him.

"The new price is six million," he finally said.

I stood up. "I guess Herr Hansen will find another buyer."

"Hold on, I'm sorry, my mistake. I remember now, yes, eight million, we have that, we can make a deal." He tried a friendly smile but the result was unsettling. "Relax and have another beer. I'm buying."

I sat back down. "Thank you, Enrique," I said graciously. "We'll do things my way this time?"

He thought about this. I could sense wheels turning furiously in his head. He wanted both the money and the coke. *Bad enough to take a chance on screwing up the deal?* He gave up trying to out-think me and took a deep breath.

"Okay, crazy *yanqui*. We'll do it your way."

Did I read him right? Does he need the coke as bad as I think? Only one way to find out.

I pointed at the duffle bag. "Put the money in my bag this time," I said.

"What difference does it make?" Enrique asked politely.

"Exactly," I said. "What difference does it make?"

Enrique considered, then shrugged. "Your way," he said.

I patted him on the shoulder. "I think you're catching on."

The setup would be the same. I liked the setting of the under-construction strip mall. I drove by to make sure nothing important had changed. The shops were closer to being done, but at least a month from completion. Longer if this was a union job.

They take their time and do things right, you know.

I drove back to the motel and rapped on Dwayne's door. Standing in the doorway, he wrinkled his nose at the alcohol on my breath. He was still upset with me, but I convinced him to join me for dinner by promising to explain my plan.

Splurging, we had lobster bisque at Joe's Stone Crab. I gave a hundred bucks to the first man I saw wearing a tuxedo and we bypassed the long line and got a good table. Dwayne was unimpressed when Jesse Weiss, an old man by this time, stopped by to chat us up.

Dwayne seemed resigned to his fate and refused to look me directly in the eye. I couldn't even get him to look at the girls in the bar. Some of them were worth pursuing, but he wanted to go over the picayune details again and again and again.

To me, over-thinking could jinx a good scheme. Nature's way always includes chaos. However, I humored him as much as I could. Noon on Saturday seemed like the right time to me, but I let him talk me into running later so there would be long shadows and dusky darkness to work with. I tried to snap him out of his mood by telling old jokes. That didn't work and neither did my attempts at finding out what he would buy with his share of the money. Car, house, boat, world travel, a girl? Some or all of the above were do-able. His spirits did not rise at the thought of any of this.

I knew, in his mind, he was back in his trailer with the shotgun under his chin hearing the loud click of that misfire.

Finally, I gave up and went to the bar to scope out the action. The cheapest girl wanted eight-hundred dollars. I was too wise and frugal to pay so much, so I slept alone that night. As a deeply sensitive man, Dwayne's mood infected me. Morose, I drank minibar beer and watched crappy TV shows until falling asleep.

Groggy and grumpy, I woke to the ringing of the motel telephone. The room was stuffy and the morning sun pierced the curtains and speared my brain. Everyone was mad at me. Becky would not return my calls, Dwayne was surly and distant, and on the phone, Stephens was abrupt and dismissive. However, the deal was on. Apparently the DEA was short of busting their monthly quota of dirt bags. My mouth tasted like something dead, but I hauled ass out of bed and made cursory efforts with a toothbrush and razor.

I drove to the strip mall where I paced the parking lot and mapped things out in my mind. I couldn't think of a good way to grab the money. This was the one worrisome part of the plan. Sometimes you give up thinking and trust in fate. If it's meant to be, then it shall be. I spent the next few days sunning myself by the pool while watching girls swim and show off their tans. My mood was dark. Dwayne barely spoke except to bring up things that could go wrong. He perfected body tone by running on the beach and lifting weights in the motel's exercise room.

Finally, the day came. The setup was simple. The goons get the keys to the truck and its load of ceramic ducks in exchange for a duffel bag stuffed with eight million in cash. If they wanted to test the stuff, the ducks easiest to reach were stuffed with cocaine paste. On cue, cops would storm the parking lot and arrest everyone. I'd get Dwayne out of the clink later. Somehow, I'd switch bags and escape with the money through a storm drain: a quarter-mile crawl through the concrete tunnels. The storm sewers were dry; at least I did not have to crawl through swampy water, alligators and debris.

On the big day, everything went per plan until the shooting started.

CHAPTER 16

Monday, August 9, 1982

Miami

Dwayne parked over my manhole. After a few minutes, the duffel bag dropped by the truck's dually tires. Hidden by the wheels, I reached from the hole and switched the heavy bags. I dropped the cash bag to the bottom, then climbed down and humped it toward daylight when automatic weapons opened up.

I heard shouting over megaphones and the roar of Dwayne's shotgun. I thought about turning back to see if I could help him, but decided he'd want me to stay with the money and make sure it got to safety. When I reached daylight, the car waited and the coast was clear. I worked through the grate, brushed off my dirty clothes, heaved the bag into the trunk of the rental car and cruised back to the room.

The big moment came when I opened the bag. After several minutes of standing and looking at it lying on the hotel bed, I gathered courage. In my estimation, the odds were 50:50 whether the bag contained money or not. I could see the future branching... In one path, I had cash and could live like a king for the rest of my life. In the other branch,

172

the bag would be stuffed with newspapers and I'd have a score to settle with Enrique.

Which would it be?

Life always seems to provide middle options where things are neither completely positive nor negative. I opened the bag and saw sheaves of neatly bundled hundreds. While riffling through the cash, I was the happiest man in the world until I found the bag's bottom stuffed with newspapers. We had one million dollars instead of eight.

When the phone rang, I picked it up and waited several minutes before Stephens stopped cussing.

"Steve, dammit, calm down and tell me the score."

"I have one agent dead and three wounded. All the dopers are dead. I have a bag full of phone books, no money and a few stupid ducks filled with dope."

"Dwayne is dead?"

"No, you idiot. Dwayne isn't a doper, he's an undercover asset. He'll spend a week in the hospital, but he'll be fine. Minor shrapnel wounds and a broken femur, that's all."

"What went wrong?"

"They opened fire. They planned to kill him and take off with the money *and* the dope. What I don't understand is why they'd do that with no money in the bag. It doesn't make sense."

The cheap bastards tried to save their measly million, but this was not the right time to educate him.

"You're right, it's senseless, but who really understands the obtuse criminal mind?"

"I want to know where you were. You're up to something. When I figure out what it is, I'll track you down, reach down your neck, rip out your heart and feed it to a starving weasel before your dying eyes."

This was a graphic image, but unoriginal. My drill sergeant said this to me many times in boot camp.

"I don't appreciate you getting my friend shot up."

"Don't pin that on me, you shit. You don't give a rat's ass for him or me or anyone except yourself. You have an angle in this and I'll figure it out sooner or later. Answer the question. Where were you when this deal went down?"

"I need to talk to Dwayne, which hospital is he in?"

This ignited another bout of profanity, but Stephens let it slip that Dwayne was at Miami General so I hung up before he could catch his breath and start more cursing.

A cop worked on a crossword puzzle outside Dwayne's room. He patted me down before letting me pass. Inside, Dwayne looked pasty and pale.

"Wilson," he said faintly.

"Dwayne," I replied.

"A cluster-fuck."

"Yeah, I know. I have bad news about the money."

Dwayne looked at me intently. He expected the worst.

"Of course. I knew it."

"We're not completely dry. They covered newspaper with cash to make it look good. We got a million."

"A million."

I couldn't tell what he thought about that. I didn't know what I thought either. It wasn't enough to retire on, but it would smooth life's rough edges for a while. He could buy a doublewide trailer, 10 acres, and a pickup truck and still have enough money to drink himself to death.

"I can get out on Thursday. Give me my cut and let me go home."

"Okay, Dwayne."

I was at loose ends; drifting through the city like a ghost. Depressed and drinking too much, I didn't have the energy to hire an escort girl to help fight the blues. I counted the money over and over. With everything added together, we had one million, one hundred and thirty-five thousand which I split right down the middle.

When Thursday came, I pulled to the front door of the hospital. In a wheelchair, they rolled Dwayne to the front door. On crutches, he hobbled to the car. I drove him to the airport and parked in front of the terminal where I handed him a first class ticket that he tucked into his coat pocket. I'd packed a canvas shoulder bag for him. I showed him the money. He didn't seem to care about the ceramic duck I thoughtfully included as a souvenir. This hurt my feelings. I handed him the shotgun shell. He looked at the dimple caused by the firing pin.

"Put that in a shotgun and try again if you get to that point. Maybe the result will be different," I said.

"You're a sick fuck."

I'd had my fill of self-pity.

"Suicide is the coward's way, you piece of shit. If you gotta go, there are plenty of noble ways to do it. Pick some evil and take it to hell with you. There is an excess of crooks, politicians, despots, morons and other assholes to pick from. Go out with both barrels blazing, your hands around the neck of some scum and a bloody trail of mayhem in your wake."

Perhaps I imagined it, but I may have penetrated his shell. He was angry, which is a far healthier emotion than despair.

"I regret the day you crossed my path, you perfidious prick."

Perfidious was a good one. With that one word I felt Dwayne would be okay.

"I have one favor to ask."

"I don't owe you anything, you treacherous bastard."

"I know." I handed him a picture of Linda. "Look in on my old lady and see if she's okay. The address is on the back."

The picture showed Linda on a horse smoking a cigar and laughing at the camera. It was one of my favorite snapshots and not just because of the way her unbuttoned flannel shirt flared in the breeze. He weighed and measured the print in the studied way of a photographer.

"Maybe I will and maybe I won't," he said finally.

I knew he would. Just as sure as I knew the reloaded shotgun shell would spread his brains on the wall if he tried it again.

Dwayne struggled from the car and threw the canvas bag over his shoulder. I watched him wrestle with the crutches and work his way into the crowd. I was ready to wave if he turned, but he didn't. I was empty.

Why did I even try to good works?

An old woman in a huge Suburban honked. I toyed with the idea of pulling her out and beating the shit out of her, but started my car and moved along instead.

I paid a private investigator run down Becky's address from her license plate number and Department of Licensing records. I found her run-down house and put a paper sack with one-hundred grand in cash on her porch and rang the doorbell. I watched as her daughter came out, looked around, spotted and picked up the bag.

At this point I felt done. Despite my inspiring speech on suicide, I considered ending it all.

What else could I do?

Over a beer at a suburban bar I decided to go back to Bolivia one last time. Face-to-face, I wanted to tell the Nazi there was no money and see for myself the doom written in his eyes. It would be an indirect suicide, but an honorable finale.

I was sick of South American airplanes, but I bought a ticket and made the trek.

CHAPTER 17

Friday, August 13, 1982

La Paz, Bolivia - Again

There I was again, dizzy and depressed, sitting in Herr Hansen's study with a suitcase on my knee. The old man looked tired and angry. He stood up, shuffled to the window and looked over the city. The sky was mostly blue with clumps of high clouds battering themselves to death against the brutal mountains.

"I don't know what people expect from an old man," he said. He turned and sat on the windowsill and stared through me. "I never killed Juden just because they were Juden. I executed communist terrorists that happened to be Juden. It was war and that was my job. If I had it to do over, perhaps I would have done things differently. But now, how can tormenting a tired old man make anything better?"

Is there anything worse than a decrepit, whining relic? We all have regrets pal, but not all of us presided over a piece of the holocaust.

"You are very, very late," he continued. I shrugged and nibbled on an irritating hangnail. "Late, and undoubtedly your expenses were extraordinary."

He motioned for Alvaro to relieve me of the suitcase. Alvaro placed it on Hansen's desk and popped the latches. He raised the top cautiously and then rotated the case so Hansen could examine the contents. His face flushed with rage.

"What is the meaning of this?" he said while waving a small bundle of bills. Ten thousand dollars. "Where is the rest of the money?"

I could have told the truth, that his money was stuffed in hardwood doors installed all across the United States, but I don't think he'd appreciate the cosmic jest.

I shrugged. His skin was ashen.

"You will bring me the rest of the money immediately."

"I'm sorry to say, Herr Hansen, there is no more money. Your shipment was lost."

Hansen shook with rage. He pulled a pair of gloves from a trouser pocket and slapped my face.

"You have my money. You will deliver my money. Are you holding out for a higher payment? Your payment will be pain and death." He emphasized each phrase with stinging slaps. The exertion left him gasping for breath. He shambled back to his chair where he sat with his chest heaving. He stared at me. I hoped for a massive coronary to claim him, but he slowly regained composure and color.

"You don't understand what this means," he said quietly.

I did understand. As I hoped, Hansen got the paste on credit with a large, overdue payment expected by unpleasant and impatient people who would invent an appropriate, creative punishment for the old man. He fanned his face with the thin bundle of money.

"I shall give you one more opportunity. Where is my money?"

I looked at him with my face as blank as I could make it.

"Very well. Alvaro, take this human filth and feed him to the rats of the sewer. If he decides to tell us about the money, then bring him back. Otherwise, I do not want wish to see him again."

With that, Hansen left the room. In spite of his defiant words, I watched a defeated man. I sat quietly while Alvaro tied my hands with a length of woolen rope.

He called in his associates; a stranger and one I'd met at the San Pedro Prison—the man with the wen on his nose. Alvaro poked me with a Luger pistol and we piled into the car. Three against one.

Was this it for me?

I felt detached and curious. Generally, I land on my feet and prevail against my enemies.

Would this be the fatal exception? My terminus?

I am not a spiritual man, but I did not believe this was my destiny.

I'm suspicious of this faith when it's held by others... The fry cook who dreams of being a country music star. The engineer dreaming of Hollywood screen-writing success. The mother clinging to the belief that her kids are smarter and more special than all the other kids in elementary school. The fat man sitting on a barstool watching pretty girls writhe on a dance floor.

The most pathetic loser has ambitions and desires, but most get ground up and spit out of the universal sausage factory.

But not me, baby.

The big machine needs me for something important, so my story does not end in Bolivia. Irrationally certain, I could relax and let things play out and that's what I did.

Alvaro sat with me in the back seat of the little sedan. The two other brutes rode in the front seat. Alvaro fingered a machete brought from the house. The handle was leather and the weathered blade reflected the cold, blue light of the pale sky. We crossed a crumbling concrete bridge and pulled over at a wide spot in the road.

An Indian woman, bearing a wool bowler hat and a large bundle on her back, walked by. She did not look our way. The trio herded me toward the middle of the bridge. I looked over the side; it was sixty feet to the soapy water. The banks were strewn with trash. It looked like people threw their dead pets over; there were bones and carcasses that looked like dogs or other animals.

Mr. Wen was careless. I took a hop and pressed him against the low railing. Off-balance, he grasped at me, but I stepped back. For an instant it looked like he might recover, but he slowly toppled over. The fall didn't kill him, but his situation was grim. His leg was bent at an unnatural angle while his pants soaked-through with blood. He screamed.

I turned to Alvaro who wore a shocked expression. Recovering, he raised the machete and brought down a killing blow. I was trained for this. If you have a choice, get close and take a nonfatal blow with your limbs instead of your body. Up close, they can't get a full swing, which reduces the effectiveness of the weapon. I skipped forward and raised my hands. The machete neatly severed my bindings. That was my good fortune.

However, a mist of blood drifted and I saw my little finger spin through the air like a crimson firework. I felt nothing, but I had enough experience with pain to know the numbness would not last. Rage bloomed. I was no longer whole. It was intolerable. My mind flooded with a tidal wave of fury.

The remaining thug wrapped arms around me as I pushed into Alvaro, but I wriggled from his grip. Alvaro, losing patience, dropped the machete and shot me with his pistol. Defying physics, I saw the bullet emerge from the barrel and traverse between us as if in slow motion. It caught me on my side just below my ribs. Again, I did not feel pain though an arctic coldness spread from the impact area.

I grabbed the machete and swung with all my might. Someone spent serious effort honing that blade. I was unable to completely sever Alvaro's arm, but it was close. Firing without effect, he stumbled against the guardrail with the gun waving in the air. I gently nudged his chest with the blade and he toppled over the railing.

I turned to the last thug. I don't know what he thought of the insane man spraying blood and cursing, but he wanted none. He ran to the car and jumped in. After making a U-turn, he tried to run me down. I dodged and I threw the machete. It bounced off the car and cascaded through the air to disappear into the thick brush that lined the ravine.

As I watched the car disappear, I felt detached. I drifted over the scene. A boy crossing the bridge led an Alpaca on a rope. He stared at me with great curiosity, but did not speak or stop to help. My poor little finger lay in the dust. I picked it up and sank to my knees.

Why do bad things happen to good men like me?

I looked over the railing. Wen had stopped screaming and Alvaro, sprawled backwards over a boulder and seriously broken, clicked his empty Luger pistol in my general direction. I tossed my finger at him.

Then my knees gave out and I passed into a black kingdom of void.

I woke with something crawling on my face. I could not raise my arms to brush it away. My eyes slowly focused. I could see I was in a clinic with a large, black fly perched on my nose. Felix the CIA spook sat on a metal chair reading a tattered Newsweek. When he saw my eyes were open, he discarded the magazine, got up and hovered over me. Fortunately, this scared the fly away.

"Wilson? You're quite a character, aren't you?"

"Yes, I am," I whispered through a dry mouth. He held up a cup with a straw and I sipped.

"Thanks," I said.

"If you're going to come down here, cause trouble and get your ass shot up, you might as well work for us. You sure you're not looking for a job?"

I toyed with the idea for a few seconds.

"No thanks. I'm done with this business."

"Suit yourself. You've made enemies."

"The Kraut?"

"No, don't worry about him, he's about done here. We're backing a new government and his free ride is revoked. I'm talking about people in Columbia and Miami who are upset with you. Do you follow?"

I nodded.

I get it. Some people don't appreciate a man living a simple, wholesome life.

"Watch your back, okay?"

"Sure. Do you know when I get out of here?"

"The doctor says you'll be on your feet in a few days. You have a few dollars in your wallet and your return ticket is still valid. We checked you in under the name Garcia. You should be all right as long as you don't dawdle. When you can walk, just hit the road. No more playing around, okay?"

"I understand, no more playing. I just want to go home."

Home. Wherever home is. Where? I don't know. Away from here.

"That's it, then. So long, Wilson."

I blinked my eyes and he was gone. I went back to my well-deserved nap.

I had many hours to think while stuck in the busy and well-run clinic. The walls were painted a sickly green and the fluorescent lighting made everything look over-exposed. The staff was friendly. I shared cigarettes with a toothless man who mopped the floors and I fell in love with the young doctor who changed my dressings. Her name was Rosa and she was married to a concrete contractor. I spent happy hours trying to convince her to dump the old man and run off to the United States with me.

I thought about lots of things, but mainly about Enrique.

Did I owe him a visit?

If I didn't do something about him, I would have to watch my back for the rest of my life.

As time went on, life seemed to be worth living again, if for no other reason than getting into Rosa's bed.

What was I doing?

I had a comfortable life on the farm with Linda. But, I felt destined for something larger. I was chosen.

I wasn't gifted with grand intellect, but I have an insatiable curiosity about how things fit together and a feeling for the tendon and sinew of human nature and enterprise. Sometimes I do things just to see if I can. I take senseless chances the way a painter might close his eyes and splash paint on a world-sized canvas—to see what might be come from the resulting mess. From my first conscious days, I would float above it all and look down at the patterns and possibilities. This was madness and mania, but we're given a scroll that stretches from birth to death. Pardon me for breaking the pen and splashing ink into the unknown margins.

I could have died on that bridge. I could feel the possibility of being crushed in the giant fist of fate and being discarded like a soiled Dixie cup. But, it didn't happen that way. I was alive to stick one of my nine fingers into the universal eye-socket.

However, missing a finger, I was unwhole. A cosmic message was sent. This adventure cost me a finger, which was one of my top-ten favorites. Gloves would never again fit properly and my career as a flamenco guitarist was truncated. Oddly, I felt like nine-tenths of a person. Regardless of my destiny, I was flesh and blood and a slave to my incomplete body. Warned by a wake-up call from the universe... Given a throbbing reminder of my mortality.

This was an inflection point. I should change my ways and embrace a more wholesome philosophy. Give up my delusions of futurity while the rest of my body parts were intact. These thoughts may have been influenced by pain-killing opiates flowing in my bloodstream.

I was supposed to be discharged on Wednesday, but on Tuesday Rosa came in and tossed me clothes. Unpleasant people asked questions about an injured gringo and she didn't think they could be stalled much longer.

She didn't care about me, but I was a risk to other patients. I could walk as long as I didn't move too quickly. At the back door, Rosa wanted to shake my hand, but I put my good hand on the back of her head and, instead, stole a kiss.

She was surprised, but a good sport... She didn't slap me until I reached for a breast under her smock. Smart. Instead of aiming for my face, she took a shot at my sore hand, which got my undivided attention.

The thrill of the stolen kiss carried me down the boulevard where I hailed a taxi. I arrived at the airport in time to catch a LAB flight to Miami. After breezing through immigration, I was soon on a plane and headed for my homeland.

CHAPTER 18

Friday, August 20, 1982

Miami – Again

I took a taxi to my private mailbox and retrieved the carton of money I'd left with the manager. Noting my heavily swaddled hand, he asked questions. I forget what story I made up, perhaps something about cutting myself while shaving. It ached because I constantly banged it against things, which made me tired and grumpy. Sometimes I felt pain or itching in the missing digit, which did not improve my mood.

With cash in hand, I asked the taxi driver to drop me at a Ford dealer where I bought a used, fire-engine-red Cobra Mustang with white racing stripes. The salesguy acted like it was no big deal to accept hundred-dollar bills counted out from my suitcase. This was Miami. Perhaps this happened every day, I don't know.

The car was an unnecessary indulgence, but I liked the raw horsepower and its great stereo. I'd never owned a high-performance car before and it was scary how fast the 427 engine could spool up. The shift knob was a grinning, stainless steel skull with ruby eyes. As a confession, that's probably the feature that compelled me to buy it.

I stopped at a pawnshop and bought an old Colt 1911 .45 and a couple of boxes of ammo. I was the king of the cosmos with four hundred thousand dollars, a .45 automatic and my new hotrod. I stowed my earthly possessions in the trunk. After buying toiletries and clothing at K-Mart, I checked into my home base, the Rest Inn. I called Becky to offer her a test ride, but as soon as she recognized my voice, she hung up. I thought my generous gift would convince her to talk to me, but I was wrong. Generally my instincts about women are accurate.

What's wrong with her?

I tried to focus on a plan for dealing with Enrique, but instead fell asleep in front of the motel TV. There would be plenty of time for planning later.

I rarely remember dreams and don't place significance in them. They are the noisy unraveling of consciousness, though a random message from the subconscious might be embedded in the cacophony. This night's dream revolved around dismembered fingers swimming upstream in a powerful river. Fingerlings swim downstream, so I was puzzled by the image. The fingerlings morphed into exhausted sperm cells seeking an elusive egg glowing like the sun. I interpreted this to mean I needed a woman, and fast.

In the morning, I drove by Becky's place and parked. I cranked up the stereo. The car came with eight-track tapes by Thin Lizzy and Deep Purple; perfect soundtracks.

I saw the curtains move, so I knew she was home. I lit a cigar and revved the engine. I disturbed the suburban peace with *Highway Star* blasting at 300 watts. Becky's daughter came out. She was about 14 and wore a denim miniskirt over ripped leggings. The outfit was completed with a leather bomber's jacket. She wore garish red lipstick and looked like big trouble in a small package. Crouched outside the passenger side window, she stared. Ignoring her, I gazed through the windshield and puffed my cigar. She leaned in, took the cigar, sucked a drag, and then tossed it in the gutter.

Have these 80's girls no shame?

"Mom wants to know what you're doing here."

"I want to take her for a ride in my new car."

"You're the guy who left the money?" I nodded yes. "Well, thanks. Mom bought me this jacket with it." It was 95 in the shade, so I didn't think she needed a jacket, but I didn't say anything. "What happened to your hand?"

I was already tired of talking about it. What's worse is I'd be explaining this mutilation for the rest of my life. I imagined resting in my coffin. Someone would surely ask: *"What happened to his hand?"*

"Bolivia. Thug. Machete. I'd rather not talk about it."

She scrunched her face.

"Mom says you're dangerous, but, to me, you look like an obsolete geezer in an antique car. Where'd you get those clothes? Were they having a half-off sale at the Saint Vincent De Paul?"

A fiery little squirt. I looked pointedly at her outfit.

"Were they having a two-for-one sale in the slut section at JC Penney's?"

She grinned at me. "What's your name, mister?"

"Glen Wilson, what's yours?"

"Angel."

"Perfect," I said. "Is your mom coming out?"

"Maybe," she answered. "How about giving me a ride to school?"

"Aren't you out of school for the summer?"

"I was bad, so I go to summer school with the retards and hoodlums. Ride?"

189

"I don't think so. You look like the kind of girl who screams rape if a guy touches her knee."

"I'm the kind of girl who laughs if a guy comes too fast."

She was full of spunky hormonal energy and attitude. I should stay a million miles away from this scary bundle of trouble.

"Shit. All right, hop in, I'll run you over."

She tore open the door, tossed in her knapsack and flopped into the passenger seat. She pressed the button and ejected Deep Purple. "Don't you have anything cool like The Stranglers or The Clash?"

I glared at her, but she was so charming I could not hold my pose.

"Tell me where we're going," I said.

We weaved through suburbia and found the school. The Ford's glass-pack exhaust system rumbled as I revved at the curb. She gave me a kiss on the cheek and jumped out without closing the door. I had to lean over and pull it closed myself. She winked and skipped away. Her classmates eyed me with fascinated horror while a pretty lady in a Jeep Wagoneer acted scandalized. This was exactly the reaction Angel hoped for.

I drove back to Becky's place and parked at the curb. After five minutes, Becky came out, locked her front door, and walked to the car.

"You passed the test," she said after falling into the seat.

"What test?" I asked as we roared off.

"It takes ten minutes to get Angel to school and get back. Longer than that and something else is going on."

"Oh."

"What did you think of Angel?"

"I think she's the kind of girl you'd better keep an eye on. Don't let her get in a car with strangers, for example."

Becky laughed. "You're no stranger. Besides, I showed her how to kick a guy in the nuts if he gets out of line."

"Great. What do you want to do?"

"It's your dime. Get me home before Angel gets out of school, that's all."

I hoped this would be a real date rather than just another trick. After driving to the Flagler Greyhound Track, we lost a few hundred dollars until I hit a hundred-to-one payoff on PuppyLuv. With that, we came out even for the day. Becky held my arm as we walked back to the car.

We pulled up in front of the school. Angel, leaning against a wall, talked with boys wearing tight jeans, silk shirts and elaborately feathered hair. They looked like trouble, but, to me, all teenage boys look like trouble. Angel squeezed into the back seat (what there was of it) and chattered about her classes. All of her teachers were morons and assholes except for her English Lit teacher who was sort of cute for an old guy. He also sounded like trouble. We pulled in front of their little house. The girls exchanged glances.

"Do you want to come in for dinner?" Angel asked. "I'm making spaghetti."

"Okay," I replied.

Their house looked as if a fashion bomb had exploded. An ironing board dominated the living room. Clothes were draped over every available surface. I don't know what was wrong with Angel's generation, but she was unembarrassed as she collected panties and bras to make a place for me on the davenport. She came from the kitchen with a plastic cup of Chianti, which she placed on a bare spot cleared on a coffee table. After flopping on the opposite side of the couch, she stared, making me uncomfortable.

"What?"

"I'm trying to figure out what kind of man gives a hundred-thousand dollars to someone he barely knows."

I shrugged. "A nice guy, I guess."

"Yeah, sure. Why are boys so pigheaded?"

Why are boys so pigheaded?

A person could write a book and only scratch the surface.

"Why do teenage girls ask stupid questions?"

Becky rescued Angel by calling for her to clear off the kitchen table. It wasn't easy to find places for the clothes and magazines and make room. Becky put steaming spaghetti and a plastic basket of garlic toast on the table. It was the first home-cooked meal I'd had in a while. Looking over the food, I toyed with the idea of asking Becky to marry me. Other than being a hooker, she was perfect. Looking over the steaming food, I figured being a hooker was a minor detail I could work around. No one's perfect.

The spaghetti was undercooked and the garlic bread cold in the middle, but we ate with gusto. The Chianti helped things slide down. Angel and Becky got along okay, unusual in my experience. Their over-dinner conversation veered into areas that made me uncomfortable, like the description of intra-uterine birth control device, but perhaps they tested me.

Angel tried to convince Becky it would be cool to spend their money on an Apple computer, whatever that was. Knowing nothing about the subject, I stayed quiet. I'd read about computers in an in-flight magazine, but didn't know what regular people would do with one. It sounded like a waste of money, but I'd just spent ten thousand dollars on a fifteen-year-old car that got six miles per gallon, so what did I know?

There were brownies for dessert eaten while sitting on the couch in front of the TV. At ten o'clock, Angel took her books out of her backpack and buried herself in homework. Becky didn't invite me to spend the night, but I was there at bedtime and she didn't tell me to go away. We made love like old married folks: a cozy and efficient coupling with her nightshirt pushed up and her panties pulled down. I slept more comfortably than I had in months.

Thus, we settled into a routine. I drove Angel to school and took Becky to the movies or the Laundromat during the day. Except for spats that flared up and blew over, we got along fine.

However, a clock ticked. Things would come to an end. Enrique was looking for me. I could feel it. I would have to deal with him or look over my shoulders for the rest of my life.

One afternoon, there was a knock at the door. It was Stephens. I invited him in and offered him a beer. He said no to the beer, but accepted a cold Coke. We sat and looked at each other.

"Was I hard to find?" I asked.

"Not too bad. That's why I'm here. The Columbians have been spreading money around. They'll be a day or so behind me."

"Contract?"

Steve nodded.

Shit. The Columbians decided I was a loose end and put a price on my head.

"How much?"

"They think you got their money. There's a hundred-grand bounty."

That was a lot. More than I could buy my way out of.

"I could leave town."

"That would slow them down."

"Why is Enrique still on the street?"

"None of his guys would talk. I can't touch him."

I was afraid of that.

Becky walked through dressed in sweat pants and a halter-top. She ignored Steve, but gave me an ugly look. She'd been listening, I guess.

"Any suggestions?" I asked.

Steve gave me a cool smile. "Nope," he said. "This is a cozy setup you have here. It's a damn shame it won't last." He stood up and walked to the door. "Thanks for the Coke."

This was Steve's way of providing a public service. He didn't care about me, but the women were in danger. I could disappear, but the girls would still be targets. Something needed to be done about Enrique.

"You're not worth dying for," Becky said.

"I know."

The next day, after I dropped Angel at school, I went back to my favorite gun shop and bought another .22 rifle and scope. I parked my Mustang and rented a generic white Ford Tempo. I found a place to park about 300 yards from the back door of Enrique's bar and, through the scope, watched people come and go. There was steady traffic in and out. Not just delivery people, but a troupe of brown-skinned young men with flashy clothes, white teeth and gold jewelry.

I didn't like the situation. I could accurately place a head shot at this range, but chances were high that the wound would not be fatal. The .22 was simply not enough weapon for the job. Enrique was always surrounded by three bruisers, which made close work a problem. I thought about the problem as I sat in the car and abraded the serial number off the rifle with a nail file.

What to do?

I still puzzled over the matter when I realized I was late to pick up Angel. I parked the rental car, switched back to my Mustang and drove to her school. She was not there. I waited for fifteen minutes, and then walked the school grounds looking for her. The only people around were staff watching me suspiciously. I drove home. Becky's Delta 88 was gone.

I waited in the car for a half hour before deciding to try the front door. It was unlocked. Inside, the place felt different. Clothes and dirty dishes were still strewn around, but not as many. A note was taped to the refrigerator. The first part was in Becky's handwriting.

Sorry Glen. We're gone and I ask you not to follow. Thanks for the money, it will give us a new start. Be well.

The last part was in Angel's sloppy scrawl.

Why are boys so pigheaded?

That was it. There was chili on the stove, still warm. I rinsed off a serving spoon and scooped up beans to fill the emptiness in my belly. I felt like a planet in eclipse. Darkness filled the kitchen and pressed against me. I wanted to be angry, but I couldn't dredge up the emotion. She was right, I should not put her and Angel in danger. Selfish, I liked our cozy, instant family, but I didn't deserve it.

I pressed a beer bottle to my throbbing head and tried to think while the day darkened to match my mood. When the door crashed open, I pulled the .45 from the back of my belt and hit the floor. Uzi bullets sprayed above my head. The shooter wore body armor, but I shot him in the knee. He fell like a sack of flour and I fired a killing shot into his neck. The air was filled with blue smoke and plaster dust. I scuttled backwards and shot the gun out of the hands of a crouching man who hopped around the corner. We looked at each other for a long second before I shot him in the eye. I had an unfair advantage because I'd had Ranger urban combat training. The army thought the future of combat included house-to-house fighting. This training came in handy when attacked by heavily-armed contract killers in the suburbs.

I heard someone batter at the back door. The deadbolt gave up and the door broke open with a crash. The intruder eased toward the kitchen. I guessed at his position and fired into the wall at leg level. He collapsed and whimpered. From floorboard creaks and whispering, I sensed there were two, maybe three more in the house. I didn't like my odds.

I poked my head around the corner and looked at the man by the back door. His fingertips scrabbled at his Uzi, but he couldn't get it. I fired into the top of his head and he stopped moving. I picked up his Uzi and stuffed the .45 in my belt. Hearing sirens, I pushed myself into a corner, made myself as small a target as possible, and waited. If the thugs went for the back door, they'd cross my line of fire.

My head throbbed and I bled from wood splinters and bullet fragments embedded in my arms and thighs. My ears rang. The overturned kettle of beans was on the floor with the spoon. I was still hungry, so I dragged it across and choked down another mouthful. This was dangerous. Because of my bandaged hand I had to put down the Uzi to handle the spoon. I didn't care. Police cars screeched to a halt in front and one of the thugs made a dash for the back door. I shot his leg and finished him with a headshot as he sprawled on the floor glaring at me.

One or two left? I was unsure. Unsafe where I was, I climbed on the stove and crouched. When a gun eased around the corner, I shot it and enjoyed the stream of Spanish curses that followed. The police shouted through a bullhorn, but my mind was scrambled and I couldn't understand the words. The usual, throw down your weapons and come out with your hands behind your head sort of rap, I'm sure.

When the first tear gas canister exploded in the living room, one of the thugs dashed toward the back door; he came around the corner with a 9mm pistol blazing. He met the same fate. I shot his leg and killed him with a headshot. This emptied the Uzi magazine so I tossed it aside.

I wasn't sure if there was one more assailant in the house, but with teargas billowing, I did not hang around to find out. I walked through the back door. My eyes watered, but I'd avoided the worst of the gas. Standing in the center of the backyard, I watched the back door. Enrique staggered out, blinded. He fell to his knees. I walked up, pressed the .45 to the center of his forehead and fired.

Then I tossed the weapon aside, sat on the grass with my fingers knitted behind my head, and waited. The first cops came around the side of the house wearing gas masks. They pushed me face down on the grass and cuffed my hands behind my back.

I lay there for a half-hour before a gas-masked figure kneeled beside me. He pulled off the mask. I was unsurprised to see Stephens. He wore a nylon DEA jacket.

"You made quite a mess of things," he said.

"You set this up, prick."

"It's cheaper than a trial and all the damn lawyers. You saved the taxpayers a lot of time and trouble."

"What do I get out of the deal? A one-way ticket to Broward prison? Killed while resisting arrest?"

"Don't be paranoid. You're one of our undercover assets. Once the medic patches you up, you can walk. Uncuff him," Stephens said to a loitering cop. We watched as crime scene tape was unfurled. The medic hacked up my pant legs and pulled twisted metal and wood fragments from my thigh. He slapped on ointment and bandages, packed his gear and walked off without saying a word. Stephens unwrapped a Snickers bar and broke it in half. He measured the pieces against each other carefully before handing me the smaller one.

"Are you looking for a job, Wilson? We can use good undercover men like you."

"You mean expendable undercover men like me. The answer is no. You'd just get my ass killed."

"We all gotta go sooner or later. The only variables are timing and method."

"I'm in no hurry." I got up and brushed grass clippings off my ass. I looked funny with blood seeping through the wrappings on my hand, fresh bandages on my legs and hacked up slacks.

"I guess this is it. I suggest you get in your Mustang and drive until the highway signs say something other than Florida."

"Sure, Steve, I'll leave you to your tropical paradise."

He escorted me to my car. We weaved through a chaotic crowd of cops and firefighters. In the car, I started the engine. It engaged with a satisfying roar.

"See you around," I said.

"If so, it'll be too soon."

The cops cleared a path through on-lookers and I eased the Mustang through the gap. I had to stop for gas in Lake Placid, Ocala and Tallahassee, but otherwise I drove non-stop and said goodbye and good riddance to Florida. As I entered Alabama, I swore I would never return to Florida.

Never, ever.

CHAPTER 19

Monday, August 30, 1982

Biloxi

My hand throbbed. I hoped it was not infected, but I was too squeamish to lift the dressing and take a look. Rivers of depression flowed in my veins. When I get this way, even in bright sunlight, darkness gathers and everything appears draped in gauzy black curtains. I wanted to pull over and shoot myself, but I didn't have the will or the energy. The bad spell would pass. They always do, eventually. Fighting my oppressive mood, I stopped for a burger at Greasy's in Biloxi. The girl behind the counter had chunky thighs and a face covered with a nasty constellation of acne.

"What exactly is a burger-burger?" I asked.

"Double patties on a French roll with grilled onions and chili. Pepto-Bismol tablets are an extra buck each."

Something about her snotty tone made me take a closer look. Her hair couldn't decide what color to be. Brown roots grew into a kitchen-sink bleach job. The pen she took my order with was chewed to the insert and her fingernails had blotches of polish on well-nibbled crowns.

She was tall for a girl, about five-foot-eight. Her thighs were packed into Wrangler jeans like supermarket hams wrapped in plastic. Her smock was dotted with brown stains. I ordered a well-done burger-burger with onion rings and sweetened ice tea.

"That's our heart-attack special," she quipped.

She cocked her head and watched to see if I got the joke.

Sometimes I can read people. Not always, but often. I could see the dusty roads of the town where she was born, the weathered shade of the run-down house she was raised in and the saggy-diaper kids she'd bear for her philandering, truck-driving common-law husband.

Her nametag said Brandi with a heart drawn over the 'i'. I held a hundred dollar bill just outside of her reach.

"What time do you go on break?" Her vision must have been weak. She squinted and tried to guess my game. "Sit down with me and I'll share my onion rings," I said.

I let her fingers brush the bill, and then let her snatch it. She noticed the denomination.

"We can't break no hundred."

"Then why don't you keep the change," I whispered.

I turned away, slid onto a plastic seat in the dining area and watched traffic pass by on Highway 10. After fifteen minutes, she dropped the tray and idled for a moment. She had not decided whether to trust me or not.

Smart girl.

My burger-burger steamed and I realized how hungry I was. Hungry for a meal and hungry for a mission. I needed a project.

"Work here long?" I asked.

"Almost a year."

"You dropped out of high school?"

201

"Yeah, it didn't seem important after I lost my baby."

"And the father?"

"He joined the Air Force. He said he'd write, but he didn't."

I handed her a napkin to blot her misty eyes and motioned for her to sit. She glanced at the parking lot, empty except for my Mustang, and toward the kitchen. This could go either way. It was the delicate balance of destiny. She sighed. Having little to lose weighed on her. She slid in and perched on the edge of the seat as if prepared for a quick getaway.

"I can rest for a minute, I guess."

"Good. What's your last name?"

"DuPris. What did you do to your hand?"

"Farm equipment accident."

"You're not from around here."

"Passing through."

"Where're you headed?"

"LA."

"LA," she repeated in a dreamy tone. "I always wanted to go to LA but I never saved up the money for bus fare. I don't suppose I'll ever get there now."

Sad. The kid was 18, much too young to give in to despair. I munched my burger-burger and studied her face. She had even features under a layer of blubber. She wasn't fat, but she was headed in that direction. I couldn't gauge her breasts, but that didn't matter. Her mind was the important thing. She seemed disconnected and aloof, like deep inside she clung to hope she might be destined for better things. Inevitably, Greasy's Burger joint would leach this out of her.

"What was your best topic in school?"

"I liked history and math," she said as if ashamed. "I read a lot. Romance novels but biographies too." She caught herself. "Look, if you're some kind of creep, then forget it. A hundred dollars ain't buying you anything off'n me."

I laughed. The kid had spirit. I finished my sandwich and slurped the last of my iced tea.

"I'm a talent scout. I see something in you, Brandi. Unrealized potential." I lifted her hair and framed her face with it. I rotated her head and studied her. She had a pouty look, but did not resist. "I have a suggestion."

"What's that?" she asked.

"Grab your purse and walk out of here with me. We'll get in my car and drive away."

"My job..."

"Believe me, Brandi. Greasy's will survive without you. They'll find someone else to serve the burger-burgers."

"Is this a sick joke?"

"Nope. Come with me to California. No strings and no games. You don't even have to sleep with me if you don't want to."

Her eyes welled with tears. She knew I'd probably rape and murder her and then toss her mutilated body in a ditch somewhere up the highway. But, she desperately wanted to believe.

"It would be a mistake to go with you, wouldn't it?"

"The mistake would be working here another minute while passing up your one and only ticket out of here."

"Really?"

"On my honor."

She dabbed her eyes with the napkin. A long silence stretched as she nibbled her fingernails and stared at the table. Finally she decided.

"I'll get my purse," she said quietly.

She insisted that we stop by her house to pick up a few things. I agreed, but gave her only five minutes.

Her house was an incredible cliché. I had no idea houses like this still existed in the 1980's. Covered with weathered clapboard, the yard was decorated with broken toys and a rusty lawn mower that had expired mid-mow. Flickering light from a television created a kaleidoscope through duct-tape repairs on the front window. I heard screaming and the sound of breaking glass. A five-year-old boy came out. He was dressed in pajama bottoms and carried a sloshing, two-liter bottle of Pepsi. He pressed his face against the car's glass. I reached over and cranked down the window.

"You're taking Patsy to California?"

He lisped because his front teeth were missing. *Calisornya* is the way he said it.

"Patsy?"

"She calls herself Brandi but her name is Patsy. I could come with you. I don't take any room and I can sleep in your trunk. You wouldn't notice me."

The kid impressed me with mature grammar, but I didn't get to where I am by trying to save the whole damned world. Still, I felt a twinge of guilt as I shook my head. Brandi/Patsy ran from the house. She turned the kid by the shoulders and gave him a kiss and a hug.

"I'm sorry baby," she said while pressing him to her heaving breasts.

She tossed a plastic bag, overflowing with clothes, in the back and slid onto the car seat. She stared straight ahead.

"Let's go," she whispered.

An old woman, screaming, stood on the porch. She threw things at my car. I watched a leather boot bounce off the hood. I popped the clutch and we raced away in a cloud of dust.

"Do you mind if I call you Patsy?" I asked.

She turned. Mascara-tracked tears streamed down her face. "Call me what you want, but don't break my heart."

As the song said, some people had hearts made to be broken.

This was not a promise I could keep, but like many others, I made it anyway.

That night, we almost made it to New Orleans. Stopping at a Circle-K store, I paid for toiletries and snacks. A few miles down the road, I checked us into a Howard Johnson's room with two double beds. She was mostly through with crying for the night, but a sniffle erupted from time-to-time. I let her use the bathroom first and she came out with a towel wrapped around her wet hair. Her cheeks were pink from scrubbing. On TV, I watched Joe Friday grumble through a Dragnet rerun.

"I know what you'll do." Her voice was quiet and resigned. "Will you please be gentle? I'm nearly a virgin."

"Sure," I said. I raised my index finger and slowly touched her kneecap. "Was that gentle enough?"

She wore a puzzled expression. "I guess so," she said.

"Good. Then get some sleep."

I locked myself in the bathroom and, courtesy of Greasy's, enjoyed a fine bowel movement. I shaved and took a long hot shower. When I came out, the room was dark. Curled in a fetal ball under her covers, she snored softly. I stared at the ceiling until unconsciousness claimed me too.

In the morning she seemed even more suspicious. When I woke, she was fully dressed and sitting in a chair. She didn't want to be raped, but had I attacked her, at least she could assign me to the proper category of pervert. The way things stood, she didn't know my intentions.

I didn't either, but at least I had stopped wanting to kill myself.

Outside, a shady walk meandered around a man-made pond. We strolled and tossed rocks at ducks. She giggled at the sight of duck's asses in the air as they foraged for food. We had breakfast in the hotel coffee shop and she wanted to order an omelet, but I made her take oatmeal instead. She glared while heaping brown sugar and raisins on her mush. I spread butter on my grits, read the newspaper, and ignored her.

After breakfast, we dashed across the highway to a Rexall Drugstore and I bought non-allergenic cosmetics and Clearasil. I made her apply the makeup before we checked out. She slathered it on like Spackle. It was too much, but I didn't want to argue about it.

I found a beauty shop and conversed with one of the stylists. Patsy offered an opinion, but we shushed her. The stylist and I agreed on a plan that started with a shoulder-length trim, then a dye job to take her hair as close to its natural brown as possible, then bleaching in sunny highlights. This took several hours, but the result was spectacular.

While waiting for the dye to set, we got manicures. The technician removed ugly, horny skin from my nine fingers. All told, the bill was three hundred dollars and we earned dirty looks from old ladies turned away from their appointments, but it was worthwhile. I tipped the stylist a hundred bucks and she loaded us up with as many free sample bottles of shampoo and conditioner as we could carry.

We spent the night in Lake Charles. It was the same scene. I got a room with two beds and watched TV while she used the bathroom. When she came out, I made her lift the phone book over her head 100 times. She held anger in her eyes, but didn't say a word while lifting that phonebook over and over.

In the morning, I made her walk a mile to an IHOP for breakfast. She wanted scrambled eggs and bacon, but I made her order mush again. She heaped on brown sugar and ate with angry little bites. On the walk back, we stopped at a dentist's office and I had a chat with him. I slowly stacked hundred dollar bills on his desk until he cancelled his appointments for the day.

He X-rayed, pried, poked, prodded, and clucked with disapproval. By the end of the day, Patsy had new fillings, bleached teeth, metal-work for improved alignment, and bottles of codeine and aspirin. My bankroll was ten thousand dollars lighter. I was lucky she didn't need crowns or bridge work. She was irritable and her jaws hurt so much that the idea of dinner left her heaving in the toilet. When I handed her the phone book, she threw it at my head and raised a welt. I picked myself off the floor, handed her the book and watched as she sullenly did her exercises. Tears streamed down her face and her jaws were locked into a grimace, but she did 100 repetitions before hitting me with the book again.

"Would it make you feel better to punch me?" She nodded. "Then have at it," I said.

She battered my chest and arms with blows, but her arms were weak and the blows bounced off. Crying, she collapsed on her bed. I covered her up and soon she slept.

The next morning, I splashed her with cold water to get her up. Her new hairstyle was ragged, but her complexion was already clearing up. I kept her away from soft drinks, greasy foods and chocolate and made her use the expensive hypoallergenic cosmetics and acne medicine. All this helped. We walked a mile and a half, but she refused to eat anything. I felt bad for her, clearly her jaws ached mercilessly and her muscles were sore.

I stopped at a bookstore and browsed, not sure what I was looking for. I found a screenplay for Cat on a Hot Tin Roof, which I had never read. In the car, we passed the book between us and traded the male and female roles. It took prodding to get her to do this, but by the end of the day she was in the spirit.

This book carried her into the next day, the heart of Texas and an improved mood. She began calling me Big Daddy. We stopped in Abilene to have her braces adjusted and she began eating again. I let her have milkshakes and icy fruit drinks which reduced the swelling in her mouth. I found a copy of the Casablanca screenplay and that got us through the rest of Texas.

She had a natural feel for the screenplay and made me laugh with various voices used to make the female characters distinctive. The car was hot and she grew comfortable; she slowly lost shyness about her body as her weight melted away. I bought more revealing clothes and she made no effort to keep all the buttons engaged. I spent the trip between Tucson and Phoenix looking more at her cleavage than the road. She grew more alluring and dangerous as the trip evolved.

We walked several miles every morning before it got too hot. Her skin firmed and I was impressed with how fast her young body sculpted and trimmed. If I worked hard, I could get her to laugh; the sweetest sound in the world.

We stopped for the night in Phoenix and the motel did not have a two-bed room available. She looked on inscrutably as I shrugged and accepted the single King. She cheerfully hummed in the shower and came out with a towel wrapped around her body. I handed her the phone book and she teased me with her eyes as she did her exercises. At 100, she dropped the book and wriggled her shoulders until the towel dropped to the floor.

She pushed me back on the bed and I came too fast the first time we made love. I redeemed myself later that night. She was not a virgin, but I don't think she'd had an attentive lover before. I showed her what all the fuss was about. We made love again in the morning and neither of us wanted to leave the comfort of our bed.

After our walk and breakfast, I took her to Fred Meyer and bought swimwear. We spent the rest of the week lounging by the pool reading movie magazines and reciting movie lines to each other from adjoining chairs. The sun tanned her skin and she sprouted into more loveliness as the days passed. She talked me into having the painful braces removed. Her teeth were still slightly buckled, but the imperfection added to her charm or perhaps I was blinded by passion.

We had feelings of regret when we checked out of the motel and continued our journey to LA. However, we were both excited about tinseltown. We didn't talk about it, but the skeleton of my plan was apparent. I designed and built a movie star. In the desert near Indio we picked her new name.

"I think you had the right idea, but Brandi won't work."

"What's the matter with it?"

"It's too cute and has already worn out its charm. Do you want a name that will soon be as obsolete as Ethel or Maude? Let's use something classy like Morgan. What do you think of Morgan French?"

"That's stupid. How about Wendi with an 'i'?"

"Morgan French it is."

She stared through sunglasses while hot desert wind swirled her hair, and then patted my hand.

"Whatever you say, Big Daddy."

CHAPTER 20

Monday, September 6, 1982

Los Angeles

The first question was where to live. We'd mingle with more Hollywood players if we stayed at the Mondrian or Chateau Marmont, but my money would run out too quickly. I set us up at the Holloway Motel because it was centrally located in West Hollywood and cheap.

The motel clerk recommended the Sport's Connection gym; I signed Morgan's membership form and made a daily appointment with a personal trainer.

She looked glam in new spandex sport attire and exercise shoes. Our tiny room looked like the aftermath of an explosion in Macy's Misses section; clothes and shopping bags covered every horizontal surface. I paid for all this with hundred dollar bills from a wad carried in my pocket.

The first of our spats was over dance school.

"I'm working out and eating like a hummingbird. Isn't that enough? Why do I need to take dance lessons?"

"Because you walk with the grace of a longshoreman. You're all knees and elbows."

At the Hollywood Dance Center, we had an appointment with Miss Peggy. Miss Peggy was thirty-five years old, thin as a twig, and the very definition of prissy. He examined Morgan as if she was a racehorse; looking at her teeth and tut-tutting at the dental work. He squeezed her calves and thighs, flicked loose skin under her arms, and chattered to himself.

"Can you touch your toes, honey?" he asked.

Morgan shrugged her shoulders. She tried but could not.

Miss Peggy glared at me. "It would be easier to turn a donkey into a unicorn," he told me with a stern look. He asked Morgan to walk for him. "She walks like a hemorrhoidal dock worker. It will be nearly impossible to get the corncob out of her ass."

"If you can't do it, I'll find someone else who likes the look of my money."

Miss Peggy caressed my cheek.

"You're cute in a primordial way. I didn't say I couldn't do it, I'm warning you that it will take a lot of expensive work."

"Do you take cash?" I asked.

"Sure, baby, Miss Peggy takes just about anything but no for an answer."

The acting coach I was equally bizarre. Barney Clark was 45 but looked 65. He had a serious problem with alcohol; we never saw him without a drink in his hand. His breath smelled like a third-world pesticide factory. However, his no-nonsense style worked well for Morgan. Also, he drank so much that I did not worry about him getting a hard-on for my girl. She was my princess and I did not intend to share her. He taught stage and body positions, character motivations, and drilled her mercilessly about hitting stage marks and creating disparate emotions out of thin air, one after another, like a machine.

The first time he slapped her butt with a yardstick, they looked at me and wondered what I would do. He hit her because she reversed lines and messed up a scene. Barney did not care if lines were flubbed or improvised as long as the actor stayed in character and the error did not derail a scene. Morgan made both errors.

"Hit her again," I said without looking up from my novel.

And he did. Morgan steamed, but forgave me over shrimp cocktail at Pinot Hollywood later that night.

Thus began our routine. I drove Morgan to the gym for her morning workout. While waiting, I sipped espresso and read Variety and the LA Times. After our workout, I took her back to the motel to enjoy the free continental breakfast.

She had private dance lessons in the afternoon, acting lessons in the early evening and we read screenplays to each other after late dinners. On weekends we watched movies at Grauman's Chinese Theatre and suburban multiplexes and trekked to Knott's Berry Farm and Disneyland where we ate popcorn and waited in 90-minute lines for five-minute rides.

Once her awakening muscles' initial soreness faded, she accepted her slavery and worked hard. I never mentioned buying her a one-way bus ticket back to Mississippi, but the thought hovered and provided motivation through long days.

She was not a natural dancer, but after a few weeks of Miss Peggy's scolding and molding she walked smoothly and the sprouting muscles in her ass gyrated fetchingly. She could produce hate and fear and joy on command. Except for premenstrual days punctuated by bouts of screaming and sobbing, her mood was pleasant.

We saw our first movie star at Musso and Franks: Carrie Fisher and entourage clustered in a corner of the bar. Morgan could not have been happier. We sent over a round of martinis and got back a smile and a wave from Carrie in return.

I upgraded my wardrobe and developed a taste for custom-fit suits, garish silk ties, and Italian loafers. I didn't go crazy; I bought three sets of clothes and wore them everywhere in various combinations. Due to generous tipping, we got to know the bartenders and waiters in all of the best hangouts like Tommy Tang's, Tuttobene, and the Flora Kitchen.

By October, she was ready for Community Theater. I made a small donation to The North Hollywood Amateur Actor's Showcase and by odd coincidence Morgan won co-lead in a play called Connie and Lois directed by Barney Collins. This play was a 90-minute cliché about two young lesbians coming of age. Morgan was terrible during rehearsals: nervous, tentative and uncomfortable with the kissing and partial nudity. Barney was apoplectic; during coaching sessions he screamed, cajoled, lectured and finally threatened to kill her with his bare hands. I hid my grin behind a newspaper as Morgan slowly came around.

The opening night show was packed; mainly due to a free ticket promotion from the sex-toy store on Santa Monica Boulevard called The Pleasure Chest. There were men in the audience, but no straight ones (except me). Morgan flubbed a few lines but smoothly recovered in-character. In fact, some of her improvisations were inspired. The show was a crowd-pleaser, though the roses and bras thrown on stage were a distraction.

The show ran a week beyond the schedule and was profitable. Morgan earned six-hundred dollars which, as her manager, I claimed and added to my stash.

Her next gig was an advertising gig as spokesperson for a waterbed store. She wore hot pants, licked a lollypop and had exactly one line, "Come to bed, baby."

This scene was used in four commercials and generated waterbed sales to members of the lesbian and schoolgirl fetish communities. It added two thousand dollars to our dwindling financial war chest.

I didn't like her career vector so I made sure the next ad campaign had hetero content. She did a photo shoot and her racy picture, kissing a used-car dealer, appeared in several Sunday newspapers. This brought in a grand. Making any kind of money was good, but we were spending ten-thousand a week on lessons and expensive dinners. As always, the choice was simple: bring in more money or cut the burn rate.

I hired a photographer to take promotional pictures. In his studio, he took traditional headshots against a gray curtain. It was gratifying; the camera loved her. The very last shot was transcendent. I gave her a sloppy kiss to smear her lipstick, and then mussed her hair. This upset her and she took a swing at me. The photographer caught the wild, violent look in her eyes.

That shot led to her first walk-on TV speaking role. The opportunity came while we sipped Perrier at Bar One. The bartender (a struggling screenwriter, of course) pointed out an associate producer of *The Jeffersons*. I bought the producer a drink and showed him Morgan's promotional postcards I carried around. He leafed through them, but asked the keep that final one.

Based on that contact, we got a call a couple of weeks later and Morgan appeared on a *The Jeffersons* episode as the neighbor's feisty sister-in-law. After editing, she was on-screen for a total of 80 radiant seconds. Before the episode aired, she did a walk-on for the *Simon and Simon* episode called Thin Air. These shows earned us four thousand dollars and her first fan mail, 17 letters including three requests for autographed pictures and a marriage proposal from a sheep rancher in Montana. To say we were thrilled would be an understatement. Her onscreen presence was remarkable. Her skin color came alive under stage lights and she was confident and professional in taking direction.

Perhaps she too good at taking direction... The *Simon and Simon* director hit on her and needed ungentle persuasion before backing off. I didn't wave my .45 around, but having it gave me confidence to stand down horny clowns like that who sniffed around my Morgan. And sniff they did. We stopped the acting lessons, but I still religiously took Morgan to the gym and made sure she didn't eat too much, so her figure was nearly perfect. She generated buzz and her star ascended.

I got her a role in a low-budget TV movie called *The Return of the Man from U.N.C.L.E.* This movie continued my problem of keeping Morgan away from pussy hounds. In this case, the problem was character actor Antony Zerbe. I broke his nose after a drunken cast party at Spago's.

In *The Return of the Man from U.N.C.L.E.*, Morgan appeared on screen for 22 seconds and spoke seven words. It didn't matter, she was good. This part led to work on another TV movie called *The Invisible Woman* with Bob Denver. Bob played his usual goofy character, but off-screen he was quiet and smart; a welcome surprise. Oddly, his college major was political science, and he had interesting things to say about Reagan and Bush. He also seemed to be happily married, so I didn't have to threaten him with my .45 to keep him away from Morgan.

The problem on this film was a producer trying to buy her. He offered fifty thousand dollars and his Porsche 924 Carrera. After I pressed the .45 against his knee he agreed to behave. At that point, I would not let Morgan go for less than 250 thousand. It was clear she was headed for greatness if we could hold things together.

From a inebriated production assistant, I bought an unauthorized copy of the *Places in the Heart* screenplay. I liked it. Working the telephone, I weaseled a meeting with an associate producer. His name was Wilton Smedley and his phone rang so much that I had trouble maintaining my train of thought.

"Would you tell your girl to hold your calls while we chat?"

He looked at me as if I'd suggested he cut off his dick with a plastic knife. I slid an 8X10 of Morgan across the desk. The photo with her hair messed up, of course. Smedley looked at it for a minute before picking up his phone and ordering his secretary to hold his calls. He offered me a cigar and I knew we would do business.

"I've read *Places* and I think it will be a hit."

"No one has read *Places*," he said coolly while directing cigar smoke toward his window.

"Okay, then I haven't read it." I tapped ash onto his carpet. "While I wasn't reading it I wasn't thinking that Morgan would make a great 'Viola'."

"We've already signed Amy Madigan for that role. Do you know anything about the movie business? This is not how casting gets done." He glanced at Morgan's picture. "She is cute, though. Can she do a southern accent?"

"Born and raised in Mississippi."

"Fine. I'll tell you what—Watson, is it?"

"Wilson."

"Okay Wilson. I'll set up your girl for an audition for Ermine."

I wasn't thrilled, but I took it.

"But, in return, I want a favor." I knew he'd ask for a weekend with Morgan in Cancun, but he surprised me. "Benton has his mind set on a funny-looking up-and-comer named Malkovich to play the blind guy. Malkovich is a pain in the ass. I don't know whether the problem is schedule, money or upside-down astrological portents and I don't care. Get Malkovich to sign for this film at union scale and Morgan gets an audition and my thumbs-up."

He retrieved a manila folder from a stack on his desk and tossed it on my lap.

We live in an age of contracts and lawyers. But, what if someone thumbs a nose at a contract? That's where enforcers and motivators come in. Like the Mafia, for example... Do what they want or they break your legs. Could persuasion be a lucrative service I could provide Hollywood?

After standing and stubbing out my cigar, I held my hand out. Smedley shook it.

"Done," I said.

Chicago

I was uncomfortable leaving Morgan behind, so I dragged her to Chicago. We bought tickets for a sparsely-attended presentation of a Steinbeck's *Of Mice and Men* at the rundown Steppenwolf Theater. Smedley was right,

Malkovich was an odd looking bird, but had a remarkable intensity and stage-presence. It was depressing that a community production troupe could be so clearly talented.

We found the backstage green room where Malkovich, with a mangy-looking velvet cape draped around his shoulders, smoked a cigarette. His thinning hair was ragged. He channeled Oscar Wilde or some other effete. Morgan instantly fell in love with him. This had nothing to do with my impulse to strangle him and leave his body to be disemboweled by wild dogs.

With so many people milling backstage, it was hard to get his undivided attention. He took a deep draught from a half-gallon bottle of burgundy and passed it on. While his hands were temporarily empty, I handed him a card that said 'Glen Wilson, Hollywood' and nothing else. This amused him.

"What brings you to our little show, Mr. Wilson?" he asked without discernable interest.

"A Place in the Heart."

"I've read it. Sentimental horseshit. Blows chunks. What about it?"

"You should do it."

"Why?" He twirled a strand of Morgan's hair around his index finger. "So I can make money? So I can get eaten alive by the Hollywood dream machine? So I can become a minnow in an endless sea instead of an Orca in our community wading pool?"

I wanted to be smooth and professional.

"So I won't smash your pretty face with a crowbar," I said smoothly and professionally.

Malkovich threw his head back and laughed. "I'll tell you what, Hollywoodman. Foot the bill for a party at the

Green Door and I'll sign your contract and play the best fucking blind man modern film has seen. Deal?"

"Deal," I replied.

I handed him a pen and he signed the papers with a casual scrawl. He stubbed out his cigarette, then stood and clapped his hands.

"Everyone. Dinner and drinks on this Hollywood dipshit. Let's celebrate our youth and good fortune."

This elicited a roar of approval and a dash for the rear door. The cast and crew squeezed into old cars and we made a motley parade to a tavern a mile or so away. At the Green Door, the bartender knew this crowd and would not accept drink orders until I peeled off an impressive stack of hundred dollar bills and placed them on the bar.

Then, beer flowed and the party kicked off. Morgan sat at Malkovich's table and they talked about character motivation and Adler methodology. Finding this dull, I cruised the room until I found chat more to my liking. A fellow named Gary Sinese and an older man (well over 30) named John Mahoney talked about the Chicago Bulls. They had a terrible season but had drafted a kid named Quinton Dailey from the University of San Francisco, so hope-sprung-eternal for the new season. After a few beers, conversation like this becomes fascinating. I was charmed by Mahoney. The drunker he got, the more his latent English accent came out.

I kept an eye on Morgan and Malkovich. They touched each other more than necessary. Morgan lit his cigarettes and made sure his beer glass was full. I wasn't jealous, but in some ways I liked the white-trash loser from Greasy's burger joint better than the beautiful and poised starlet I'd created. I smoked cigars and watched the crowd dwindle as the night progressed. Mahoney had a day job as a hospital orderly, so

220

he excused himself early. Sinese moved to the bar and started drinking samples of each of the varieties of Scotch. I nearly nodded off before a pretty brunette joined us. Drinking a cola, she looked like the only sober customer in the bar.

"You're Glen? I'm Glenn too."

I nodded in greeting.

"Is that your girl?" she asked.

I nodded. "Morgan."

"Is that her real name?"

"It is now."

"Will you let her fuck my husband?"

"Husband?"

"Yes, I married him last year. He's a genius, you know."

"That word gets tossed around a lot."

"I agree, but it applies."

"He isn't much to look at."

"I know, I can't explain it either. So, will you answer my question?"

"Yes, I will answer your question and no, I will not let him fuck her."

"In that case, we don't have a problem. Is your girl good?"

"Yes, and she gets better every day. She gets an audition for A Place in the Heart if Malkovich signs on."

She nodded. "I was hoping it would be something like that. Texas?"

I nodded.

"Okay. He's doing a play in New York before he can join the film crew. True West. Sam Shephard. It's rather good."

A bad idea popped into my head. If you haven't noticed, this happens from time to time.

"Shall we get out of here and find someplace to talk privately?"

I'd felt better if she pretended to consider the idea, but she answered quickly. "I don't think so, Hollywood," she said. Standing up, she tossed the strap of her purse over her shoulder. "See you around."

"Yeah, see ya."

She left me alone with my darkening mood, a warm pitcher of beer and the first signs of a headache waiting in the wings. I watched Morgan and Malkovich exchange Tennessee Williams lines from *Streetcar*. This was more intimate than the sex Glenn worried over. Malkovich had a peaceful intensity and delivered lines with casual passion between drags on his cigarette. He was better, half-drunk and talking off the top of his head, than anyone I'd ever seen. I wanted to be him, not me. Further, I wanted to be anyone but me.

"Last call," said the bartender.

Malkovich's wife pulled him up by his collar. "Let's go home, maestro."

He shrugged to Morgan, then spun around and engulfed Glenn in a clumsy hug.

"Whatever you say, pooh."

Morgan stared at them. They wandered off, giggling.

I watched her watch him.

"He's really good."

Already I was tired of people telling me how good Malkovich was. Sure, he's immensely talented and destined for wealth and international fame. So what?

I settled the tab with the bartender.

"How could so few drink thirteen hundred bucks worth of booze?" I asked.

The bartender shrugged.

"Sinese likes single-malts."

I walked up to Sinese.

"You're paying for the rest yourself, pal," I said in passing.

Bleary-eyed, he slid off his barstool.

"Then I guess I'm done," he said while draining the shot glass.

We gave him a ride to his apartment, then made our way downtown to our hotel. I was too drunk to make out with Morgan, so we fell in bed and slept like the dead.

Los Angeles

While traveling back home, Morgan didn't say much. She kept to herself, read a script and dozed. I drank Bloody Marys and stared out the window. We picked up my Mustang at LAX and drove straight to Smedley's office. After parking on Wilshire, we weaved through drunks and tourists and walked to the office. Smedley's receptionist waved us through. I tossed the Malkovich contract on his desk.

"What's this?" he asked.

"Malkovich," I replied.

"Yeah. You got it?"

"Yes, I got it."

"I forgot, what do I owe you? Shelby will cut you a check."

"The deal was an audition for Places in the Heart. Ermine."

"Okay. I remember." He leaned back in his leather chair. "Go," he said.

"Now?" Morgan protested.

"I don't have all day, let's see what you got."

I had the illegal script photocopy in my valise, but Morgan, with a disgusted look on her face, waved it away.

"My, don't you two look nice together," she said defiantly.

Smedley leaned back in his chair.

"I'm impressed. Can you do it with Texas Panhandle? Put more south in your mouth?"

Morgan closed her eyes and took a breath. She recited the line again. I give him credit: Smedley was perceptive. After walking around his desk, he cupped her chin in his skeletal fist and rotated her face. I wanted to offer a magnifying glass or dental mirror, but held my tongue.

"You understand the set up. You're at the dance and slimy Wayne has been screwing around on his wife. Give me smirky sarcasm."

"My—don't you two look nice together," Morgan spat, smoldering.

She nailed it. Smedley took her in from crooked lower teeth to the chipped red toenail paint protruding from her sandals.

"Okay, you're good. Let's have a look at you," he said, motioning for her to remove her jacket.

She dropped the jacket and rotated slowly while Smedley gazed at her. As she twirled, she gave me an evil glare. She wore tight jeans and a yellow Polka Dot blouse. The best thing about her was how sexy she was when angry. She had an irresistible, pouty expression.

"Well shit," Smedley said. "I like you so it's too damn bad I signed Toni Hudson for Ermine."

Now *I* was angry. I didn't reach for the .45, but this took discipline. The clever man sensed immanent bloodshed, so he quickly riffled through papers on his desk.

"Let me see what else I have. How about Footloose? Herb Ross is signed to direct and it's going to be big. Can you dance? Wanna go to Utah?"

I was prepared to press my point, but realized, after all, I did not want Morgan filming in a remote location with horndog Malkovich. *Footloose* sounded good, so we set up an audition and Morgan doubled up on dancing lessons. The next few months were a blur. She did a month of filming in Utah. Most of her performances were edited out, but you can see her in the high school dance scene at the end. We got paid, so it was okay. After that she did more television and music videos.

Footloose was a hit and royalty money started coming in. With the authority of her power of attorney, I invested her money in a small house in the hills above Malibu and a share in a strip mall being built on the site of an orange grove near Anaheim. Bored with the scene, I stopped following her around. The hours on the set were the picture of tedium; endless time spent moving equipment and twiddling the sound and lighting. The studios sent a car for her and I drove around LA in my Mustang. Smedley gave me jobs running contracts and coaxing signatures from reluctant actors and producers. One of my biggest fears is boredom. When I'm bored, trouble seeks me out.

CHAPTER 21

Thursday, November 18, 1982

Los Angeles

It is a cliché that everyone in LA has a screenplay: every taxi driver, doorman, waiter and pool cleaner has a manuscript, a treatment and an elevator pitch.

With all this competition, why was I compelled to join the madness?

Because of all the crap made into movies, that's why. We watched a string of crappy films including *Grease 2*, *The Slumber Party Massacre*, *Boogeyman 2*, *Doctor Detroit*, and *The Sting 2*. For every good movie like *Blade Runner* and *Eddie and the Cruisers*, there were ten stinkers. Any idiot could write a script better than barf-fests like *Cross Country*, *Disconnected or The Trail of the Pink Panther*, for cripes sake.

So, I started my screenplay.

The Dope Dealer
By Glen Wilson

FADE IN:

INT. HOTEL SUITE -- AFTERNOON

GARY WALTERS is a tall, handsome man dressed in a white suit with thick gold chains around his neck and garish rings on his fingers. He is fit and intelligent. He holds a cigarette in his left hand, which is missing the little finger. There are three other people in the room, FREEWAY RICK, a husky black man, PENELOPE, a beautiful Blonde, and PACO, a lithe Mexican who guards the door. A briefcase packed with cash is open on a coffee table. FREEWAY RICK dips a long fingernail into a bag of coke and snorts the contents. He is pleased with the excellent quality of the Bolivian cocaine.

FREEWAY RICK
This is primo shit. Perhaps you'll tell me where you got it...

GARY WALTERS
I already told you: Bolivia.

FREEWAY RICK
My Columbian shit comes from the Cartel. You look like a Fed. CIA? (chuckling) That stands for Cocaine Import Agency.

FREEWAY RICK pulls a huge automatic pistol from his jacket.

FREEWAY RICK (CONT'D)
Perhaps I cap your ass and keep the dope AND the money, CIA-man.

GARY WALTERS
I'm a businessman trying to make a buck, just like you.

FREEWAY RICK
(Angry)
You'll never be like me, you fuck. Nobody is like me.

Lazily, he aims the automatic. There is a snap and FREEWAY RICK has a startled look on his face. In close-up, a dribble of blood emits from his mouth. The camera pulls back to show PENELOPE holding a smoking derringer. She points it at PACO, who freezes as he reachs into his suit for his gun. GARY WALTERS reaches over and plucks a bundle of cash out of the briefcase.

GARY WALTERS
(To PACO)
I have no quarrel with you, *hermano*. Walk away.

GARY WALTERS throws the cash to PACO who snags it neatly out of the air. PACO slips the bundle into an inner pocket and brushes off his suit jacket. PACO nods and slips out the door. PENELOPE slowly moves the gun until it's pointed at GARY, who casually takes a drag from his cigarette.

GARY WALTERS (CONT'D)
Don't even bother. If you intended to shoot me, I'd already be dead.

PENELOPE
You have a lot of confidence for a man about to lose his product, his cash and his life, all at once.

Slowly, GARY stands up. He closes the briefcase on the cash and repacks the cocaine into a sport bag.

GARY WALTERS
Let's start our partnership by going somewhere and getting properly introduced. You like Vegas, Miss...?

PENELOPE
Penelope. It turns out I like Las Vegas quite a lot.

GARY WALTERS
I thought you might.

GARY throws the strap of the sport bag over his shoulder and lifts the briefcase. He holds out his arm for PENELOPE. She drops her gun into her handbag and walks around the couch to take his arm. They exit the room.

INT. HOTEL HALLWAY -- AFTERNOON

PENELOPE
I hope you're good in bed.

Ken Coffman

GARY WALTERS
(Laughing)
And I hope you're not wearing a padded bra.

FADE OUT:

Thus began my masterwork, at that time, the best screenplay on the market. When I should have been watching Morgan, I hunched over an IBM Selectric typewriter, drinking, smoking and perfecting my manuscript. At first, I saw myself playing the main character, and then figured it would be better to get someone like Clint Eastwood or Sean Connery to play opposite Morgan, who would play Penelope, of course. I had fun with the story, mixing my experience in the dope business with paranoid fantasies about the CIA and the DEA.

I paid a proofreader a hundred bucks to review the manuscript and she said it was the best screenplay she'd seen in a decade. I didn't ask how many screenplays she'd seen. She was competent, but had eight cats, bad breath and a drinking problem (she favored large plastic cups filled with syrupy sloe gin on the rocks) so I didn't hang around much. While working, she wore an old bathrobe and was careless with the sash. I saw more sagging gray flesh than I needed to.

Morgan didn't like the fate of the female lead character, but otherwise thought it no worse than other scripts she worked with. She'd been reading scripts like *Adventures of the Tijuana Tarzan II* and *Robin Hood vs. The Three Musketeers* so her judgment didn't count for much. I registered *The Dope Dealer* with The Writer's Guild and made twenty photocopies to send to agents all over town. Then I patiently waited for contract offers to roll in.

I couldn't find an agent who would work on spec, so I paid a guy. He got me a meeting with Larry Peters who produced a series of low budget films with titles like *So Many Titties and So Little Time* and *Little Red Riding Whore*. We met at a tiny Century City office sandwiched between a used clothing store and a Chinese dry cleaner. The meeting didn't go well.

"Great script, eh?" I suggested.

He leaned back in his chair and rubbed his eyes.

"Screenwriting is a craft. You learn it by studying and paying dues. Writing, rewriting and rewriting again. Go to film school, work around sets, read a lot of scripts, then you'll be ready to write a screenplay, okay?"

"I didn't just fall off the strawberry truck. I know my way around. This script will make a great movie with the right leading actor like Roger Moore or Sly Stallone. A blockbuster."

"Assuming crap like this ever gets made, you'll be lucky to get Eric Estrada or Mark Harmon. Here's information for you, a good screenplay is more than a bunch of tired clichés strung together. And you insult the director and actors when you try to their job for them. Remove the camera instructions and emotional reactions."

"Alright, if the script has some problems, I'll fix them. Tell me what to do."

Peters covered his face with his hands.

"Where do I start? First of all, your characters all have the same voice; they have no individuality. The dialog is clunky and wooden. There are too many expensive locations and tricky special effects shots so the movie couldn't be made on a reasonable budget. Finally, the CIA won't allow themselves to be presented in such a negative manner. They'll get the IRS to find something in your tax return or

Ken Coffman

the LA cops will beat the shit out of you and lock you up for assaulting a cop. Do the world a favor and go back to Pocatello and forget about making movies. Your girlfriend is cute, but, as a writer, you stink."

I tried to be calm and professional, but my blood pressure peaked. Peters sensed this, because he tried to soften the blow.

"Look, Wilson, I feel for you, I really do. My next movie is called *Dick Wadd, Private Detective*. You think I'm proud of that? I have screenplays too, seven of them. I can't get them made either. And they're good ones like *Alien* meets *Godzilla* with high school kids saving the world. A guaranteed hit if I can finalize Japanese financing. Look, let's have a drink."

"Most films are pure trash, why can't I just slip this one into the flow of sewage?"

"That's not the way Hollywood works. Hollywood starts with a great screenplay and then turns it into offal. Get it?"

I wanted to hate Peters, but I didn't have the energy. The drink was a good idea. He pulled a bottle of Cutty Sark from his desk drawer and we sipped in silence until I had enough and went home feeling depressed and lethargic.

Morgan and I watched *Metropolis* twice in a moldy old theater on a rainy Monday morning. We were the only people in the audience except for the projectionist who came out once the film started and shared a box of cold fried chicken and mumbled endless quirky comments about filmmaking technique.

When I woke the next day, I was consumed with a new screenplay idea. 1984 was coming and I was obsessed with a mixture of *Atlas Shrugged*, *Close Encounters of the Third Kind* and Fritz Lang's *Metropolis*. My story was about one woman's doomed war against corporate groupthink and totalitarianism.

I took inspiration from watching dust motes drift in alternating stripes of blinding light when car headlights slipped through a cleft in my curtains. I lost track of time. Morgan kept me alive with hot dogs, corn chips and beer. I worked every waking hour. Toward the end, I slept with my head on the typewriter and refused to leave the room except when the need to shit became unbearable. I pissed in 2-liter plastic soda bottles like a truck driver.

By the time I typed FADE TO BLACK followed by THE END, I'd poured my heart and soul into 275 pages of sex, adventure, wry humor, objectivist philosophy and existential despair. I was unshaven, wearing stinking, filthy clothes, and suffering from a massive headache. My skin felt waxy and oily; loose on my bones like old canvas. Trails of charred cigarette butts abused the hardwood surface of my desk. One smoldered as I watched.

There was no doubt in my mind this was the best screenplay since *Gone with the Wind*. I had the feeling I'd created my life's work and was now free to die. I don't know how long I sat with the manuscript on my lap with my mind adrift with possibilities.

While I slept, Morgan took the manuscript to the library and made ten copies. One went to Larry Peters. It took a few days, but he called, so I paid him a visit. He looked tired. Screenplays were stacked on his desk. Idly, I counted them. 17.

"Shit, Glen," he said, "there's only one thing I hate more than a terrible screenplay and that's a terrific one that will never be made."

"Won't get made?"

"First of all, I'm stunned. It's outstanding. The female lead is so good everyone would kill to play her. Kathleen, Shirley, Faye, any of them. Some of the scenes were incredible, like the robot battle and when she throws that hammer into the big video screen. Magnificent, glorious imagery."

"Thanks. Why won't it get made?"

"The dialog is witty and snappy and I loved the cyborg dog."

"Why won't it get made?"

"The way you mixed Greek mythology with Spaghetti Western sensibility... Outrageous and original, mind-blowing, I loved it."

"Quit blowing smoke up my ass and tell me why it won't get made."

Peters deflated and rotated his chair so he could stare through his dirty window at shadows passing on the sidewalk. Outside, a black guy in a fur hat peddled maps to the stars homes.

"All the underground scenes would be cheap to film, I give you credit for that. But the battles and the exotic locations? Too expensive. This thing would cost a hundred-million to film properly. No one is going to spend anything like that for a space opera. And 275 pages? That's over four hours. It's too long. It's genius, but it ain't gonna get made, end of story."

Part of me wanted to scream and beat him to death with his typewriter. Tear his eyes from their sockets and crush his testicles with my boots. But, another part of me knew he was right. Dead right.

"I'm sorry, Glen. If you're light on cash, I'll write an option for a hundred bucks."

"No, I'm okay."

I stood and stubbed out my cigarette in an ashtray on his desk.

"Glen, I hate to be stupid, but…"

"Spit it out."

"I'd be honored if you'd autograph my copy and let me keep it."

I was touched. My previous autograph requests were on Army discharge papers and an IRS settlement I'd signed before joining the underground economy. I signed and walked out. I visualized an epic struggle to get an agent, endless sales pitches to film company executives, battles to reduce screen time and cost, quibbling over dialog and the hacked-up, hackneyed mess would come from the nether end of the Hollywood dream machine.

I didn't need the aggravation. In retrospect, I should have taken the hundred bucks. We weren't broke, but all of our money was tied up in investments. I only had a few thousand dollars of walking-around money left. I didn't feel like driving so I wandered around on foot.

The air was in inversion and the sky was obscured by smog the consistency of brown gravy. I was hungry so I stopped at Musso and Franks. I had to cough up a hundred dollars to get them to seat me at a small table in a corner by the bar.

I sipped martinis and ordered a rack of lamb with mint sauce. Meat, potatoes and booze to feed my mood. I wasn't angry and I wasn't sad. I didn't know what I was. After a couple of martinis, I wouldn't worry about figuring it all out. On the verge of being sick, I had an annoying scratch at the back of my throat. I was feverish. My brain was still partly in the monochrome world of my screenplay. The light and color of the real world was flat and washed-out in comparison. I liked the characters in my screenplay better than any of the real people I knew. This is probably the definition of a sociopath.

The word kenophobia popped into my mind and I thought about it. A pathological fear of the void, that's it means. In a way, it's a fear that nothing exists and therefore nothing matters. This did not scare me, probably another sign of severe mental disorder, but I could not summon the energy to be upset about it.

I finished my dinner. As long as I ordered drinks, the waiters left me alone as other patrons came and went. I'm not sure how long I sat there before I noticed Morgan's laughter in the mix of clattering plates and chattering gossip.

At first, I thought I was hallucinating. I couldn't see her, but I could see an actor she'd been working with and the back of the head of a man in a suit bearing a precision haircut that shouted lawyer. I recognized her hand and understood the implicit intimacy as she stroked the actor's arm with gilded fingernails.

I thought about how I felt about this. I should feel betrayed and jealous, but these emotions didn't kindle. I waved the waiter over and ordered them a round of drinks. When the drinks were delivered, I raised my glass in toast. Morgan leaned over and I enjoyed the waves of emotion that washed over her face. Once she re-attained composure, she bravely waved for me to join them.

When I stood up, I found out how drunk I was. The restaurant yawed and tilted under my feet in a disturbing manner. The actor, whose name escapes me, reminded me of a low-budget Cary Grant. He offered to slide out so I could sit by Morgan, but I waved him away and collapsed into the booth.

I wanted to hate the lawyer, but he told a story about a well-known actress with a proclivity for teen-aged boys (several at once) and a young pop singer who surgically altered his face to match his sister. It's impossible to hate a man with great stories like these.

The actor exchanged worried glances with Morgan and kept his mouth shut. I admired his sense of self-preservation. Besides, the lawyer picked up my dinner bill and saved me a couple hundred bucks. I wanted to bear his children. I wasn't sure where I left my car, but they wouldn't let me drive anyway. Morgan and her boyfriend left to work with their film's dialog coach and I give them credit for not touching while they were in my sight. The lawyer dropped me at home where I heaved up nasty glops of partially digested lamb and booze before flopping into bed.

I woke with a nasty headache. The tickle in the back of my throat turned into a raging throat infection and my head felt three times larger than normal. After finishing a big project, the body knows it's useless and falls prey to disease. I wanted to die but I didn't have the energy to turn on the gas and strike a match.

I chewed aspirin and forced myself to drink cup after cup of black tea. Again, I lost track of time. When I tried to read, I could not focus on the words. I switched between the few channels picked up with the TV's rabbit ear antenna.

After a week, there came a knock on the door. I was unsurprised to find the lawyer standing in my doorway. He brought a pair of large men, former LA Ram linebackers, I assumed. When I let him in, he came to the point.

Handing over legal papers, he said, "These revoke your power of attorney over Miss French's affairs."

I motioned for something to write with and he handed me a gold Cross pen. I signed the papers where indicated with X's and pushed the papers back. He was taken aback as if he expected it necessary for the linebackers to sack me before I would cooperate.

After looking over my signatures to see if I signed as Howard the Duck or something, he spoke again.

"Morgan is not asking for anything of yours. According to her rough accounting, you took 360 thousand dollars she earned over the last nine months. We would like to get back as much of that money as possible without unpleasantness. She will allow you to keep your car and personal belongings if you'll remit everything else."

Morgan didn't mention the three hundred thousand dollars I spent on her dental work, acting and dance lessons, hair stylist, expensive clothing that adorned her now-slender frame or the expensive portrait studio sessions. There was more, but my thinking was fuzzy. It is a Hollywood cliché that the starlet's svengali will steal her money.

I used her power of attorney to buy property, but I put everything in her name. I pulled a shoebox off the top shelf in the closet and tossed it on the kitchen table. While the lawyer looked through the papers, I prepared another cup of tea. The box's content documented a small fortune in receipts, deeds and titles. I'd already had a profitable offer on a strip of land bought on her behalf in Orange County, but I was holding out for a higher return.

If she held onto everything I bought her, she'd be a millionaire in five years. She could afford to stop working, have babies and get fat. After he looked over each piece of paper, front and back, he leaned back in his chair.

"It's possible Miss French misjudged you, Mr. Wilson."

"Perhaps so," I replied before collapsing into a coughing fit.

"It appears some of your money is in these holdings…"

"Screw it, take everything and go."

He stuffed the papers back in the box and stood. I thought I saw a flicker of sympathy on the face of one of his linebackers, but the connection was fleeting and possibly imaginary.

"Shall I call you a doctor?"

"Send the coroner in a week if the neighbors complain about an odor," I said between tortured gasps for air. He wanted to shake my hand but I waved him away. "Let me die in peace," I whispered.

The next day, I thought about hanging myself, but by the time I had energy to attempt it, I felt better and changed my mind.

I remember my last conversation with Morgan. She called late in the morning and for some reason I picked up the phone.

"Wilson here."

"Glen, its Morgan."

"Hey babe."

I could not describe my mood. I was not angry. I didn't own her and I didn't care about the money. If my destiny was to die destitute and alone, then so be it. It did not seem like a lover leaving. The situation felt like more like a daughter growing up and going her own way.

"I want to say I'm sorry."

"There is nothing to be sorry for. We had good times."

"How can repay you for all you've done for me?"

"I didn't do anything for you. We brought out things that were always inside you."

"But you were my guide, my coach and my drill sergeant."

"Look Morgan, let's not get all sloppy, okay? It's time for you to go one direction and me to go another. The situation could be better, but life is like that sometimes."

"I owe you something. I could sign over some of the property. Or, maybe you'd like to fuck a movie star one last time? We could go away to Catalina for the weekend and I could bring a friend if a two-some would light up your marquee. Whatever pleases you, Glen. Please say yes. For me."

The two-girl image was tempting. However, I was still in the suburbs of disease. I imagined my nose running endlessly while I coughed up chunks of my lungs. The reality would never match the vision.

"I appreciate that, I really do. But, I'll pass."

"Shit, Glen, I'm trying. The scales are unbalanced. Let's not leave things this way."

"Just say goodbye."

"What about your screenplay? Someone will come to their senses and buy it."

"Take the photocopies and throw them in the aqueduct."

"Damn you, Big Daddy. Okay. we'll do this your way. I hate to ask, but can I come over and get my clothes?"

"The rent is paid until Friday. I'll be gone in the morning. Come by anytime after that. There is one thing you can tell me."

"Anything."

"What exactly is a burger-burger?"

"What?"

"You heard me."

Silence stretched on the line.

"Double patties on a French roll with grilled onions and chili. Pepto-Bismol tablets are an extra buck each. A well-done burger-burger with onion rings and sweetened ice tea is called our heart-attack special."

Together, we laughed as I pressed the phone button to disconnect the call. I was not crying, but a histamine attack left me wheezing and teary. I blew my nose in a towel and wiped my face. The only thing in the refrigerator was a diet Pepsi. I didn't want it, but drank it anyway.

That night, I dreamed of economics. The money machine slowly turned and carried a man along or crushed him with its power. When I was in Europe, I noticed most people could not afford to buy homes. They drove tiny little plastic cars because the fuel was so expensive. This meant they had plenty of money for smaller purchases like clothes, fashion accessories and parties all week long. It was not better or worse than the way we lived, but different. I had a vision of our future, of thinking machines and low-cost luxury items anyone could afford.

I could get rich. Making money is no secret. Figure out something that moves commerce's big wheel and you will be rewarded. However, in the end, there's something better than being rich and that's the knowledge you can make money when you need it and you don't need to worry about it. That's freedom money can't buy. Think in terms of independence and liberty, not in accounting terms of dollars and cents, and you'll be happier than any rich man.

The next morning, I evaluated my situation. Counting all my assets, I had just over $7,000 and a Rolex I could hock for a few hundred bucks. I had the Mustang if I could remember where I parked it.

Why did I walk away from Morgan's money?

Partly to mess with her head.

There would be many times she would regret her lack of trust and wish we still shared ice cream while reading screenplays to each other. There are worse legacies.

Truth be told, I was bored with her and the Hollywood scene. If this town was too dumb to recognize the genius of my screenplay, then they could go straight to hell; I would find better things to do. Besides, if you don't challenge yourself and reset everything back to zero on occasion, then how will you know what you're made of?

My Mustang had been towed and it cost me a ten-dollar taxi ride and $125 to extract it from impound. I took a long piss at an Enco station in San Fernando; a proper goodbye to the City of Lost Angels.

After driving through the flat and boring farmlands of central California, I cut over on Highway 152 to Gilroy and arrived in Santa Clara late in the evening. I ordered greasy tacos from an RV converted into a rolling Mexican kitchen. After a short argument to prove to the cook I was not a cop, he produced Carta Blanca *cervesas* from an ice chest hidden under blankets.

I tried to find Highway 17 North and got lost in a rough part of town where I noticed gang-bangers with tire irons breaking the windows of an old Honda Civic. On a whim, I turned back. The Mexicans were brutes but not stupid. They recognized the swagger of a man bearing a firearm.

"*Suficiente, amigos.*" That's enough, my friends.

Their eyes bored into me as I leaned against a brick building inspecting my fingernails. The rear window of the Civic was still intact. They smashed it. One of the boys scrawled a quick tag on the car with spray paint, and then slowly sauntered to their low-rider pickup idling at the curb.

The driver flipped me the finger as he drove away. High school kids joyriding and having fun on a school night.

The Civic driver Civic unfolded himself from the driver's seat. He was a tall Indian wearing a turban wrapped around his head. If my memory could be trusted, the turban meant he was a Sikh.

"Many thanks to you, sir," he said. "I am Ranjit Singh and I owe you a great debt for saving me."

"What are you doing in this part of town? It's not safe."

"I was lost."

"No shit," I replied, before walking back to my car.

"Sir, my headlamps are inoperative, can I further trouble you for a lift? I don't have cash with me, but I can pay you when I reach my home. Please, sir."

I'd stopped on a whim. I wasn't looking for a friend. But, I was in no hurry. In fact, I did not know where I was going, so why not? I motioned for him to jump in.

His home was a rundown rambler in Cupertino's working-class outskirts. He chattered nervously during the ride. He was from Jammu, a small city in northern India. His father was a banker and Ranjit was a student at Stanford studying computer science, whatever that was. As far as I knew, computers were big boxes with Christmas lights on cheap SciFi movies.

Ranjit insisted I drink tea with him before hitting the freeway. In no hurry, I accepted. The house was a mess; there were disassembled TVs, radios and unidentifiable electronic parts everywhere. With my mug of tea in hand, Ranjit led me to the garage where three scruffy-looking young men stunk up the place with soldering pencils. A tall punk named Steve got up and stretched his back. He shook my hand and showed me the boxes being built. I was unimpressed by the useless suitcase-sized things with blinking lights and toggle switches. You could type on a keyboard and characters would appear in green lettering on a video screen. Big deal.

I liked the kid; he was enthusiastic and sharp. He spoke a mile-a-minute in terms I could not follow. Complementary symmetry metal oxide semiconductors? Microprocessor chips? 4.77 Megahertz? Dynamic random access memory? Ranjit went on and on about something called Arpanet and insisted I memorize a funny-looking string of numbers he called an address.

None of this meant anything to me, but he said I could send electronic mail from a military base or government office. I couldn't think of a reason to do that, but I humored him. Then he showed me a thing he called a spreadsheet where numbers could be entered into boxes and manipulated. Added, subtracted and multiplied. Mathematical models could quickly calculate results. I'd done balance sheets and kept track of rental income and expenses with a pencil on legal pads, so I appreciated the implication of this electronic automation. Then Steve asked a key question.

"Do you have any cash?"

Thus I became an investor in SCS, the Solar Computer System Company. I hocked my Rolex and scraped together $7500 and bought in. Steve became a legendary Silicon Valley icon and Ranjit, after cashing in for 100 million dollars, went back to India to create a software company. They were good people who never forgot my faith and finance.

A few weeks later, when I got back on the highway headed north, I had a hundred dollars, a half tank of gas, and paperwork wrapped in a plastic bag in the bottom of my toolbox that granted me 5% ownership of SCS.

Steel Waters

I was, if I ever cared to cash in, quite a rich man. However, being a millionaire, while interesting, is not an end goal. It's better is to travel the world and lead an interesting life.

While my old Mustang took me through Stockton, Sacramento and Redding, my determination intensified and solidified. It will drive me until the day my body is planted in the ground and the universal sausage machine figures out how to rotate without me.

EPILOGUE

Friday, December 31, 1982

California - Oregon

Traveling north, I pushed the car hard though central California and into the Siskiyou mountains. The Mustang had a lot of power, which was great for passing RV's on upgrades, but the lumbering beasts passed *me* when I stopped for gasoline every hundred miles or so. Like a speed demon, I roared through little towns called Mount Shasta, Weed and Yreka. I wasn't going anywhere in particular, so I don't know why I hurried.

I decided to look in on Linda.

My driveway was blocked with a new gate sporting signs that included Beware of Dog, Posted: No Trespassing, No Hunting and Private Property, Beat It. I left the Mustang idling and leaned on the gate. The house still looked like its spine was broken, but bore a new coat of paint. The roof was a patchwork puzzle of old and new asphalt shingles. The shiny, new, hardwood front door looked out of place.

Gray smoke oozed from the chimney. Rudely, a pack of dogs barked at me. I recognized Dwayne's walk and was unsurprised when he came out on the porch with his arm around Linda. I wasn't jealous until I noticed the way he cradled my double-barreled shotgun. Not his. Mine. That wasn't right. I felt violated.

Oh let me take my chances on the Wall Of Death...

Dwayne, chewing on a buttermilk biscuit, walked to the gate.

"Glen," he said.

"Dwayne," I replied. "Did you go back to Coos Bay and make that carpenter an offer he couldn't refuse for one of the doors?"

"That's none of your fucking business," he said.

I looked over the field toward Modine's place. I could see his missus staring at me with a hand shielding her eyes from the slanting afternoon light. It seemed like she spat in my direction before disappearing in her house, but she was too far away to be sure.

It wasn't their time of day, but I imagined meadowlarks taunting me. The alpacas, nosing a bale of alfalfa hay, didn't even look up. I never liked the damned things anyway.

"Things are okay around here?"

"They were until you drove up my driveway," he said.

"Any chance you'll invite me in for supper?"

"Linda still bears a grudge."

I watched a dirt-caked tomcat strut to the porch and drop a limp rodent at Linda's feet. Did one of my ceramic ducks sit on the porch's near corner? From this distance, I could not be sure. She picked up the filthy cat and petted it.

"I thought I'd stop by and see if things are under control."

"And now that you know..."

Ken Coffman

Glen Wilson can take a hint, particularly when offered by a large, unfriendly man holding a 12 gauge shotgun.

"See ya."

I turned to go.

"Wait," Linda said.

She dropped the cat and went in the house. When she returned, she carried a brown sandwich bag.

"I saved something for you," she said.

I got back in the Mustang and rolled slowly on Dead Indian Road. I'd made a big circle from LA to Bolivia to Miami and Coos Bay and LA and back again. I was permanently marked by a lost finger. I screwed an old Nazi and created a movie star. Instead, I could have spent my time on earth painting the house and replacing shingles.

Good things happened. Bad things happened. Was it worthwhile? At the bottom of the balance sheet, was the grand total positive or negative, written in black or red? In answer, my ghostly finger throbbed. When I got to the I-5 interchange, I took the northbound onramp and pointed the car toward Seattle.

Just north of Grants Pass, I stopped at the Heaven on Earth restaurant where I walked around back and pissed in the old outhouse. After finishing my business, I bought a Styrofoam cup of coffee from Christine and took it to my car. Looking at Linda's paper bag, I wondered. If it was filled with dog shit, I would not be surprised. I opened it.

It held a sandwich made with thick slices of homemade bread, still frozen in the middle. I was hungry, but did I dare eat it? I opened the waxed paper and lifted the bread. Modine's turkey. She'd made it the way *she* liked with thick mayonnaise, slices of jalapeno pepper and jellied cranberry. I laughed and threw the damned thing out the window.

A crow, much less fussy than me, cautiously hopped over and pecked at it. After sampling the turkey and finding it to his liking, he stared at me.

"Ha," he said.

I started the car and continued north.

THE END